93249

ON LINE

MONTVALE PUBLIC LIBRARY, N.J.

P9-AOU-177

Duncker, Patricia,
1951-

The deadly space
between.

$23.95

DATE			

BAKER & TAYLOR

MONTVALE PUBLIC LIBRARY

THE
DEADLY
SPACE
BETWEEN

Also by Patricia Duncker

THE DOCTOR

HALLUCINATING FOUCAULT

MONSIEUR SHOUSHANA'S LEMON TREES

THE DEADLY SPACE BETWEEN

Patricia Duncker

An Imprint of HarperCollinsPublishers

Originally published in Great Britain by Picador,
an imprint of Pan Macmillan Ltd.

THE DEADLY SPACE BETWEEN. Copyright © 2002 by
Patricia Duncker. All rights reserved. Printed in the
United States of America. No part of this book may be
used or reproduced in any manner whatsoever without
written permission except in the case of brief quotations embodied in critical articles and reviews. For
information address HarperCollins Publishers Inc.,
10 East 53rd Street, New York, NY 10022.

HarperCollins books may be purchased for
educational, business, or sales promotional use.
For information please write: Special Markets
Department, HarperCollins Publishers Inc.
10 East 53rd Street, New York, NY 10022.

FIRST U.S. EDITION

Library of Congress Cataloging-in-Publication Data
has been applied for.

ISBN 0-06-008593-2

02 03 04 05 06 RRD 10 9 8 7 6 5 4 3 2 1

For S.J.D.

What moral lesson can be drawn from the story of Oedipus, the favourite subject of such a number of tragedies? – The gods impel him on, and, led imperiously by blind fate, though perfectly innocent, he is fearfully punished, with all his hapless race, for a crime in which his will had no part.

Mary Wollstonecraft

Death of the Father would deprive literature of many of its pleasures. If there is no longer a Father, why tell stories? Doesn't every narrative lead back to Oedipus?

Roland Barthes

To pass from a normal nature to him one must cross 'the deadly space between.' And this is best done by indirection.

Herman Melville

1
MEMORY

She came home smelling of cigarettes. She didn't smoke.
So either she sat in a place where everyone else smoked, or
she was going out with someone who did. Someone who
smoked bitter, foreign cigarettes. Someone I hadn't met.
Someone I had never seen. Where did she go? I began
asking myself questions. Endless staff association meet-
ings? She was no longer chairwoman. The Art Group
Collective? This had been dormant since the last exhibition.
The pub? Which pub? She never went to the pub. She never
met her friends in the pub. She met them in restaurants. If
she intended to meet them she told me where she would be
in advance, or she rang from the restaurant itself, warning
me that she would not be back for supper. Yet she came
home late, smelling of cigarettes. She must be going out
with someone who smokes.

It began in October, three weeks after my eighteenth
birthday, the year I was preparing for my A-level exams.
The wind was increasing, leaving damp leaves in piles
down the pathways. She came home after dark. Once a
week at first, on different days, then more often than that,
late, often slightly anxious, jittery, excited. She kissed me

quickly and asked me what homework I had to prepare. Then she flung her bags into the corner of her studio, that long room of shadows and gaunt spaces all along the back of the house, and made off into the kitchen. I heard the radio, the sound of water bursting from the taps, and the fridge door, opening, closing, again and again.

The smell of cigarettes, passing, incriminating, pungent, the smell I could taste, just for a moment, when she held me in her arms.

*

I can't remember any other house. I have always lived here in this draughty, comfortable, mid-Victorian mass of red brick and white gables. I have always played in the attics, come in at dusk from the long garden, knees stained green with moss. I marked the trees with my knife as a child and watched the bark ooze round the cuts as the years passed. I saw the white shed rot, turn green and black at the corners and finally end up on one of the Guy Fawkes bonfires. I killed woodlice on the tiles in the back porch, watching the remaining carapaces, squat like small tanks, scuttle into the cracked skirting boards for safety. And it was I who warned her when the greying stained floor above the cellar was rotten and dangerous.

My childhood is a long peaceful memory of rain. An English childhood of respectable suburbs, minor events and a pale stream of drizzle, punctuated by the odd June day of green lawns, pale sunshine, the sound of mowers cruising through damp grass, croquet and daisies.

This is my first experience of sex. I fell in love with the neighbour's daughter when I was five and she was seven. I followed her about down the prickly trails in the next-door garden, which was wilder than our garden and flowered weeds, turbulent, unchecked, unkempt. The girl accepted my adoration as a form of homage that was legitimate and deserved. My mother was obscurely disapproving. Then, one day, when I was playing with my tractor in the long grass, the neighbour's daughter declared, 'Let's show our bottoms!' and pulled down her plain white panties. She sat down flat on the grass with her legs apart and presented me with a surprising, narrow pink slit. I stared at it amazed. She assured me that I could lick it if I wanted to, but that I had to promise not to tell and that it would be our secret. I wasn't sure that I did want to, but I said that I might reconsider the situation on Sunday afternoon. This was my first sexual excuse, an attempt to buy time. She pulled her pants back up and stormed off to her room in a huff. She didn't make her offer twice. I forgot all about the incident until, years later, after the family had moved away and I was about ten years old, my mother told me that the child's father, a paediatric physician, had been jailed for abusing his patients. He was also accused by his daughters, one after another, as they grew up. I asked what abuse meant, fearing that it might involve whipping. She said that it was fiddling with children in a way you shouldn't. I asked whether that involved licking other people down there. She stared at me and said that she supposed it might. I said nothing more, but was very pleased that I hadn't taken up the neighbour's daughter on her kind offer. It was clearly a game that led straight to jail.

Other people had grandparents. I didn't. When I reached the plastic animal and model weapons stage I asked my mother why. Other people's grandparents were a great source of Lego battleships and red-eyed dinosaurs. She hesitated a little, then told me part of the truth. They were serious, religious people. She had been very wild when she was younger. She had not been married to my father. Her parents had not been able to accept her decision to keep

3

the child. She was speaking to me. But she still said 'the child' as if I were royalty and she had to use the third person. Or as if I were someone else. The Christian charity of her parents' religion did not extend to children that were loved, but not legal. I didn't understand this. No, she never wrote to them and they never wrote to her. No, they never sent Christmas or birthday cards. Then, oddly, as if she were imparting a mighty revelation, she told me that some things, sometimes, could never be forgiven. Somehow I knew that she was no longer talking about my grandparents. She was thinking of someone else.

'Remember that,' she retorted, as if we had been having an argument.

I promised to remember every word and dropped my demands for grandparents. In fact, I was simply disappointed that the new model laser kit, with coloured ray firing equipment and optional sound effects, was now for ever beyond my grasp if no grandparental contribution could be expected. Children's desires are very material. Food, cuddles, guns.

Fortunately I was blessed with aunts. Aunt Luce was like a ship in full sail, layers of clothes in great gusts of colour, billowing around her. Aunt Luce invented new combinations of colour. She specialized in fabrics for women prancing down catwalks and rich people's furnishings. She made money, big money, out of cottons, silks, velours, crêpes, cheesecloth, felts, linens and rolls of 100 per cent acrylic. Everything she did was wholesale, generous, vast. She bought me a rocking horse. She was a great source of plastic and metallic equipment, some of which produced giant bangs. She did not disapprove of items which could realistically imitate mass slaughter in the way that my mother did. But her generosity stopped short of the animated laser gun.

4

From my earliest days I remember the smells of lipstick and independence, her frequent visits in a Volvo estate with the back flattened by rolls of fabric, huge cylinders of colour, an Arabian cave piled in the boot. I remember her house. She had blinds, not curtains, in Bauhaus patterns and a completely white kitchen.

Aunt Luce lived with another woman who was even younger than my mother and who therefore must have been at least twenty-five years younger than Aunt Luce. She was stocky and flushed and turned an even deeper shade of pink whenever she initiated a conversation. This made everyone smile. Aunt Luce's companion was called Liberty. I once asked her about her odd name. We were putting a new chain on my bicycle, sitting with our bums sunk in damp gravel out on the front drive. Our fingers were covered in oil. I scraped at the dirt caked under the back mudguard and it came showering down in little flakes. She explained.

'My parents were flower children. They bought a small-holding near Hebden Bridge but never managed to grow anything successfully. I was born there. I was born at home. They wouldn't risk the hospital. They educated me at home too, which wasn't so usual then. Calling me Liberty was meant to symbolize the fact that I lived outside the capitalist state. Theoretically, at any rate.'

I shook my head doubtfully, wondering if this evil state was located in South Yorkshire.

'But did you want to live outside the capitalist state?'

'Dunno. They did.'

There was a pause. Then she said:

'I don't think my name's silly. One of their friends had a daughter called Ince. And we used to play. It was only when I was twelve or thereabouts that I discovered that it was short for Incense. And her second name was Rainbow. No hope there.'

I sat twirling the toecaps on my pedals.

'She called me Tobias. I wonder why.'

'Maybe your grandfather was Tobias. No, on second thoughts, given what Luce says about your grandparents she wouldn't want to name you after him. Maybe your father is called Tobias.'

'I don't know what my father's called.'

'Ask her. He can't have been the Angel Gabriel.'

'He could be. I've never seen him.'

Liberty realized that she was submerged in unknown family waters and changed the conversation.

But I did sometimes wonder if I had ever seen my father. When I dredged the silt at the bottom of my memories I was aware of an event which had terrified my mother. I must have been about four or five at the time. She had received a phone call, and upon hearing the voice, flung the machine against the wall. I stood open-mouthed in the hallway, while she ripped the wire out of the skirting board. Then she spun round in search of me, snatched me up onto the hall chair and forced my arms back into the woollen lining of my anorak so that I began screaming. Ignoring my yells, she strapped me into the stained child's seat in the Renault 4 and roared away down the road. I howled all the way with fright and pain. I can remember howling, but I can't remember where we went.

And this is the moment I can remember clearly.

We are hidden away with Aunt Luce. Someone is at the door. Aunt Luce locks us into a cupboard in the hall, which she calls 'Deep Cloaks'. There is a gap under the door and a zigzag series of holes to aerate the cupboard. We are crouched in a tangle of shoes and plastic covers from the dry-cleaners. There is a terrible reek of mothballs. I have my nose in the sleeve of a real fur coat. My mother is stifling my every breath. Her hand is clamped over my mouth. Her breath is a sequence of hot gasps. I am terrified because she is frightened. The front door is to the right of the cupboard. The doorbell sounds again and again. Now Aunt Luce is opening the door. She tells lies.

'She isn't here. I would have thought that you would know better than to look for her now. And I won't have you in this house. If you don't leave I shall call the police. Go away.' Her voice rises. 'I said, go away at once.'

I hear a low voice. This voice is too low and too quiet for me to distinguish the words. This voice is calm, patient, firm. I see a pair of black shoes with a dotted swirling pattern pierced in leather. My mother now has one hand on my head, pushing me down, the other around my waist, clutching me to her chest. I am convinced that I am going to sneeze. I want to sneeze. Aunt Luce is shrieking.

'Get out. Get out. Get Out.'

And then the voices recede. For no reason that I can ever explain I am certain that this man is my father. But I never ask. I say nothing.

Years later there is another incident, which I never forget. It is summer. I am ten years old. We are having tea on the back lawn. My aunts are visiting. Liberty is making me a daisy chain. She slits each stem with a thumbnail and threads the flowers through. Aunt Luce already has two lots of fluttering daisies attached to her left ankle. My mother is wearing a necklace of flowers. Liberty has made me a white and gold crown. She sets it on my blonde straight crop. I look like an Aryan Cleopatra.

'You're all ready to worship Dionysus,' Liberty exclaims.

'Goodness,' says my mother, 'that's the sort of thing his father would have said.'

'Oh, that's the sort of thing he said, is it?' snaps Aunt Luce, her voice suddenly dangerous. My mother glares at her. Everyone is silent, embarrassed.

Aunt Luce knows something. But not enough. And she feels that she ought to have been told. Liberty doesn't know. She hasn't been told. I will never be told. My mother hasn't refused to tell me. She has just never created the conditions within which it would be possible to ask. But I searched for Dionysus in her *Dictionary of Greek and Roman Myths*. He is the god of wine and ecstasy. Worship him, and you run mad, cannibal, murderous.

Aunt Luce made it clear, for reasons I could never quite grasp when I was small, that the existence of Liberty was one of the living imperatives that had transformed us into a family and in part, the cause of our continuing solidarity. She was fond of saying that we all had the honour to be family scandals. She described our lives, unrepentantly, as a sequence of delicious, deliberate disgraces. She urged me to keep up the family tradition of colourful infamy.

'Put it all in the papers if you can,' she said, 'or better still, go on television. Two minutes of television is worth six columns of print.'

Aunt Luce helped out with donations for holidays, special projects, major repair works and colossal financial undertakings; like updating the bicycle and the computer, re-roofing the studio and purchasing the car, second-hand, but with very low mileage. She gave us money, gifts without interest and apparently without strings, for any adventure which required large sums. She never offered her opinions until she was asked, but always made it clear when she was desperate to hand out her views, like an oracle, blessed with an excess of prophecy. She had a pointed arresting face, like a whippet. When my mother talked she would sit, reflective and intent, on the edge of her chair, with her clothes settling around her, waiting for the right moment to intervene. If Liberty wanted to say something Aunt Luce would hold up her hand like a traffic policeman until the young woman's blushes had subsided. Whenever Luce and Liberty came to visit I brought them everything I had invented or drawn and stood there expectant, craving their approval.

This triangle of women, Aunt Luce, Liberty and my mother, was like a companionable Greek chorus. They were all the family I had. But there was another, disapproving chorus, offstage, which dared to comment on our private acts. I followed the scandals and disputes at second hand, absorbing the fact that we were not independent, autonomous, a little Amazon republic with a son to inherit the kingdom. Everything we did was watched. Family quarrels, always, finally, boil down to arguments about money. I imagined that we were cut off without a penny. This seemed Victorian and final, yet new outrages were always taking place, elsewhere, at regular intervals. Here was a history of share certificates in my mother's name, which nevertheless required my grandmother's signature to release them from fiscal bondage. Permission was angrily withheld. Aunt Luce was the messenger. I saw the tall, peculiar form of Aunt Luce, smouldering in the doorway, holding a letter.

'Outrageous! How dare she?'

It was my unseen grandmother who dared. Here stood Aunt Luce, elegant, intolerant and enraged, in the midst of an indiscreet waterfall of abuse, in which my name was mentioned, several times, while my mother brewed tea, murmuring replies to my aunt's threats.

'Why won't they sign? Is it because they don't like me?'

I asked, interrupting the kitchen discussion of my grandmother's iniquity. They swivelled round in their seats to stare at me.

'It isn't because they don't like you. They've only ever seen you once. They don't know you.' My mother tried to be reassuring.

'I want to know why they never see us and why they write angry letters.'

Aunt Luce burst out laughing.

'Your grandmother is my sister,' she cried, 'she loathes other people and she loves writing angry letters and making scenes. Listen, my dear, you may not have a grandmother, but you have been spared the discomfort of a dozen teatime scenes. My sister sits in a cloud of righteousness over her cheap Darjeeling and Mr Kipling's fairy cakes, criticizing other people, that is, other righteous people. The lower classes are de facto not righteous, and therefore beneath contempt. We ought to be grateful for her persecution. At least she takes notice of us. She has never had the misfortune to be in the wrong and is therefore perpetually on the attack. She has the right, not only to judge other people, but also to comment, with great candour from her position of Olympian rectitude, on their morals and behaviour. She thinks that being rude, which is the same thing as being right, is one of the cardinal virtues. Her New Year's resolution is to make more enemies.'

My mother sat grinning at Aunt Luce, who was now well into her stride, cigarette alight and aloft, clearing the harbour bar of restraint.

'One step off the narrow path of lower-middle-class morality, which is all recycled paper napkins and malice, and, my dear, you are doomed. You can never be visited. You can only be vilified.'

She stared at me speculatively.

'Thank God you don't look like her – or indeed, him,' said Aunt Luce, sighing. I wondered what would have happened if I had done. And concluded that I would not have been loved.

Everyone commented on the resemblance between my mother and myself. There's no doubt whose son you are, Aunt Luce always exclaimed emphatically, when she had not seen me for several weeks. And we were strikingly alike: short, straight, blonde hair, like a couple of Nordic heroes, pale freckled skins which burned easily, and the same grey-blue eyes. I looked into her face and saw the reassuring mirror of my own. All the hair on her body and on mine was ash-blonde, almost white. Our hands were slightly square. But by the time I was sixteen I could enclose her hand in my own. I was already as tall as she was. Our hands were the same shape, the same wide nails, the same fair skin, the same frank grip. She had painter's hands, stained, strong hands, working hands. I loved watching her cleaning her brushes. They were expensive and she took good care of them. But these were the only things she ever cleaned carefully. From time to time I saw her scraping the thick chunk of glass she used for a palette and leaving huge, caked slabs of colour. My hands were smooth and untouched. I had the hands of a rich, spoilt woman. She had a man's hands. Neither of us ever wore any jewellery, any rings.

I never had any pets. I never asked for rabbits or hamsters. Pets teach children the lessons of love and loss. I didn't need them. She was enough. The smell of her body, a sharp, florid, tacky perfume and the eternal whiff of linseed oil, dominated the house. Until I was fourteen, fifteen, sometimes even well after that, she came to my room every night, to kiss me goodnight. I saw the shadow of her hair, the curving line of her smile, still marking her cheek, felt the cold prod of her nose as she bent to kiss me. She kissed me on the forehead, the cheek, the mouth, she ran her lips gently down the curve of my neck. I felt our likeness in the dark. She tasted of paint. Her breasts brushed heavy against my chest. Sometimes she lay down beside me and held me in her arms until I was asleep. Once when I awoke in the morning she was still there, shivering, fully dressed, her eyes gummed together with exhaustion, fighting me for possession of the duvet. We squabbled crossly as if we were both children.

We were often mistaken for brother and sister. A man in the car park asked us whether our parents had paid. In giggling conspiracy we disclaimed all knowledge as to where our parents had gone. Then she went shopping. I sat in the car and we saved 80p for two hours. I found our likeness reassuring, a promise that she would give me the recognition and love which I feared would not always, as of right, be mine.

I inherited her concentration and discipline; we could both occupy ourselves peacefully for hours without speaking. But I did not have her gift for laughter and I minded the mess she made. I tidied up after her. I did all the washing up she left. I scrubbed the sink with Vim. I scoured the kitchen floor. Without me the kitchen would probably have become a health hazard filled with rotting food and crawling beasts. Sometimes, despite all my efforts, this happened anyway. When I did clean up she always kissed me, thanked me, but never changed her ways. Her room was a cavern of old clothes, abandoned washing, painting materials, scraps of cloth purloined from Aunt Luce for a collage experiment which didn't work, and several huge buckets of coloured sand. She never made the bed. She once told Aunt Luce, who was amused rather than disapproving, that she only changed the sheets when she stuck to them. I changed mine once a week. I did all the washing. I loathed hanging out her clothes. I did this even if it was frosty, just to air them. I was afraid of her underwear, which I stuffed into the machine, one load once a month, and avoided examining too closely. I even disliked touching her wet jeans and shirts, smart ones for work, shabby ones for painting. In those days I was prim, prurient, afraid of her zest for grime. She seemed to love matter, textures, odours, liquids, slime, in quite physical and visceral ways. I was a little afraid of all those things.

*

In every way, the child of a gifted artist labours under a terrible disadvantage. You live under the shadow of a tidemark on the wall, an unobtainable level of excellence, which remains there, accusing, just out of reach. Everything you produce is derivative, worked in another's colours. I never escaped the sensation that she was the original and I was the copy: second-hand, second-rate. I haunted her studio in order to be close to her. The room smelt of turpentine, linseed oil, glue, varnish and fixative. She had several huge chests, immovable, paint-spattered, which had been constructed to hold architectural drawings. These chests took up the entire wall backing onto the living room. They loomed out into the space. The handles of the drawers were often sticky with gum or wet paint mixed with sand. I was unable to open the drawers, which were too heavy for me when I was small. And when I was strong enough to peer into them I discovered that there was one which she kept locked.

She had a huge easel, but didn't always use it; sometimes she just stuck paper up on the wall with masking tape and painted on that. Sometimes she leaned huge canvases against the structure and negotiated paint at knee-level. There was nothing mysterious about her methods. She spent a long time preparing her canvas in the traditional manner, with layers of rabbit's foot glue, transparent substances, the texture of egg white. Then her ground wash, faint, light, pale, then her underpaint. Here she varied her colours. She never drew directly onto the canvas at all. She worked her designs in curtains of paint, each one falling over the canvas, layer after layer, deepening, changing. She soaked her brushes in plastic Vittel bottles with the tops chopped off. But these weren't her only tools. The kitchen was next door to her studio. She used the kitchen knives, the fish slice, the pastry brushes, the rolling pin, sheets of tin, her bare hands and forearms, the tips of her fingers and her clenched fists. Once she unpicked her jeans and used the frayed bottoms to create a repeated, fan-shaped pattern. She worked with appalling, inflexible intensity, always on more than one canvas at once, the radio blaring on the window sill. She never worked in silence. She worked every day. Even when she came home, tired out from teaching. I admired her readiness to make herself filthy, but was alarmed by the fact that whatever she cooked tasted of acrylic, glue or turps. The paintings probably tasted of elderly food. I was never quite at ease with her carelessness. I could not resist eliminating the trails she left behind her.

Her style was described by sexist critics as masculine. Or at least, she said they were sexist. She worked on a grand scale; huge abstracts, dense, knotted surfaces, worked and reworked, the paint thick and edible. When I was small she sometimes allowed me to play with the paint on one corner of the canvas. Sometimes she integrated my ideas. I longed to become her apprentice, gazing up at the huge geometric masses, their shifting volumes and uncompromising, monolithic intensity. Whenever she sold a picture she took me out to dinner. Not to a local wine bar, tandoori or McDonald's, but to an expensive restaurant in the city, with real white tablecloths and napkins, where the waiters spoke French and she ordered snails, sizzling in individual craters, like smoking bombs, the kind of restaurant where there was never any background music and everyone spent a long time gazing at huge ledgers with the wine list handwritten inside. No ordinary cheque card was ever sufficient to cover the bill and she paid with her American Express. Once there was a knife fight just outside. I remember the wail of police sirens and the manager losing his temper.

'Shall we go and look?' I demanded.

'Nonsense. If somebody's dead we can read all about it tomorrow. Look at your salmon. It's much more important to eat well than to watch fights.'

Reluctantly, I attacked the fish.

'Listen,' she said, addressing my lust for the sensational directly, 'I'd go on eating – no matter what. Even if History was passing in the street.'

I immediately envisaged History as a giant chariot, covered in garlands, with a mob trailing behind.

*

She taught part-time at the local art college. This was not a particularly distinguished institution, her colleagues were much given to espousing passing fads. One year everyone had to work with bricks and cardboard boxes. But a year later the apotheosis of modernity was sculptures in concrete. A group of Easter Island look-alikes on the same scale as the originals won the end-of-year award. They proved impossible to transport and became a permanent fixture outside the sculpture studio. Then they went out of fashion, and like much civic art, became an awesome and indestructible warning against temporary enthusiasms. They attracted graffiti, red rubber noses and giant penises during the festive season.

My mother was in charge of the painting studio. She was convinced by the ideology of art in the community, and even organized a live paint-in, which anyone could attend. The deeply courageous, a happy few among the public, actually took part. Much against the better judgement of her immediate boss, she set up several huge wall-painting projects along the motorway and in the shopping centre with her students. One of them caused a public scandal. It was a giant frieze of dancing, copulating couples, all uncannily alike. The design was censored for overt eroticism, rather than androgyny, quite unsuitable for a car-park wall overlooking the main entrance at Safeway, and had to be withdrawn. She reworked the plan, excising the frolicking nudes and including portraits of the local drug pushers in their silver Mitsubishis. The car park was one of their night haunts. There was a public phone box, which they used in the early days when they began to frequent the suburb. Later on, when they all had their own mobile phones, they still parked by the phone box, talking into their receivers. Thus the fresco became a surreal public icon, a tribute to the men selling death beneath their own warning images. Neither the public arts committee on the Tory council nor the dealers ever noticed. But her students knew. They were converts to her ideology. Her students loved her. She had a talent for subversion.

*

Aunt Luce told her, in my hearing, that if she was serious about being heterosexual, then she ought to find herself a man.

She had two affairs which I could remember, or knew about for certain. One man was a younger colleague at the college called Jo, who was there on a one-year teaching assistantship. He was tall, with spiky hair cut close, and rows of vicious-looking earrings rising up the side of his reddening lobes. He was her immediate junior colleague. She was supposed to be showing him the ropes. When she promoted him, very shortly after his arrival, to the official position of lover there was a muted frisson of scandal in the staff common room. He took to staying over on Friday and Saturday nights. I liked the new lover, who was cheerful, offhand and made the Weetabix lorry off the back of the packet to amuse me. Then Jo came home with a DIY kite in a box and we stitched it up so that it floated like a dragon over the bracken and horseshit on the common, with the three of us rushing after it, far below, tugging the invisible floating wire and shrieking. As a sexual presence Jo was good-natured, irresponsible. He walked about the house stark naked, to my astonished delight, referred to his penis as his 'donger' and played two of her reggae records, *Black Uhuru* and *The Harder They Come*, until they wore out. He helped me with my homework, and promised to take me to a punk concert, where the band pissed on the stage and then into the audience, but never did. I was bitterly disappointed.

Liberty liked him and Aunt Luce didn't. He was never allowed to share the studio. He moved on to another college at the end of the year and rang once to say that he loathed it and that he missed us. Then we never heard from him again. She seemed a little sad for a week or so after his departure. There was more muttering in the staff common room. The scandal blew over, although, like all scandals, it was never quite forgotten.

The other lover was a more sinister affair. I can only just remember him. I must have been about four years old. Aunt Luce was never even allowed to know of his existence. He was never named, never mentioned. Sometimes I wondered if he had ever been there. He was an older man with a large car and a butterfly tattoo on his forearm. I caught sight of the tattoo on the first morning that the man was still there when I woke up. The man is shaving, with the bathroom door ajar. The bathroom is at the top of the stairs; a long, thin, converted corner of a much larger room. The moulded leaves of the cornice circle three sides of the walls, nuzzling the ceiling and nurturing cobwebs, then vanish suddenly into the blank, undecorated fourth wall. I stand, gazing at the light wavering across the walls, splintering against the cornice, guttering on the water in the bath. This is a very early memory. His mouth gapes as he draws the razor carefully across his upper lip. His forearms are dense with black hair and there, in the midst of the foliage, as if struggling free, is a butterfly, a dark blue butterfly with a touch of darkening red, thick lines, larger than life, shimmering in the watery light. This is what I remember, the man's gaping mouth and the fluttering, extraordinary tattoo.

But I know, I have always known, that neither of these men is my father.

*

When you live, always, in the same house, with the same suburban landscape cradling your memories, one year becomes another. It is hard to remember whether it was that year, the same year I bought my first bicycle, the year the willow tree blew down and the men came to cut it up with chainsaws, and it was rotten inside, crumbling, yellow dust, and how extraordinary that it hadn't blown down before. I measured out my life not in years, but in events. That was the year of the art teacher lover and the dragon kite. That was the year she bought a new car, with a handout from Aunt Luce, second-hand, but new really. When I was five the neighbour's daughter asked me to lick that suggestive pink slit between her legs. And further back, that was the year of the man with the butterfly tattoo, the year my mother sold three of the giant blood-red monoliths and I drank a whole half glass of champagne. I remember that year.

That was how I remembered things.

There were some things to which I could attach a precise date, a date like a luminous marker, an orange buoy on a grey sea. Some dates I planned in advance. I made a pact with myself. I would ask her when I was twelve. I would ask her on her birthday. She was born on August 1st. We were always on holiday for her birthday. And because we were never at home, but in exceptional circumstances, it was easier to make exceptional demands. And to the mysterious Oedipal question – who was my father? – when I had no birthmarks, no memories, no purple swaddling to identify my origins, the reply was bound to be exceptional. But she responded by breaking all the classical rules. She laughed. She shouted with laughter. She hugged me. She unsteadied my dignity while I wobbled in red shorts: pompous, egotistical, righteous, white-faced, demanding my rights, the right to know, the right to identity, the birthright, my inheritance.

But she laughed and laughed, her straight gold hair, her breasts, laughing, shaking.

Then she declared that she had often wondered if I was ever going to ask directly and had considered proposing the Archangel Gabriel. No, my father was quite real. She giggled a little more. I felt utterly ridiculous.

'He was much older than I was, very sexy, rich and married. I never met his wife. But I noticed his wedding ring.'

'Do I resemble my father?'

'No, mercifully, not at all. You look like me.'

'Have I ever met my father?'

'No, not to my knowledge. You never have.'

'Do you still see him?'

'No. Never.'

This was an astute question because it brought my father into the present and she looked at me, surprised, no longer laughing.

'Were you very, very young at the time?'

'Yes, fifteen. Three years older than you are now.'

'Did you really truly love him? As much as you do Aunt Luce?'

'That's my business.'

'Did he ask you to marry him?'

'How could he, twit? He was already married. And I was under age.'

And here she closed the conversation by sidling off to the kitchen, that stranger's kitchen in the beach house, where we could never find the cutlery, the salad servers, the bottle opener, the plug for the TV aerial, the pump for the lilo. And I didn't ask again.

But she made it up to me. We spent all the days and all the nights together at the beach house. By day we scoured the beaches, whatever the weather, searching for unusual stones, skulls, driftwood, shells, bones picked clean by the sea. We took huge collections home in boxes and the smell of the sea dawdled in her studio for weeks. By night we slept together in the huge sagging bed, curled around one another like sunburned clams.

I had her full attention. I needed no one else.

*

She was careless with her own money. She was generous with my pocket money. If she saw something she liked or wanted, she bought it: a food processor, a new CD system, a Kelim rug, in a sale, but it was still £700 and she paid in cash, an old smuggler's trunk with a broken iron lock, which she repaired herself and used to store her rolls of canvas, a naturalist's cabinet in which she amassed objects for still life studies, flints, bird's bones, crystals, a thirteen-speed mountain bike I had coveted, a pair of Indian cushions with tiny mirrors, thick, stitched threads and tassels at each corner. She never hesitated. She spent money as if she was a rich woman.

But she never bothered with the everyday things. The light in the hall was never mended. Every new bulb fused at once. She never rang the electrician. The white shed in the garden had rotted, leaving the croquet hoops and mallets rusting and exposed. She didn't bring them inside. The neighbours said it was a shame, to have such nice things and to allow them to deteriorate. The hedges were never clipped and grew to fabulous heights. The neighbours complained. They were deprived of light. She climbed up a stepladder, cut back the hedge and shaped the top. I heard her singing as she did it. When the neighbours came home they were faced with a large prick and balls and two suggestive green breasts, carved in privet all along the top of the hedge. The penis blew over in October and she

21

lopped it off. She never employed a gardener. But she never did the garden. The windows needed repainting. The sills on the south side were crumbling with damp rot. In every room one of the sash cords hung frayed like an unsuccessful hangman's rope. She didn't bother. She didn't care. And it wasn't that she couldn't afford it. Although sometimes she said that she couldn't. If it was a lean time Aunt Luce would have paid. She couldn't be bothered to ring up the builder, the plumber, the electrician. Yet the one thing she always had mended at once was the telephone.

She never looked into the stack of free daily papers which accumulated in a pile of woolly dust behind the door. But she wouldn't throw them out and she wouldn't let me do so. She hardly ever hoovered and whenever I did the housework she told me I was wonderful: that I was a thoughtful man, a man who noticed dirt, scoured work-tops, plumped up cushions. But I could feel her smirking, sensed her smothered laughter when she said those things. Somewhere, in some other place, there was another kind of man. One I wasn't like. One she liked better.

When I was very young I suffered from appalling, violent jealousies and made scenes. I hated it when she settled down with the phone, sinking into the big smelly sofa, pulling the rugs round her legs, shutting herself off from me to listen, to talk. She gossiped about people I didn't know, had never seen. Her voice rose and echoed. She laughed; there was a gurgle humming in her throat. I loitered in the kitchen with the door ajar, an inefficient spy, hearing every third or fourth word, bitter and angry. She had a secret life that was not mine, about which I knew nothing.

Yet she was always aware of me. She read my face like a landscape. I saw my shadowed surfaces and animated planes reflected in her own. You should get out on your bike more often, go to the club at the pool, make more friends. You can bring them home if you like. Why don't you bring them home? I survived at school by resisting the pack, never answering in class, getting the top marks silently, secretly. They only picked on me once. A group of them, in the lavatory. I knew who the ringleader was. I never answered their taunts. I just waited, waited for him to make his move. Then I stabbed his hand with a compass. After that they called me Sparafucile, after the assassin in the comic. But they left me alone.

What filled my life was books, books, books. I read my way across great plains of irrelevant trivia, occasionally striking gold. I preferred fantastic Empire Stories to Tolkien or *Star Wars*. I wanted to read about the adventures of brave English heroes, in khaki shorts, pushing through undergrowth filled with snakes, followed by lines of native bearers, uncovering secret caves with gleaming, precious seams of stone. I liked suspense. I also liked the big-breasted black women, who had magic knowledge and unbounded power at their fingertips, but who were always left regretfully in Africa to inherit their father's kingdoms. The English heroes of Empire returned to the quiet, damp lawns, pale sunshine, croquet and daisies, to houses smelling of roses and lavender, to quiet women in white dresses and the discreet clink of crockery in the distance. The huge black breasts of the lost African queens were an initiation ritual, a ravine traversed in the mind and only dimly remembered in all their uneventful lives to come.

*

It was October. My bedroom was at the top of the house, tucked into the peeling white gable. I hung damp towels on the radiator under the window and looked out down the street. Our front garden was overgrown with browning dying buddleia, a dwarf conifer which, unbidden, had magnified itself to giant size, a camellia sheltered in the lee of the porch, a hedge of eleagnus which had never flourished and remained in a stunted condition of disappointment. The banks of evergreen darkened the bay window of the sitting room. The only point from which the entire, quiet, suburban street was visible was my bedroom window. There was never anything to see. I could always hear the distant ebb and flow of shrieking children. I never saw them. The husbands came home every weekday after dark, washed their cars on fine Sundays, even in the winter if there was no frost. The neighbours marched their dogs forth to the commons. A flicker of gorse marked the end of cultivated domesticity over a hundred yards away. The view never, never changed.

It began in October. I was perched in my bedroom translating French for my S-level exams. I was the only candidate. One of the passages was very mysterious.

> *J'appelle* Triangle arithmétique, *une figure dont la con-struction est telle. Je mène d'un point quelconque, G, deux lignes perpendiculaires l'une à l'autre, GV, GL, dans chacune desquelles je prends tant que je veux de parties égales et continue, à commencer par G que je nomme 1, 2, 3, etc; et ces nombres sont* les exposants *des divisions des lignes.*

> I have named the following construction the Arithmetical Triangle. From a random point, G, let there be two perpendicular lines, GV, GL from each of which I take equal sections and continue, beginning with G, which I call 1, 2, 3, etc and these numbers are the 'exposants' of the divisions of the lines.

I ceased to translate. Idly, I began to draw the mathematical figure described in the text. Then I heard her voice, calling, calling from the bottom of the stairs. I did not move. She was going out. I shouted back, a noncommittal assent. I heard the door clamp shut behind her. Then, automatically, I rose and stood at the window looking down the street. She appeared in the fading grey light beyond the shadows of the evergreens. The orange lamps were already shimmering in the dimness. Her boots rapped the concrete. She never carried a handbag. I saw her hair, bobbed short like a 1920s good-time girl, swinging gently in the orange glare. I raised my hand to my own head. I imagined her hair in my hands. She walked past her own car, peering briefly into the back seat. Then she looked up and quickened her stride. I followed the line of her gaze. From the angle of the window I was secure at the apex of the triangle, watching her flicker across the void, converging on the obscure point, fixed, unseen. There was a slight movement, a hand descending. And my gaze came to rest on the figure in the coming dark.

I saw the other man for the first time. He leaned against a heavy black car, a panzer with giant rutted wheels, bull bars and special plates. At first I could make no sense at all of the male shape, and understood only details, a loose black suit, very short grey hair, it shone slightly, a man like any other man, larger perhaps, no, much larger, I can see that now as he moves, a barrel chest, a heavy step as he turns to gaze at the woman coming. Then he looks up. He is clean-shaven, fifty years old, maybe more. His face is heavy, white, as if he is wearing an actor's mask. I am too far away to see his eyes. Then he raises his hand to his lips. He is smoking. So this is the man whose smell engulfs her body. This is the man, whose hands, reeking of nicotine, enclose hers. This is the man whose voice displaces hers, drowns her out. This is the man whose outline bulks in the doorway. This is the man whose weight crushes her ribs. This is the man who opens her secrets. This is the man she loves.

> *Ensuite je joins les points de la première division qui sont dans chacune des deux lignes par une autre ligne qui forme un triangle dont elle est* la base.
>
> Then I join the points of the first division which are in each of the two lines by another line which forms the base of the triangle.

I crumbled over the French translation. I knew I was going to be sick, a hot wave of acid rose up from my stomach. But when I reached the lavatory nothing came, just raw waves of wretchedness. I sat there gripping the bowl that I had carefully cleaned earlier in the day, feeling lonely and cold.

She came home late that night, smelling of cigarettes.

I knew I would always remember that night as the first sighting. It was October. I was eighteen. I had never been separated from her. I had never left home.

*

It was a great mystery to me why this huge, heavy man with the black car was never introduced. I had a fairly clear memory of her other lovers and of the friends who appeared on rare occasions. She always brought them home. Indeed, I had the distinct impression that I was the acid test they had to pass. My inspection was a sort of initiation ritual. She was proud of me. She said so. She boasted how clever I was. If I liked the look of her companions, and she never misread my unspoken judgements, they were warmly welcomed through the external foliage and over the threshold. Usually, I did like them, although I persuaded myself that I had been wary of the man with the butterfly tattoo. She had no very close friends outside the Amazonian triangle. When she went out, it was either to attend public functions or to do something – eat, discuss, raise money – with a group. No one took precedence over me. She held others at a distance. But she used to tell me about her work, her fears, her plans. Like all children confronting adult confidences, I didn't always understand what she said, but I hoarded every word. I was intensely jealous of our quiet evenings snuggled together, half asleep, in front of an unsuitably violent thriller on the television. We were like a comfortably married pair, confident of each other's silences, weaknesses and rhythms. Apart from the great mystery of my origins and my alienated grandparents, I had never been aware of anything hidden, unspoken, taboo. So why did this man remain her open, but unacknowledged secret? If I had wanted to raise the matter I would have had to make a scene. She gave me no opportunity to ask.

I no longer had to be in school every day. Sometimes I came home early in the afternoon, smelling the fumes of coal fires already lit, hanging in the damp air. If she was still at college I listened to the messages on her answerphone. Her French friends of frequent phone calls and illegible postcards, ringing from the rooms dark with woodsmoke, antiques, and dim, ancestral memories of generations and generations.

'Ecoute, Isobel – c'est moi, Françoise. Tu me rappelles? J'ai déjà des idées pour Noël. Bisous, bisous à toi et Toby . . .'

The woman at the gallery who exhibited her work, and occasionally sold giant canvases for thousands, sharp-toothed, aggressive, much criticized by Aunt Luce: *'I may have a lead on that gallery in Cologne. After that huge success in Munich we mustn't let Germany go off the boil . . . call me back asap . . .'*

Aunt Luce herself, resplendent, confident, on the crest of another huge financial connection: *'Can you both come to dinner next Saturday? Let me know. Liberty and I are definitely off to New York at the beginning of November. It's all fixed and I can't wait to tell you . . .'*

. . . and at last, the voice I had waited to hear, feared to hear recorded, fixed, implicated in demand. *'Hello,'* – a pause, he doesn't say her name – *'I'm still in the lab . . .'*

He's a scientist, then. Or a doctor? A pathologist? A coroner? What laboratory? Where? A hospital? A research institute, a university? Where? Does he live here? Or in London?

'I'm here till eight. Call me.'

Instinctively, I look at my watch. It is nearly three. She is not here. She will not be back until after six. Will she listen to the messages immediately? Usually she never does. Has she started doing that, hoping to hear him? Does he ring her at work? When she hears his voice, will she ring him back at once? 07710 283 180. This is his mobile number. I have neither his address nor his name. I have no concrete information. I do not hesitate. I sit down on the floor beside the phone, listening to the sizzle of the rewinding tape, watching the red light winking steadily, fluttering through her book of numbers, addresses. I have never done this before. She is not methodical. She writes new names on empty pages, any empty page, regardless of the alphabetical letters embossed on the serrated edge.

There is no detectable pattern in her collection of names, numbers, addresses. It is quite arbitrary, slapped down at any angle. Here are the names of people I do not know, have never seen. I have never been interested before. Some names are crossed out, written again elsewhere, but still not under the apparently correct letter. There are numbers floating free, without locations or identities. Some have initials attached to them. I stare at blank initials, which hide everything, even the sex. It must be an institute, a hospital. I search the entire book for official addresses. I note the London numbers, which have no names attached. In desperation, for it is now nearly four o'clock, I ring one of these at random. It is a dry-cleaning service, impatient to know another number, the number on my green ticket, without which they can tell me nothing. Coat, jacket, trousers? What make? What colour? In despair I give up. I lean against the wall. Then listen to the tape again.

The voice is steady, confident, unhurried. This is some-one who is not afraid, neither of the answerphone nor of the tape. But, I realize this on the third hearing, from the question implicit in his tone, he had expected her to be there. He had missed her. Just missed her? When had he rung? He doesn't say. And our answerphone doesn't record the time of the messages. So she knows he would ring? Has he rung often before? Why didn't I know? Why wasn't I told? The boy on the floor, leaning against the comfort-able tattered wallpaper of the hallway, is very near to tears. Obscurely, I feel shut out and betrayed. The prickle of tears begins at the back of my eyes, then slithers on down my face. The woman I love is slipping away. I no longer know her. She is no longer mine.

I raise my hand to the rewind button. The answering

machine is switched off. The phone suddenly rings. I jump backward, discovered, appalled. I stare at the clattering, vibrating phone, incapable of touching it again. I am absolutely certain that it is her lover, that vast, obscure and crushing presence, invisible, all-seeing, who is waiting, smirking with contempt on the other end. It rings and rings. I cower beside it, enraged and hysterical. Suddenly it is all over.

I spent the rest of that afternoon grappling with an unseen from a Greek treatise on mathematics. The language of mathematics is biblical. Let A be equal to B. Let there be light. I found myself writing like the scribes, translating the prophets. It was a language of power. Henceforth the necessary characteristics of an axiom are: (i) That it should be self-evident; that its truth should be immediately accepted without proof. (ii) That it should be fundamental; that is, that its truth should not be derivable from any other truth more simple than itself. (iii) That it should supply a basis for the establishment of further truths. An axiom then, is a self-evident truth, which neither requires nor is capable of proof, but which serves as a foundation for further reasoning. I sat up, awash with a gust of clarity. The language of mathematics is very beautiful. My mother loves another man.

I hear the door bang behind her. She has seen my bicycle, my new bicycle, the one she bought for my eighteenth birthday, shoved inside the gate. She shouts up the stairs. I do not reply. She goes into the kitchen. She turns on the radio. It is well after six. I hear the news headlines, floating up the landing. She opens the fridge. I hear the plastic rattle of the crisper. Electric with tension, I go down the staircase. All the bronze stair-rods are green with iron oxide, this banister loose, shaking, the carpet worn to brown threads. I see the world too close, as if I had swallowed hallucinogenic drugs. She pauses, smiling in the kitchen doorway, her old, habitual, generous wide smile, full of pleasure to see me. I am well above her height now, next year I will be taller still. Her blonde straight hair, my own is the same, swings as she turns to fling the courgettes into the sink. I cannot take my eyes off the red winking light on the answerphone in the hallway. The number four glints steadily. Four messages. But she is asking about my mathematics homework. She is telling me about another argument with her head of department about the studio budget. She is opening a bottle of mineral water, she is handing me the garlic, the one sharp knife we still possess and the chopping board. She hasn't even looked at the answerphone. She doesn't care.

Like a murderer, convinced that the corpse will be discovered any minute, my gaze is fixed on the glittering, revelatory red light.

In the midst of a quite different story she suddenly asks if there were any calls. No, I didn't take any, but there were messages left on the machine. I cut the garlic, which is stinging my bitten cuticles, into tiny unsuitable quadrilaterals. She adds mixed dried herbs from a plastic sachet, gives the courgettes one more stir then bounds off down the hall. Why do you seem so young? You aren't old enough to be my mother. The radio is still on, so she turns up the sound on the tape. All the voices to which I have listened, again and again, crackle and echo in the steam. I stand there, staring into the filthy sink. The French gutturals, the gallery owner's twang, Aunt Luce's breezy chatter, and then the pause, before that last voice begins, firm, unhurried, confident.

'I'm here till eight. Call me.'

She is still smiling as she races for the courgettes. It's OK. Nothing urgent. As she slithers past me, pressed against the table, I catch the unmistakable, incriminating, pungent stench of cigarettes.

2
LABORATORY

'Toby! Can you come downstairs for a moment? One of my friends is here and I'd like you to meet him.'

I was practically a recluse. At school I had pitched camp in the library and risked the accusations of 'teacher's fucking arse-lick'. I didn't stop working, but I had started to cut lessons. This enhanced my reputation with the back of the class. My form tutor threatened to write to my mother. I said, go ahead, do it. It was the first time I had been openly rude to one of my teachers. She stopped dead in the corridor and stared at me. I sneered slightly and bolted for home. My moment of rebellion had come at last. But I wasn't waiting for Iso when she came back from college. I was no longer downstairs, patrolling the corridors and the kitchen, watching out for her. I had retreated to my attic. And she had not noticed. I stood up carefully. Even her voice made me feel resentful, irritated.

'Toby! Did you hear me? Come down.'

She was coming up the stairs. The figure behind her loomed in the dark at the bottom. His outline suggested the Minotaur, metamorphosed completely into man, irre-futably male, yet unequivocally bestial. She dwindled into pathos beside him. How do you do died on my lips. The man was very, very still. I felt him watching me creep down the staircase, reading my body rather than my face. My mother took my arm and led me down to him as if I was a virgin bride. Then he reached out, one huge white hand, and took mine in his. His hand felt like that of a reptile, cool, smooth, dry. I returned the handshake, transfixed with curiosity, fascination and alarm. He was wearing at least three gold rings. I said, 'You're the scientist.'

The man dropped his hand and flicked the ash on his cigarette into her brass umbrella stand.

'That's right,' he said.

I felt like a justified spy. It was the same slow, firm voice that I had heard on the tape. I tried to take him in at once. I couldn't. There was too much of him there. He had already occupied too much of me. I gaze into this man's hooded eyes. His gaze is steady, pale and grey. He has the eyes of a wolf. The curtain has gone up on the action. The play can begin.

But what was my role? My lines? Who was waiting in the wings, following the text, ready to prompt me now? I stood tongue-tied, gazing at the Minotaur, who returned my stare in the shadow of the dim staircase, unhurried, amused. I perceived the compliment, and blushed. He thinks I'm like her. He thinks that I too am beautiful. I drew myself up straighter. I know who you are. I have seen you before. But this is the first time that you see me. This man does not care. I watch the great hand rising, the cigarette gently clenched. This is how a man looks at a girl he owns, her face, her thighs, her throat. His gaze is slow, obscene.

But the moment passed. My mother is talking. She is bored, wants to go out. She is utterly unworried by our first charged glares at one another.

'We're going out, sweetheart. Do you mind? There's still some chicken from last night in the fridge. Just heat it up. Nothing but yoghurt for pudding.'

She is grappling with her coat. He doesn't help her.

'I haven't even introduced you. This is Roehm. We've known each other since God knows when. How did you find out that he was a scientist? Did I tell you? I don't think I did tell you. Can you answer the phone? Your aunt might be back. She left a message yesterday. I rang from work but she was out and Liberty had no idea. If she does ring tell her that tomorrow is fine . . .'

She is combing her hair. She is the Lorelei, her siren power bobbed. She is diminished beside this man.

'You'd like to go, wouldn't you? It won't interfere with your homework. You've got bags of time over the weekend and anyway you don't go out enough. Sometimes I wonder what on earth you do up there.'

She flashed her smile of intimate complicity at my reflection in the mirror, littered with shadows.

'Luce is off to New York in November and won't be back until a bit before Christmas. Did I tell you? She's got a new contract. It's wonderful news . . .'

Now she is leaning up the stairs to kiss me. I bend down towards her. The huge man she has called Roehm stands absolutely still, sinister, unhurried. I feel compromised and angered by his size, his gaze. It is as if he absorbs all the light around him. Sweat gathers in my armpits, my fingers are chilly. In the empty spaces of the darkening house the central heating clicks on, the gas thuds alight. In this man's presence nothing seems natural between my mother and myself.

I formulated a curious sentence in my mind, each word carved and precise. This man is my mother's lover. And then there it was, engraved on the murky wallpaper behind his dense black presence, at once so enthralling and so monstrous. This man is my mother's lover. I tried to make sense of the triangle we formed in the hallway. There she stands, combing her hair and watching me, not herself, in the mirror. Roehm stands before the sentence I have written on the wall. The sentence remains, fixed, accusatory, but without concrete meaning and suddenly repeating itself without end. This man, this man.

'Turned to stone, have you?'

Here is her warm breath on my cheek, loving, chiding, relaxed. This is no big deal for her. They are going out. I have to eat the chicken, answer the phone. I have no lines to speak. But I have to walk about the stage.

Then Roehm speaks, transforming the temperature of the air around him.

'I'm sorry that you aren't coming with us tonight. I'll ring you next week.'

My mother is watching him, smiling. It is as if he is making an improper assignation in public, disregarding her. She doesn't see it that way. She is nodding, grinning. Her lover is making an effort. He has acknowledged her son. But she is surprised. It's too soon. She wouldn't have suggested this. Nevertheless, she is determined to be pleased. Roehm nods, offhand. She bounds out in front of him. The porch door crunches shut and I am left sitting on the bottom step of the stairs in the dingy light from the last bulb left that still works.

The first meeting was over. I found that I was shaking slightly. I began to finger my own emotions, to turn them over and look at the unpatterned side, as if they had been rare carpets. I was angry, insecure, obscurely humiliated. But why? The scene had passed off in a matter of minutes. I had looked into this man's face. I now knew who he was and I would know him again. But what was it that

I felt? With her, it was simple. A peaceful steady torrent of demand. I love, I need, I want. Give, give, give. This man's sexual presence, obtrusive, peculiar, still lurked in the empty shadow of the stairs.

I sat looking at jealousy, naming the emotion for the first time. I had been excluded, given second place. This was the meaning of jealousy. I was being given Iago's job, 'and I – his Lordship's ancient'. What will happen to the three of us? Why are there three? I turned the tarot cards over in my mind, seeing, again and again, not my mother whom I had expected to see, but this man's face. Then I learned something, sudden and peculiar. I was not jealous of the Minotaur's grasp upon my mother's body. I was jealous for myself. Why have you chosen her, and not me? I wanted her place.

Was this jealousy? I could not decipher the unpatterned side of things.

I turned back to look at Roehm's promise: *I'll ring you next week*. It was Friday night. A desert plain of homework unfurled before me. Two days of waiting and saying nothing. What if he didn't ring on Monday? I was at school in the mornings, on Monday I would be home by twelve. Next week suddenly became five, possibly even six days of suspended time. I rushed up the stairs and slammed the door. My Stratford poster of *The Taming of the Shrew* with Katarina pushing a tiny pink Fiat in her muddy wedding dress shivered slightly in its frame.

My room now appeared before me like an adolescent pit of discarded identities. There were the old pop posters, plastic *Star Wars* models, even a one-eyed bear lolling in the corner on the bottom shelf. I sat on the bed, pulling my duvet around me, trying to imagine my mother making love to the man she called Roehm. Everything I knew about sex had been gleaned in the boys' lavatory at school, both from the walls and from the passing inmates. The underground lavatory was the theatre for assiduous masturbation sessions in which I had never taken part out of fear that my prick would not be sufficiently admired to gain admittance to the inner circle. But what I learned in the lower depths was confirmed by one or two very strange sites on the Internet. If all I had seen was true, then I couldn't make sense of the difference in size between my mother and her lover. He would cover her like a bull. I felt a gust of nausea sweeping up my gullet.

I threw the duvet aside and sat down in front of my computer. The screen-save goldfish wobbled past, bubbles rising from their stupid mouths.

Press Return.
Microsoft Internet Explorer.
Return to Main Menu.
Wordsearch. http://www.whoswho.com.
Enter name.
How does he spell his name?
R-H-E-R-M?
R-E-R-M?
R-Ö-H-M?
R-O-E-H-M?
Enter name.
Searching.

In fact I had no idea how his name was written. *Oh God, there's pages of them.* It was like searching the jungle in the dark. I decided to look at the ones that sounded convincingly Germanic. I was puzzled by his accent. He spoke perfect English, but was obviously foreign.

RÖHM, Ernst
ROHMER, Eric
ROEHM, Gustave

Here goes.

RÖHM, Ernst (1887–1934) Hitler's SA Chief of Staff in the early 1930s. 1906 Maximilian Grammar School-Abitur. Fought in the First World War. Wounded three times. Promoted to rank of Captain in 1917. General Staff in 1918. Disillusionment with post-war society, Treaty of Versailles, etc. Spring 1919, Röhm joined the Freikorps Epp. Supporter of right-wing parliamentary and extreme nationalist organizations in Bavaria. German Workers' Party. First meeting with Hitler, 1920. NSDAP.

What's that? Must be the Nazis.

Autumn 1923, Beer Hall Putsch.

Why'd they try to take over a beer hall?

Röhm's dismissal from the army and a 15-month jail sentence. Release 1st April 1924. Hitler still in prison. Orders Röhm to form the SA, April 1925. He withdraws from the NSDAP and from active politics. Military adviser in Bolivia from 1928 until 1930.

They're always finding elderly Nazis in South America.

September 1930 Reichstag Elections. Hitler recalls Röhm as SA Chief of Staff from 1st January 1931. SA attracts 800,000 members in 2 years. Street terror and propaganda.

Hitler's thugs, I suppose. We did all this for GCSE History. Can't remember the beer hall business. I expect it's crucial.

Röhm's ambition: the SA as a nucleus for a people's army. Hitler consolidates his power in the state. Röhm's homosexual circle and their excesses. Click here for detailed information.

39

Ah, all this is coming back to me. But Hitler knew all along that Röhm was homosexual. It was only used as an excuse to get rid of him. Anyway, there's something seriously queer about the Nazis, even our English teacher said so. Does this interest me? Yes, it does rather.
Scroll down.

> June, 1934. 'Night of the Long Knives': Röhm was arrested and, after refusing an invitation to commit suicide, shot dead in Munich's Stadelheim prison on 1st July 1934 by the SS.

So much for Röhm. But imagine issuing invitations for suicide. We are having a suicide party tonight. Please wear appropriate clothing and bring your own weapons. Next?

> ROHMER, Eric (1920—) French film director.

Can't be right? My Night at Maud's, Claire's Knee? Knee? None of this is relevant.

> EARLY CAREER / BIBLIOGRAPHY / ON-LINE INTERVIEWS / SUMMARIES OF HIS FILMS: Delicate interpretation of the novella by Heinrich von Kleist *Die Marquise von O.* Directed by Eric Rohmer who also wrote the screenplay (1975) Janus Artemis Films du Losange & United Artists Starring Edith Clever and Bruno Ganz, 102 minutes.

Kleist? Oh yes, we're doing one of his plays for A-level. I didn't know he wrote short stories. He's difficult. Feels very modern. Not nineteenth century at all. Thomas Mann admired his style. That's a bad sign.

> Aristocratic Marquise von O. finds herself pregnant but retains no memory of ever having been seduced. She is repudiated by her family. Advertises for the father of her child.

Advertises? That's as bad as issuing suicide invitations.

Distraught, handsome army officer arrives. She refuses to
speak to him. Her final capitulation. 'Why did you repulse
me as if I were the devil?' 'Because when you first came to
me, I took you for an angel.'

This is nothing but Prussians with crazy codes of honour.

Latest project . . .

Scroll down.

ROEHM, Gustave (1755–1786) eighteenth-century Swiss
botanist. Alpine explorer. Lost during the first successful ascent of Mont Blanc. Jacques Balmat, mountaineer
and crystal-hunter, Michel-Gabriel Paccard, native of
Chamonix and the region's first physician together with
Gustave Roehm decided to find a route to the summit
of Mont Blanc. On the afternoon of 7th August 1786,
they departed from La Prieuré in the valley, bivouacked
between two rocks at the top of the Montagne de la Côte
and began their attempt on the summit at 4 am the next
day. Their progress crossing the glacier was followed by
telescope. Dr Paccard lost his hat on top of the Rochers
Rouge. They attacked the final slope at 6.12 pm and
reached the summit at 6.23. They took some measure-
ments and began the descent at 6.57 pm. Gustave Roehm
was lost in one of the crevasses on the Grand Plateau. His
body was never recovered. Balmat returned to La Prieuré
the following day leading Paccard, who was snowblind,
by the hand.

Roehm's research on glaciology and his development
with his friend Horace-Bénédict de Saussure of such meas-
uring instruments as the hair hygrometer had considerable
influence on Alpine exploration in the period.

FURTHER READING: Roehm, Gustave, *Alpine Plants:*

Their Varieties and Habitats. Abridged and translated by Katherine Holroyd, Cambridge University Press, 1977 (Original Edition, 1782, 2 vols)

NEXT PAGE Click here to continue.

It's not worth it. Nazis, film directors and a man lost in ice. Who is this man she calls Roehm?

*

I climbed back into bed, fully clothed and alarmingly aroused. Why? The search had yielded nothing. I was no closer to finding out who Roehm was. I lay flat on my stomach until the heat had passed away. I was forced to do the one thing I found difficult. I was forced to wait.

*

I monitored every phone call that came in and went out of the house. This was easy to do. The phone had an illuminated green panel, which gave the last number that had called. But the days came and went. He never rang. Luce was constantly in touch, full of her latest, greatest coup. Her textile designs had been chosen, more or less en masse, by an Anglo-French *maison de coûture*, Lewis and Gautrin. The deal was through. The entire spring collection would be awash with her colours. The show was being presented, first in Paris, then in London and finally in New York. We were all going to be millionaires. I heard my mother laughing in the hallway, then moving away as she fiddled in the studio, cradling the phone on her shoulder.

Roehm did not ring. Neither her nor me.

On Thursday she was late back. I had cooked dinner for both of us and eaten mine. I didn't get up when she came into the sitting room, where I was sunk into the sofa, eating crisps and watching mindless murders on the television.

'Hello, darling. Mmmmm, gross. Crisps.' She swallowed a handful and sat down on my right leg.

'Get off. You're crushing me.'

'Sorry.' She watched the car chase and the shoot-out. Her right breast hung across my line of vision, cutting off half the screen.

'Move. I can't see.'

'Aren't we irritable?'

She pushed me over and lay down beside me. She smelt of turps and linseed oil, but not of cigarettes. I put my arm around her, longing to touch her breast. I had never touched a woman's breast. Now that she was with Roehm it was easier to look at her simply as a woman and not as my mother. I did some sums, lying there with her in my arms. I was eighteen. She was thirty-three. It was as if the gap between us had suddenly, dramatically narrowed. She took another handful of crisps and stuffed them into her mouth. I leaned over and kissed her ear.

'My sweet love, am I forgiven for missing supper?'

I laid my head on her shoulder and watched her right nipple, swollen and rising beneath the wool. Then the phone rang. She rolled onto the floor, scattering crisps, and sauntered into the hall. It was eleven twenty on Thursday night. She came back into the room, her eyes still fixed on the television.

'It's Roehm. For you.'

My mouth went dry. She took my place on the sofa and seized the packet of crisps.

'Hello.'

There was a long pause at the other end as if he had already vanished.

'Hello?' I said again.

'Would tomorrow suit you?' The same cool, slow voice, disengaged, indifferent.

'Yes.'

'Good. Meet me at seven thirty in the Earl of Rochester, Old Compton Street. Your mother knows where that is. She tells me that you like the food in L'Escargot.'

'Yeah. I do. OK.'

'Fine. See you tomorrow, then.'

Click. Hummmmm. Roehm disappeared. I put the phone back in its cradle and bit my lip. When I looked around the door I saw that she had settled down into the hollow I had left and eaten all the crisps. She scrunched the empty bag, disappointed.

'Have we got any more?' She looked up, childish, demanding.

'I'll go and see. You haven't eaten any supper, have you?'

'No.'

I went off to light the gas, shaking my head free of her image. She didn't ask what I had arranged with Roehm. I wanted to tell her, to boast. She never gave me an opening.

*

Old Compton Street was not like any other street in Soho. I realized, with a flash of curiosity and panic, as I looked into the video store, that this was London's gay ghetto. It was a cold wet night, but the street was illuminated, ready, en fête. All the red bulbs flashed and glared around a bevy of leather men suggestively wielding chains and whips on cover after cover of the lurid, empty boxes. There were one or two videos with images of women, some flaunting buttocks and breasts, others wearing uniforms reminiscent of the Waffen SS. I looked inside. A man bristling with silver jewellery and tattoos smiled at my hesitation.

'Hi there,' he said, 'can I help you?'

I fled down the road, looking for the pub. It was an ordinary Victorian pub with stained glass and tiles. Inside the music was turned down to levels that made conversation possible. All the men behind the bar wore white T-shirts and had shaved heads. Every single face turned towards me when I came in; the polished bar reflected my reddening cheeks. I noticed my school scarf with a twinge of horror. I looked like a boy in one of Gide's novels, much too young and unwittingly asking for it. There was no sign of Roehm.

'Yes, darling? What can I get for you?'

The man behind the bar was brisk and knowing. He wasn't young. There were very few young men in the pub. I muttered, 'A half of Flowers.' The beer appeared before me. I had intended to guzzle it down and then wait outside, but he vanished away to serve someone else while I was still fumbling for the money. I was completely unnerved by the fact that the men didn't just take you in and look away as locals do when you enter their strange, flyblown cafes. A good many of them just went on staring. I leaned on the bar, mortified. I couldn't face the mirror and so began reading the cocktail suggestions and the notices about Happy Hour. A man in a checked shirt and leather trousers with thongs up the sides caught my elbow as he pushed past.

'Sorry, love.'

He turned sideways and smiled. He had a heavy florid face and a wide smile.

'New girl here, aren't you?'

I nodded, turning even redder. It seemed to me that

everyone was listening and I was too self-conscious to speak.

'What's your name?' He settled onto the stool beside me.

'Toby.'

'You on your own?'

'No. Well, sort of . . . I'm waiting for someone.'

He gave me an amused, private smile. But he was neither threatening nor unfriendly. I began to relax.

'I see.'

He paused, smiled again.

'Maybe I'm the man you've been waiting for?'

I was terribly serious. I took everything seriously. While it was happening I didn't even realize that I was being picked up.

'I don't think so. He's called Roehm.'

My companion burst out laughing.

'Well, at least you know his name already.'

I felt another rush of panic and tried to catch the barman's eye. I still hadn't paid. The red-checked man read my mind.

'I've already bought you that one. Drink up and let me buy you another.' He turned back to the bar and waved to the nearest white T-shirted tattooed arm and shaved head. I was suddenly aware of Roehm standing behind me. The red-checked shirt had seen him first.

'Whoops. Here's your date. Looks like Big Daddy's here.'

'Good evening.'

Roehm simply occupied all the space around us. There he was, like a Zeppelin slowly inflating.

'Just keeping your seat warm for you. And Toby entertained.'

The two men actually shook hands, meeting each other's

eyes. Both were unworried and calm. Someone shut the outer door and the cold dark gust which had licked in behind Roehm settled about him.

'We've met, haven't we?' said the man who had been chatting me up, but had never given me his name.

'Yes,' said Roehm, 'we have. I hope we'll meet again.'

'Oh, we shall. I'll see to that.'

The stranger stroked my cheek reassuringly as if I was a nervous horse, then slipped away. I had no time to draw back or speak. I was left gazing into Roehm's heavy white face and grey eyes. He looked patient and amused. He didn't say anything. I gulped down my beer and stared. He was wearing a huge leather trenchcoat with padded shoulders, which made him even larger than he actually was.

'Are you hungry?' he asked at last.

'Yes. I think so.'

'Come, then.'

Roehm nodded to the bar staff, one of whom saluted, and then strolled out of the Earl of Rochester. I trailed calong behind him, like a tug attached to an Atlantic cruiser. On the street, groups of men gathered and talked, their breath forming smoky gusts in the frosty air. The tarmac glittered beneath their feet as if they were walking in pools of red and gold. Roehm waited for me to catch up.

'Did you really know that man?'

'Yes. After a fashion. We met in that club over there.'

I saw a blue neon sign curved over a tacky black doorway.

VERITABLE CUIR

MEN ONLY

I stood, open-mouthed with surprise, puzzled by the name in French. Then I realized that it was a joke. Roehm smiled slightly, enjoying my discomfort.

'I'll take you one day. You're over eighteen. You'd be quite a hit.'

He made it sound like a day trip to the Asterix theme park. I didn't like Roehm's smile. His smile, private, ambiguous, amused, was the perfect echo of the smile on the face of the man we had left behind. I was angry and confused. If Roehm was queer then what was he doing with my mother? If she knew he was queer then what was she doing with him? I sank into a cantankerous adolescent silence. I hated ambiguity, indecision and muddles, including those of my own making. I had wanted to find out who this man was, but he appeared to be a dozen different things. The bizarre thought actually crossed my mind: he's a completely unsuitable candidate to be my stepfather. Neither Luce nor the social services would give their approval.

Roehm coasted easily through the stealthy narrow alleys. I could smell burning fat and greasy pots; the odours rushed out from the lighted kitchen doorways. A cook leaned against the dustbins. I could just see a pile of plates and pans, stacked in the chaos behind him. Roehm paused and asked him for a light. While he leaned forward, concentrating on the flame, I stared at Roehm's illuminated face behind the huge cupped hand. There was an odd fluidity in his heavy features, as if there were no bones beneath the skin. I stared at his rings. He wore a gold signet ring on the third finger of his right hand. The emblem was blurred. The next ring had a pattern of interlocking leaves, also rubbed and worn. The third was a wedding ring, perfectly plain, made of reddish old gold. He looked into my eyes, spread out his hand and extended it towards me.

'They're family rings. I wear them all the time, so that I don't lose them. Even in the lab. If I need to, I wear gloves.'

It seemed amazing that he actually had a family of any

kind. He indicated the signet ring with the obliterated crest and laughed.

'There's our coat of arms. As you can see, we've practically faded into obscurity.'

I peered at his hairless white fingers and the smooth bulk of his hands. Chain-smokers usually have yellowed fingers; Roehm's hands were perfect, white.

'You don't smoke, do you?' He offered me his cigarettes. I shook my head. 'But that's not because your mother won't let you, is it?' Roehm chuckled to himself. He was remembering something. Then he slid his arm through mine, as if we were two girls exchanging confidences. It was a very intimate gesture. I felt like a reluctant courtier, being drawn closer to the monarch and implicated in the royal conspiracies, much against my better judgement. But I did not pull away from him, nor did I resist.

'Look,' said Roehm.

We turned out of the murky back passages and found ourselves in Chinatown. The restaurants were hung with giant red lanterns trailing golden tassels and long comic dragons hanging from the pointed eaves, glimmering red and fierce in the night air. I stared into the bulging eyes and fine painted teeth of the nearest monster.

'It's a festival,' said Roehm.

I drew closer to him and looked up. Above us, like great gleaming moons, the lanterns swarmed, tier upon tier, looming and swaying above the people who pressed past on the road. The smell of gunpowder rose from the pavements. I heard the sharp crack of fireworks let off by children, a sequence of small explosions, random, dangerous. But above the whiplash of firecrackers, the music was techno, a bizarre throbbing pulse, at odds with the lanterns and the soaring dragons.

'We won't eat here,' said Roehm.

He had the art of creating a secure circle around him, as firm and clear as if he had drawn the macrocosm in chalk before him on the gleaming roadway. I felt as if I had acquired a particularly lethal bodyguard who was armed to the teeth beneath his black leather coat and loose suits. Roehm always wore loose clothes so that his exact size and shape remained imprecise. His outline was comfortable, rumpled. He could become larger if he wished; there was room inside his clothes. My arm felt like a twig against the great trunk of his sleeve. He consolidated his hold upon me.

'Come,' said Roehm.

I trotted along beside him, intimidated, bewitched. Suddenly he turned inside an almost invisible doorway, pushing back the leather curtain, and we found ourselves in a hushed French space with no music, smelling of herbs, wine and money. It was a familiar smell. This was where I had come with my mother over a year ago, after the big sales in the gallery in Germany. The head waiter wore evening dress. We were whisked into a corner surrounded by mirrors and art deco coils of green glass. I saw Roehm reflected into infinity, gradually decreasing in size. He took my jacket from my shoulders as if I were a woman, and placed me where he could watch the restaurant and I could only see him. On his way back from the coat stand he paused and peered into the tank, where beautiful speckled fish circulated sadly in a mass of maidenhair weed and pumped oxygen, waiting to be chosen by one of the customers. There were lobsters and giant crayfish waving their pincers and whiskers gently on the bottom. In one corner the crabs were piled one upon the other, like crashed tanks.

Roehm looked back at our table and smiled.

How can I describe his face? He was heavy rather than fat. His cheeks were oddly white, as if he never saw the sun. There were long black hairs in his nostrils, but his skin was smooth and strange, as if he never had to shave. His hair was grey and clipped very short. He smelt of cinnamon and cigarettes. I tried to fix his image in my memory, but something always escaped me.

The menu and the wine list, as I had remembered, were handwritten. I looked around over the crisp white napkins stiffened into bishops' mitres and the array of wine glasses lined up for battle. The waiter removed our plates. Then I noticed that we had come in through a back door, a secret entrance. Behind me was the front of the restaurant with a reception desk and a couple of men in a refrigerated glass box, opening oysters and arranging shellfish on huge tiered platters banked with crushed ice and sliced lemons. Roehm was decrypting the menu. I couldn't understand the handwriting.

'Want any help?' He looked up.

'Yes, I do. You can tell me what all this means. But I also want to know how you met my mother.' This came out more sharply than I had intended, as if I was the *juge d'instruction* beginning my inquiry. Roehm laughed.

'I bought one of her pictures. And I liked it so much that I went back to the gallery and bought another. And then another.'

I listened, open-mouthed. He owned somewhere with walls. He became more and more corporeal before my eyes. Something that had stood, solid and messy in my mother's studio, had been translated into an object on his walls. The thing had undergone a double metamorphosis. To us it had become money, and then, on Roehm's walls, it had become art. He had purchased her work and therefore wanted to meet the artist. This was a twist I had never considered.

'Which ones?' I asked, amazed.

'Do you remember her white paintings? The ice mono-liths. Different textures of white. Huge things, uncanny, vast.' His rings flickered as he drew the paintings in the air. I followed the glowing line of the cigarette. 'Well, I bought eight of those.'

I thought, he must own chateaux, castles with great halls and wide staircases. I didn't say anything, but Roehm added,

'You need a lot of high spaces to show them off.'

'She's doing some more. They sold very well in Germany.'

'I know. That's where I bought them.'

'Oh,' I paused, stared at the menu, 'and you came to find her just because you liked her paintings?'

'That's almost right. I thought I had recognized her in her paintings.'

This was beyond me. How could he recognize someone he had never met? Something was wrong. 'This is Roehm. We've known each other since God knows when.' When? The waiter arrived. Roehm ordered snails for both of us, followed by *salade aux anchois, rôti de porc*, a 1992 burgundy, *un grand Badoit, et un cendrier. 'J'ai le droit de fumer ici? Merci.'* I faltered along behind him. He spoke flawless French with no accent whatsoever.

'How many languages do you speak?'

My interrogation began again. I decided that I was not going to be battered into submission quite so easily.

'As many as you do. And the same ones. My Italian is very rudimentary.'

Roehm then began to ask me about my studies and my reading. We still studied literature at my school. But it was considered an extravagance and was under perpetual threat from the Cuts. I was wary of Roehm's questions. He was very interested in what I had read. But why? At first I was careful, guarded, even monosyllabic. I had learned not to admit to the possession of too much knowledge. It was safer to be ignorant, belligerent and philistine. But Roehm's manner was gentle and encouraging and the wine untied my tongue. He had already read everything I mentioned. His grey eyes and white face appeared to shift and soften. I had been reading Camus. The other students in my A-level French class were all girls, who had disliked *L'Étranger* for its chilly racism and misogyny. They had written angry essays, which got good marks. I went home and read all his other books. I dared not confess to this at school. Only pooftahs liked reading. And so my cautiously held opinions poured out for the first time. I had just read Camus's *Le Premier Homme*. Roehm said he hadn't read that.

'Tell me about it,' said Roehm.

'The manuscript was with him in the car crash when he was killed in 1960. It wasn't published until 1994. I saw his daughter, Catherine Camus, speaking about the book on French television. When we were in the Alps. My mother has friends who have a chalet above Chamonix. She was painting those great white canvases that you bought. Just the small-scale versions. She works them up to the bigger scale later. When she's home. Of course the publication of a new, unknown novel by Camus would be a big thing, a major literary event. But the interviewer didn't really want to talk about literature. He asked the daughter what the great man was like in private life. She looked puzzled and confused and said, "I don't know how to answer that. He was my father. *C'était mon papa.*" I found her simplicity electrifying. She said that Camus's emotional feelings were perhaps more present in this book than any other. She's right. I thought that Camus was, I don't know, a cold writer. He had a ruthless, chilly sort of intellect. Which is always evident in all his books. Even as terrifying a book as *La Peste*. You say you like that one best. I'm surprised. It's a heroic book. And you don't strike me as the sort of person who would go in for heroism.'

Roehm laughed. I pounded on, astounded by my own loquacity.

'I want to read books that make me think, pull me up short, put my life in question. Camus made me think, but he wasn't moving. You don't feel his books. You think about them. But this one made me so sad. Really sad. Sad enough to cry. *Le Premier Homme* is about his childhood in Algeria, his mother, his poor neighbourhood, the life of those times. Like a lost world. There are so many worlds you can never get back. Some worlds you can only find again in memories. He was like me, he was brought up by women in a woman's household. And so he was closer to women. He never had a father, and I didn't either. At least Catherine Camus could remember him. Some of the scenes are so vivid, that I can taste them now: killing the hen for Christmas, the children mixing poisons, the old Arabs in their cafes. They're just ordinary poor lives. But he describes them with such passion. I revised my opinion of Camus as a result of reading that book. I'll read every other account of childhood and test it against what he wrote. It's like a glimpse into his workshop. Or like watching her in the studio. All his notes, sketches, the illegible words in brackets – I loved all the loose ends, the rawness of an unfinished book. It was like touching how he thought, how he worked. Catherine Camus said that he would have edited out all these passionate, personal feelings because he was so private and reserved. Well, if he'd have done that, then I'm glad he never finished the book. As it stands, it's finished. Read it. Tell me what you think.'

'Thank you,' said Roehm, 'I will.'

He never interrupted me, nor patronized me. He had

the listening gift. I gabbled on. Suddenly I wanted to tell him everything I had ever thought or ever known. I began telling him about my hideout in the library at school. About the way I had to hide my books to stop people ripping out the pages. About the thugs in my class who had menaced me because I liked reading, the teachers who were a mixed pack of wolves, some of them as violent as the students they attempted to educate. One of the sports masters was suspended for attacking a pupil. Everyone agreed that knocking that particular child unconscious was the best thing he could have done and at least the teacher was strong enough to protect himself. The parents were summoned, but they never came. My French mistress was very beautiful. She had been threatened by some of the older boys who were wearing Bobby Kennedy masks when they did it. It happened just outside the school. She was unlocking her car. They surrounded her. Jostled her. Pushed her against the wing mirror, so hard that it broke off. Other people were witnesses. Nobody tried to stop them.

'The bitch needs a good fuck.'

'Go on. Give it to her.'

'Fuck the Bitch, Fuck the Bitch.'

'She wants a good big one up her.'

Behind the masks the voices were unrecognizable, but we all knew who they were. The incident was reported in the local paper. Everyone was questioned. No one talked.

The violence which simmered just below the surface of suburbia was generated by boredom and drugs. I never took drugs for the not very creditable reason that everybody else did and I was determined not to belong, but to be different. Everything was on offer in the changing rooms, even crack, at a good price. Periodically there were sudden staff swoops and searches, and some of the fourth-formers, the well-known pushers, were expelled. Drugs were egalitarian and casually crossed all the class bound-aries. Drugs were cool. It was the done thing to be out of your head from time to time. No one regarded drugs as criminal. They were an essential leisure activity. It was a crime to be bookish, clever, a pooftah, or to have a middle-class accent. It was still worse to be black. None of this could be policed, contained or controlled. Sometimes the teachers fell ill, gave up, went home early or absented themselves without notice, if disciplining their classes proved too exhausting and too dangerous. There were numerous cases of arson. Someone started a fire in the bike sheds and it was only the smell of burning rubber which alerted the caretaker. Everything was chained down and locked up. Otherwise it would have been stolen and sold.

Roehm's face shimmered behind a dense cloud of ciga-rette smoke. He listened with absolute attention. He made no comment.

'My school's like a police state where the militia can't really control the underworld. There are more of us than there are of them. They may have more power, but we have more information.'

'And what's your strategy for survival in all this? Apart from the bunker in the library?'

'Well, there are always a few of us who want to work. Doesn't do to sit at the front, though, mid-class is safer. It's OK now that I'm in the sixth. Everything's calmer. I steer clear of the more aggressive gangs. Don't go outside during break. Don't take showers after PE. It's safer to go home filthy. I fought once. I stabbed one of them with a compass. He's still got the scar. But we even talk to each other sometimes now. If they know you'll fight they'll leave you alone. And they realize I'm not a snitch. I didn't say anything after they threatened to rape my French teacher. I vary my route to school. I don't leave my bike in the sheds. I lock it up behind the paper shop. Jess lets me do that. They're Pakis. And I used to do one of his morning rounds when I was younger. Then I help them scrub the graffiti off the shop windows and walls. Sometimes we have to paint it over. You can still see the swastikas, but only very faintly now. I walk the last half-mile or so to school. But I even vary that route. I haven't been beaten up for over two years. There are girl gangs too. But they only pick on other girls.'

'I don't think that your mother knows anything about this.'

'No, she doesn't. I wouldn't tell her. She'd be worried. And then she might get in touch with the school. She thinks you can change things by protesting and making a fuss. That would only make life hell for me. Word gets around. If the parents kick up, the children get done over. I've seen it happen. Anyway, she wouldn't understand. They don't have discipline problems at the college. Everybody's there because they want to be.'

'But she does worry about you. She says you don't appear to have any friends.'

I suddenly resented this. I didn't like her talking about me to Roehm. If I had no friends it was my business.

'I'm OK. I keep busy.'

My bottom lip set into a tight line.

Roehm reached across the table and stroked my face. I drew back at once. We had been in the restaurant for hours, and I was sweating, but his touch was still cool and dry. I felt his rings on my skin, sharp, chilly and cold. He frightened me a little, yet I wanted him to touch me again.

'Don't be angry with her for loving you. She tries not to be possessive.'

I wanted her to be possessive. I gazed at Roehm and suddenly hated him for all the confidences I had poured onto the emptying plates between us. Just because a man listens carefully doesn't mean that you have to gush secrets for hours on end, as if you were sitting in a confessional. He's not my doctor or a psychotherapist. So I got bullied at school. Lots of people get bullied. It's nothing special and I've come out all right. Roehm watched me closely. I realized that he knew what I was thinking.

'Then perhaps we can be friends,' he offered, his voice slow, unhurried.

'Maybe. I don't know.'

I wasn't taking any prisoners. I had said too much already. Roehm threw a bridge across the table towards me.

'Would you like to see where I work? I have to close down one of the experiments.'

We were contemplating the cheese board. My curiosity got the better of me.

'The lab?'

'It's not far.'

'OK.'

It would have been taking a risk to sound excessively enthusiastic. Roehm was too strange a man for me to take any risks.

We left the restaurant in Soho well after ten. Roehm paid in cash. The streets were still bright with voices and music and the air smelt of boiling fat. The Dragon festival, now in full swing, had drawn crowds, musicians, street vendors selling imitation Rolex watches, leather hats and African jewellery. I saw a gaggle of children playing with phosphorescent yo-yos. The glowing yellow circles spun and danced in the dark. Roehm took hold of me again as if I had been arrested and marched me up Charing Cross Road. Some of the shops were still open. Roehm paused to look into Borders Books. There was an exhibition on

Switzerland and the Alps. He pointed out images of the ibex and the chamois.

'We used to hunt them. They're protected species now. That's the summer coat of the chamois. They have a brown stripe down their backs and those dark bands on either side of their muzzles. The hunting lodges had their horns stuck up all over the walls. At one point we hunted them practically to extinction.'

I suddenly realized that this was the longest speech I had ever heard Roehm make.

'You used to hunt?'

'Yes. Disgraceful, isn't it?'

'I don't know.'

'That's what your mother says.'

'Oh, she's very ecological. Where did you hunt?'

'Switzerland. In the mountains.'

'With a gun?'

Roehm laughed. 'Yes, of course. When I was your age I used to set traps too.'

'So you can shoot?'

'To kill. Every time. With all sorts of guns. I grew up in those mountains.' He indicated an Arctic-looking range of ice peaks on the cover of a book about rock-climbing. 'My father used to take me with him on his climbs, when he came back from the war.'

I stood wondering which war he meant. Roehm was absorbed by the display in the window.

'Look. Heinrich Harrer's book, *The White Spider*, *Die Weisse Spinne*. So that's been reprinted. I'll get it for you in German. It's the classic account of the ascent of the Eiger. The North Face. So many people were killed on that face they called it the Mordwand, rather than the Nordwand.'

'When was it climbed?'

'Successfully? In 1938. A joint rope of Austrians and

Germans. Harrer was one of the victorious four. The Nazis exploited their success for publicity purposes. The ascent of the North Face presented Aryan manhood at its zenith. They were congratulated by Hitler. Harrer doesn't mention any of that.'

'How could he avoid it?'

'He just leaves it out. He doesn't tell his reader that he was a member of the SS either. He says other things that are true. Ordinary people don't usually understand mountaineers. They don't understand why we do it in the first place. But the mountains are the most beautiful pure space I have ever known. The rock face, snow, ice, the avalanches and the storms, they bring you face to face with the limits of who you are. You are stripped of all pettiness. The mountain reduces you to simplicity. That's a very liberating thing.'

He stopped.

'Go on,' I said.

Roehm smiled slightly. 'Why are you so fascinated?'

We marched past the YMCA.

I suddenly felt childish and naive. Never in my life had I ever wanted to hunt, shoot or fish. I loathed outdoor sports. I had barely learned to ski. I had never played football for pleasure. In fact I had never done anything that men were supposed to do. I hardly ever went to pubs. I had never had a girlfriend. And so far as our trips to the mountains were concerned, only Liberty actually enjoyed skiing or snowboarding with the French entourage. My mother spent her time walking in the snow, then struggling back to the chalet to paint what she had seen. When we returned from the morning walk I just sat in my mother's room, reading. Luce enjoyed the endless aperitifs and actually drank cocktails at lunchtime. She then settled down to spend the afternoons channel-hopping on satellite television. Her favourite foreign channels were Spain and the United Arab Emirates: Spain because the women paraded about in revealing clothes wiggling their breasts and bottoms in a permanent sensual fit that looked very odd, and the Arab states because they broadcast public prayers and had long stretches of the Koran simply pasted up on the screen. Luce found the koranic script very soothing. She said that an hour or two of the Koran was like having a hot bath and she dozed off in front of the descending scroll. We enjoyed the fresh air and the views. No one had ever felt driven to climb one of the mountains. And no one ever went hunting.

Yet I found it hard to imagine Roehm as part of a milieu that dressed up in furs and strode across cols and glaciers, tracking ibex and chamois. His skin was too perfect, too white, too smooth. He smelt of indoors.

We turned up Gower Street. Now the pavements were empty. Roehm increased his stride. I realized that I was in fact only a head shorter than he and that I could keep pace easily. It was his overall size that diminished me. Beside him I was insubstantial, like a thin thread of ectoplasm, easily dissolved. Roehm squeezed my arm gently, acknowledging my hesitation. He always appeared to know things, without being told, and it was this uncanny intuition, even sympathy, that increased my confidence in him. Everyone loves someone who listens, but the quality of his attention was in itself seductive. He persuaded me that, under his surveillance, I could never come to harm. Yet he was not in himself an altogether safe presence. I felt that no amount of explanation would ever quite tell me who he was. I did not and never would have quite enough information.

'You're not tired? It's just here.'

'No. I want to see where you work.'

It was as if he was presenting me with a gift. We turned suddenly into the side gates of a hospital. The porter on duty simply nodded at Roehm, who produced a set of keys and opened the first door. We strode onto a long out-stretched corridor of polished green linoleum as if we were visiting politicians arriving on the carpet. Now it was the Minotaur who led me on, into the heart of the labyrinth.

Hospitals always smell the same. We could have been anywhere. I followed him past the trolleys heaped with soiled linen and rooms furnished with pinboards and com-puters. The lights were on, the computers were running, the in trays were full and the papers neatly stacked. But there was no sign of the night staff. We saw no one. Wherever we went, the long empty spaces hung before us, antiseptic and void. Roehm suddenly turned down a staircase and we began the long descent, one landing, then another. I heard his shoes clicking like dog's claws on the polished floors. Again, we saw no one. The staircases were deserted. At last we stood before a pair of green double doors. The sign simply said:

UNIVERSITY COLLEGE HOSPITAL
DEPARTMENT OF BIOLOGY
EXPERIMENTAL LABORATORIES
AUTHORIZED PERSONNEL ONLY

And underneath, glowing yellow and black, was the radiation-warning symbol. Roehm used two different keys to unlock the doors. Inside, beyond green barriers, I could hear a dense high-pitched hum. There were no obvious overhead lights, but the space, a vibrating echo of endless low ceilings reaching away into the dark, glowed fluores-cent green. It was unbearably warm and humid. Great glass walls contained swirling funnels of green. My eyes adjusted to the half-dark. I stumbled against the hot pipes, which ran along the bottoms of the huge glass tanks. The floor was damp. Everything smelt of damp ferns and moss, like a tropical forest. I gazed at each plant as we walked past. They appeared to consist of endless varieties of begonia, some speckled, some semi-succulent, others with a deep, furry green sheen on the surface of the leaves. There were leaves shaped like arrowheads or covered in golden spots, and some were huge with arteries spreading out like fingers on an open hand. Nothing flowered. There was nothing in the giant glass tanks but oozing, seething green.

Shouldn't everything be labelled? I looked for labels, but there were none. The smell of wet compost was over-powering. I stripped off my coat, jacket and pullover. There was a humidity gauge in a glass box, running with condensation, the needle tracing a steady purple line across the turning graph paper inside the still, damp world. I heard the timbre of Roehm's shoes change as they hit the surface of the floor. We were in another part of his under-world. He was walking on concrete. And now I could clearly hear the humming throb of the generators, pushing out slabs of wet heat.

'Tropical temperatures. We keep them constant,' said Roehm, fingering more keys as we came to another door. All the keys were for Chubb locks. They looked exactly alike. This time there was a red eye winking above the lock. The door was wired against intruders. I gulped down a viscous cloud of damp air and tasted stale water at the back of my throat and in my lungs.

Inside the second door was a thick dark space. I remained outside in the sweating green while Roehm felt for a light. Before me gleamed a sombre crescent of gold over one desk and the pale blue of a lighted computer swung round to greet us. Something behind glass scuttled and jerked. I couldn't easily make sense of the objects before me. Here is a desk full of papers and computer printouts. Everything on it is connected with work. There are bound reports and a laser printer. There are no photo-graphs. There is a pile of graphs, which have been amended in red pen. There is a book with a German title and many torn scraps of paper marking the place at intervals. There is another humidity gauge. It is almost as hot as the long glass world of green, but not quite. There is more air and a strange smell. We are being watched. The computer displays rows of different coloured figures. There is a telephone covered in Post-it stickers. Something hums, something ceaselessly hums. Everything is floating in tanks, except for this thing. What is it? It has raw chewed branches on which to clamber and sawdust on the floor. It drinks water. What is it? It has a large cage. It has huge eyes encircled with darkness. It is watching, not me, but Roehm.

'That's a ring-tailed lemur.'

Roehm was amused by my startled face. My own imagination had betrayed me. I had assumed that he worked with smoking phials of blood and laser beams, with frightening technology, glittering chrome tubes and robots, but never with living things, not plants and animals. Roehm did not seem to be part of the living world. I had imagined his laboratory as an automated machine, like a car assembly line or an arms factory. Yet all around me living things seethed and scuttled as I approached the cages and glass tanks. There was a faint smell of urine and rotting vegetables. It was unbearably hot. I found myself looking into the single unblinking eye of an iguana. I tugged at my shirt. Roehm settled down to watch the stately process of figures, line after line, marching down the blue screen.

'You've never studied biological sciences, have you?' He gazed calmly at the steady flood of figures.

'Maths, French, German, English. I took my French A-level last summer.' I recited parts of my recently completed

UCAS form and stared back into the horrified eyes of the ring-tailed lemur. I tried to identify some of the animals. Something scrabbled into a hutch. It stank of fresh urine.

'Just rabbits,' said Roehm.

He knew where I was in the laboratory without looking round.

'Do you kill them?'

'Are you involved in the animal rights campaign?'

'My mother is.'

'I know.'

'Does she know what you do?'

'She's never been here. And you know better.'

I surprised myself. A rush of pleasure made my fingers tingle. He had given me something special, a secret shared. The rabbit cowered in his hutch. I addressed the creature's shaking ears.

'Tough luck, punk.'

Roehm laughed out loud behind me.

There are walls of grey cabinets and here each one is labelled. Dates, coded letters. It's like the *X-Files*. Nothing so simple as the alphabet. You'd have to know what you were looking for. Roehm's hand closes over the mouse. I stare at his rings. He has slipped my jacket over the back of his swivel chair. He is still wearing his black leather greatcoat. He is perfectly cool. He is like the salamander. He lives in fire and ice. There is a square white sink, immaculately clean, with long-handled taps, like the ones they have in hospital operating theatres. To the left of the sink stand two waste bins with flip-top lids. One says ORGANIC WASTE. The other just says WASTE FOR SHREDDING. There is a large box of white plastic gloves, each pair individually sealed as if they were food on an aeroplane. The light remains dull, green. I peer into the retreating gloom. The laboratory appears to recede, long lines of shelves, desks, cages, tanks. There is a row of green overalls hanging on pegs. The smell is growing stronger. Further away, beyond the gold crescent on Roehm's desk, I can see more glass tanks with oxygen bubbling up in streams. I dare not venture deeper into his strange kingdom.

Roehm stands up, stretches. All the creatures flee into corners, terrified. Laboratory animals are usually bored, morose, unmoving. But these creatures seem to know that they are all doomed and fear their murderer's every gesture. How do they know that he is going to torture and kill them?

'You do genetics, don't you?'

'In a manner of speaking. Even you must have heard of global warming, Toby.'

It is the first time that he has used my name. I stare back at his huge hands. He has not smoked for over an hour.

'Well, we are experimenting with strains of plants and animal life that will resist intense heat and cold. Living things that can survive in fire and ice.'

He speaks slowly, unhurried.

'We must be ready for either. For the ice, or the fire next time.'

I imagine a vast army of monsters, built like Frankenstein's original creature, all of whom have the same gigantic paranoid eyes of the ring-tailed lemur. Roehm's printer sucks and buzzes in the gloom. He takes each sheet from the tray as it comes out, face up, and folds it away in a leather portfolio, which zips up all round, so that it is sealed.

'Come,' says Roehm, 'let's go.'

But we don't go back. We go on, deeper and deeper into the sweating green gloom. Roehm unlocks and relocks door after door, never hesitating over the identical keys. Here are luminous eels flickering in the oxygenated tanks; some of them glow strangely as we stride past, others dive for their artificial caverns. I gaze at Roehm's heavy, smooth white cheek. He smiles slightly. I am sweating. Everything appears to be afraid of Roehm. We burst through an aluminium grille into the chill and brightness of an underground car park. Roehm relocks the last door behind us. There is nothing written on this door. It could have led to a service unit, a staircase or a lavatory. I look at my watch. It is almost midnight.

'I could catch the last train if we rush.'

'I'll drive you home.'

'It'll take hours.'

'Get in.'

The car was oddly spartan inside. Roehm's choice of food and wine suggested sybaritic wealth on a Roman scale. But he had no extras. No radio, no phone. And the thing made no sound, neither without nor within. We said very little to each other. He drove fast. I scanned the road for dead eels, lemurs, rabbits. London seemed alien, strange. The suburbs dropped away beneath the motorway. When we reached my mother's house Roehm pulled up short of the gate on the far side in the same place where I had first identified the car. We got out and stood next to one another, leaning against the panzer. Roehm was very relaxed. His weight appeared to menace the car. He lit a cigarette. He seemed in no hurry to be gone. I lingered, getting colder. My sensations were obscure. I didn't want to leave him.

'Thanks for the lift. I could have caught the last train.'

'I know. But your mother would have worried.'

She wouldn't even have noticed. She was always late. She had no sense of time.

'I looked up your plates. They're French. 74. That's the Haute-Savoie. Where we go skiing. Where Françoise has her chalet in the mountains.'

Roehm chuckled.

'Oh, you looked that up, did you? Find out anything else?'

'No.'

I blushed, but he wasn't looking at me. He was looking at the house.

'I'm the director of another research institute over there. Near Chamonix. Where you go for your winter holidays.'

'Do you want to come in? She's still up. Her lights are on.'

'No. She's not expecting me.'

It began to rain.

'OK. Well . . . thanks for supper. And for showing me your lab. It was great. Goodnight.'

'Come here, Toby.'

Roehm unhurriedly flicked his cigarette away into the drizzling suburban dark and placed his right hand on my neck. I felt the eerie chill of his rings. His touch was very cold and slow. I had never been so close to him. He smelled of tobacco and cinnamon. His face loomed, white and blank, close to mine. He suddenly appeared to occupy more space than he had done all evening, like a cartoon drawn on an ever larger scale.

'You're very like her,' said Roehm softly.

I didn't move.

'So everyone says.'

Then he kissed me, a soft, cold kiss on my lips. I stood still and frozen, longing for him to take hold of me. But he only smiled slightly, and turned away, nodding his goodnight. I ran across the road and into the house. I didn't hear the car start. I didn't look behind me.

3

BONFIRE

I dreamed about him that night. I saw him in the laboratory, but there were no more walls, no doors, no locked spaces.

He is standing by his illuminated computer in a drenched and streaming torrent of thick green, a sinister vegetable green. The plants rustle and gleam all around him, fresh, succulent and suggestive. There is an evil smell of rotting compost. I look carefully into the shifting, glistening vegetation and see the terrified mass of eyes, dilated, feral, all fixed upon him. I am the only person who is not afraid. Roehm's gaze holds me in thrall. His glare is fertile with intent, but he is waiting, waiting for me to make the first move. I remember his kiss, that stealthy, gentle kiss, the taste of his cigarettes and his cold lips. He is waiting for my permission, my invitation. It is up to me. And in my dream I see myself as if I am two people. And one is pressed, sweating, terrified, against the damp slab of heat and the other, supple, erotic, a boy sure of his power to entice and to possess, reaches out a hand towards this strange and powerful man whose gaze never ebbs, whose attention, predatory and passionate, is all my own. It is my desire that you should come to me, come to me. You who are all to me, call to me. I reach out for you, for your arms, for your cold kisses and your cold, cold, golden love. Give me your cold love and free me from the kingdom of this world, from this endless thriving green. I see myself, erect and untouched, pushing towards him through the ensnaring green. Roehm does not move, but he smiles, eerie, suggestive, ambiguous, triumphant. And then I know that I love this man, that he has come back for me, that he has never forgotten me. It is my desire that you should come for me. And I am unafraid.

I woke in the half-light sweating and trembling, the damp flood of semen drenching the sheet. I sat up feeling sick, and swallowed the stale water left on my desk. As the dream receded I felt dizzy, filthy and ashamed. Roehm had simply kissed me goodnight, yet that was enough to unleash a sombre gust of queer fantasies. I heard the school thugs hissing 'faggot' and shivered. Her bedroom light was still on as I crept down the corridor to the bathroom. I looked at my watch. Not yet 5 a.m. I pushed her door open, just a little.

She had her mattress on the floor with a giant Indian bedspread suspended from the ceiling above, like a rajah's tent. Her nightlight was an illuminated plastic banana, now elderly and peeling, but still operational. She was asleep, her fingers clenched around the book. She had been reading *The Talented Mr Ripley*. The cover illustration was of a handsome young man in an Italian straw hat. I looked down at her sleeping face. Her hair was damp with sweat about her ears, her nightshirt tight across her breasts. I turned off the light. She stirred slightly and the room gradually shifted from black to grey and finally to orange as the streetlights leered through her open curtains. I waited until the darkness had cleared from my eyes, then abandoned her to her own unconscious terrors. I shuffled up the last flight of stairs. My bed smelt of unconsummated sex. The smell was disgusting. I ripped off the sheets and flung them into the corner. Then I pulled my sleeping bag out of the suitcase stowed under the bed and climbed into a blue nylon cocoon. After that I didn't dream again, but slept on, exhausted and inert, until midday.

She had left me a note on the kitchen table.

Gone shopping. Don't forget that we're invited to Luce's tonight. Hope you had a good time with Roehm.

I thought about the eyes of the animals in Roehm's lab and decided not to tell her that I'd been there. There was a Greenpeace protest poster on the back of the kitchen door, which denounced experiments on laboratory animals. I had ceased to notice the tragic rabbit with electrodes riveted to his skull. He had become part of our daily furniture. I now dismissed the creature and her ethics of pity. I would neither betray nor condemn whatever happened in the experimental tanks and the hot green underworld I had unwittingly entered. What Roehm did with his rabbits was his own business.

But she never asked where we had been, what we had done. I prepared a cautious story about the restaurant and Chinatown, but was never required to stand centre stage and deliver the script. She brushed me off with a handful of clichés.

'You had a good time?'

'Oh, I'm pleased about that.'

'The food's always excellent at L'Escargot.'

'He's a nice man, isn't he?'

Nice was the very last word any sane person would use to describe Roehm. Nice people were simply not on that scale.

'I dreamed about him last night,' I said, suddenly spiteful, courting a reaction.

'Oh, did you?' She walked out of the kitchen and locked herself in the downstairs lavatory.

At last, I had drawn blood.

*

Luce's house looked different. I couldn't work out how or why. Here were the patterned cobblestones and the bower of ferns, neatly cut back for the winter, the tiny trimmed evergreens and the bank of Dutch bulbs, recently mulched, and all professionally cultivated by the landscape design team. No one ever pottered in Luce's garden. It was kept under control by uniformed officials. The original creator of her courtyard landscapes had enriched his portfolio of ideas by a visit to Japan. The bamboo was strategically placed in relation to a group of stones and a still pool containing three lilies and a flotilla of psychotic carp. They circled endlessly, staring. The light over the front door signalled the end of the Japanese theme. Here beginneth modernism. One of the architects who built the Centre Pompidou at Beaubourg had also designed Luce's house. The interior was all parquet floors and huge service tubes suspended from the ceiling, even in her abattoir kitchen. Luce owned a painting by Tamara de Lempicka, which represented two women intertwined. The figures also contrived to look like steel tubes. The place bristled with burglar alarms. There was one just inside the door. You had thirty seconds to switch the thing off before the entire house exploded with wailing sirens and the security service employed to watch the house from all angles, at all times, arrived in military-style armoured cars. There were tiny red eyes in the corners of every room which followed you around even when the alarm was supposedly at rest. The red eyes also operated outside the house. One of them was trained on the carp pool. I looked at Luce's house and at the lady herself, sunk into her raw silk white sofa, and wondered how I could have spent my life with women.

It was as if they talked in secret codes, like Freemasons. Luce, Iso and Liberty settled down to look at one another, to observe shifts, changes, tiny lines, hardening around the eyes, the gentle sea tides of each other's appearance. They studied one another carefully, in case one of them needed instant rescue, but was unable to voice her plea. If all was well within their kingdom they would begin to build their conversational card houses. Each of them added another card to the edifice and even when they contradicted one another they never disputed the point or began an argument, because that would interfere with the programme of steady construction. They simply picked up the opposing point of view and ran with that. The link in the chain was always more important than either the subject or their differences. I had never noticed how the women talked before. It all seemed unnecessarily complex and pointless.

I made all the usual gestures, reported on my A-level work, opened the wine, carried the sizzling prawns to the table. But I noticed the silences in Iso's chatter. She had no intention of telling them about Roehm. We did not even need to discuss this. If she said nothing then he remained our secret.

Our hidden complicity gave me an odd rush of pleasure. But I was now outside the triangle of women, observing them and their carefully tended trellis of love, which they built across their divisions. Luce boasted of her forthcoming certain triumphs in Paris and America. Her unspoken assertions were suddenly clearer to me than they had ever been and so was the fact that they were addressed primarily to Iso.

'There's a spring showcase of British fashions and British designs on at the Arches. Next year's collections. You will both come, won't you? I've got your invites here. And some more for the people at the gallery. I think it would be wonderful to hold a show at the gallery, Iso. When you've hung the next exhibition. But that's a long-term plan. The Arches will be mostly dealers and people in the trade, but I've got a whole section of my stuff being presented. Two young women who want to make themselves rich and famous. Don't we all? They've got talent, but no backing. I didn't charge my usual. Should've, I suppose. But they're great girls and no one gave me a hand when I was starting out. We all need a leg-up sometimes. Especially when you're young. Beauty doesn't always pay the bills, does it, Iso?'

'I needed you,' replied my mother simply and all three women exchanged a long look of intimate sympathy. It was as if they were completing a quadrille. No one else knew the steps of the dance nor did anyone see how they circled one another. Why had I never seen this? Luce was profligate in her love and reassurance. She never counted the cost. I am doing all this for you. I make money so that I can protect you, provide for you, care for you. Liberty and I were included in her largesse. We too were her beneficiaries. But the person my great-aunt loved most in all the world was my mother.

'Your mother was an awkward bugger when she was your age, Toby. She never admitted that she needed anybody then.' Luce waved her cigarette in the air, then puffed like a dragon. 'Who'd like a chocolate?'

Liberty leaned her elbows on the table and sniffed the perfumed deadliness of her Poire Williams.

'Did you get this in France, Luce?'

'Well, they don't sell it here.'

Luce turned to Iso.

'Do you remember when we were in Normandy, and we'd rented that dreadful draughty house, and Toby was at the bucket and spade stage of seaside holidays and we were bored out of our minds and that old codger offered to take us round the Normandy landings? And I was all for it, well, anything to get off that beach, and you said, "No thanks, I don't want to take my son on a tour of bellicose arte-facts," and I was so desperate that I said, "Nonsense, the boy needs a thorough grounding in murder techniques." And you made a scene, right there in front of the antique war veteran who was all but sporting rows of D-Day medals.'

'I remember. Oh my God, I remember.'

'And you shrieked a lot of mad statements about nuclear weapons, Greenham Common and the *force de frappe*, replete with statistics, while the dear old hero gibbered on about sacrifice and our boys and so I trudged all round a bloody museum, full of dotty jingoistic balderdash, being polite to a sad old man who'd left most of his friends behind in French graveyards and couldn't forget them. And when I escaped I bought you the bottle of Poire Williams to make up for being tyrannical.'

'And that's the last of the Poire Williams.' Liberty drained her glass. 'Have some Calvados instead, Toby. It'll awaken your fighting spirit.'

'Don't encourage his masculinity. We've kept it under wraps till now. Iso, my sweet,' Luce turned to my mother, 'we must arrange our trip to France at New Year.'

'I haven't got my diary, Luce.'

She was making excuses, backing off. Luce didn't see it. But I did.

We drove home from the overflowing supper table well after midnight. Iso was slightly drunk. I offered to drive. Encouraged by a crime report in the local paper, I'd been practising up and down our road when she wasn't there. Two children, aged six and eight, had stolen a Mercedes. They were both too small to drive the car alone, but one stood on the seat and clutched the wheel and the other worked the pedals. They had got as far as the motorway before the police and the social workers caught up with them.

'You don't even have a learner's licence, Toby, and I haven't put you on the insurance.'

'I drove the tractor last summer in Cornwall.'

'That was in a field, not on a road.'

'I'm eighteen.'

'OK, OK. So get yourself a provisional licence and I'll teach you to drive. But not tonight.'

Iso swerved.

'You're pissed.'

'So're you.'

We stopped at a red light. The roads were empty, evil in the orange glow. Why had I never seen how streetlights unmasked the dark? Why did I, suddenly, unbidden, long for nights without cities or stars? The car jerked away from the kerb.

'Keep an eye out for the fuzzies,' Iso giggled.

'If you lose your licence, you're screwed.'

'Don't tempt fate.'

We pulled off the dual carriageway onto the slip roads curling out towards our suburb. I squinted into the polluted gardens spinning past.

'We could've stayed over at Luce's.'

'Yeah, we could've.'

'Iso, why didn't you say anything about Roehm?'

Suddenly she was sharper, sober, listening.

'Why didn't you? You were out with him till all hours last night.'

I had not expected her to attack me so directly.

'But it's up to you to tell Luce and Liberty if you've got a boyfriend. I'm not going out with him. You are.'

'Well, you could've fooled me. It was nearly two when you came in.'

She was shaking with anger.

'You'd missed the last train. I was worried sick.'

'Why? You've never worried before. You knew who I was with.'

'Oh God, you don't notice anything, do you?'

I waited before I answered this. What should I have noticed? We turned into the avenue of nearly barren trees.

'You knew where I was. Why are you so upset?'

She stamped on the brakes and the car stopped dead some fifty yards short of the house. The back tyres skidded slightly into a bank of wet leaves and rain speckled the windscreen. Then the engine stalled. She turned off the lights. We were jutting out into the road like a beached ship.

She turned towards me.

'Look, Toby. I haven't said anything to Luce because I know she won't approve of Roehm. She's going to America. Leave it till she gets back. OK, so I'm a coward. But I can't face Luce.'

I was genuinely mystified.

'Why should she be cross?'

'Maybe you haven't registered the fact, but Roehm is even older than Luce is.'

'So what?'

'Luce hates Germans.'

'No, she doesn't. And anyway, he isn't German, he's Swiss.'

'What do you know about him?' she yelled. 'You know nothing whatsoever.'

Then she sat silent, biting her lip.

'Oh, shut it, Toby. I'm going to bed.'

She banged the car door shut, leaving the keys swinging in the ignition. I sat still for a moment, astonished. Iso was rarely so irrational. The wind plucked at my sleeve as I leaned on the window, shivering slightly. I locked up the car and went straight up to my room. She had slammed the front door with all her force. Some of the beading on the architrave had come adrift. I snapped it off.

Hours later I awoke to hear her steps in the dark, mounting the staircase, pushing the door open, crossing the boards. She trod on one of my trainers, kicked it aside, and muttered 'Shit' to herself as she did so.

'Toby? You awake?'

'I am now.'

'I'm sorry.'

'I know. Doesn't matter. Come to bed.'

'No. I'd fall asleep. I can't.'

But she stood there, her shadow increasing the volume of dark in the room.

'Goodnight, then.' I turned over.

Did she feel dismissed, pushed away? I listened carefully to every creak and echo on the descending stairs.

*

We sat waiting for the show to begin. It was as if we were sitting in a theatre expectantly watching the footlights, spots and chandeliers. The Arches had once been a railway shunting shed for old stock under the nineteenth-century vaults near King's Cross. The venue was long and thin. All the audience were equally close to the stage and the back wall was covered with obscure graffiti, huge coloured block letters, the sort you always see on trains and bridges, but which you can never quite read. We were perched on the rim of a dais, just a little higher than the first two rows. The programmes were covered in glittering silver spangles, tiny shiny triangles, which the girls in my school stuck to their cheeks when they wanted to make an impact at the disco. I had loitered outside the disco on several occasions. I wanted to watch the girls. I watched them going in through the dark doorway. I watched their skirts stretched tight across their opulent backsides. But I had never bought a ticket and I had never been inside. The spangles came off in my hands.

The seasonal fashion shows appeared to exist in a vacuum, suspended outside time. It was the beginning of November and we were to see the spring collection, a mass of light, bright colours and short, swirling skirts, while the external world faced a descending curtain of wet leaves and the increasing dark.

'I rather like that,' said Iso, 'it gives you hope.'

There was free white wine and cheese squares laid out in the foyer. The sausages topped with real cubes of pineapple vanished at once. Iso and I wolfed the last lot as if we hadn't eaten for months, grinning at each other. There was peace once more between us. She had not seen Roehm for over a week. She was never late home and the panzer did not appear in our street. I checked the answerphone several times a day. In his absence the old intimacy reasserted itself. We were friends again. We never mentioned Roehm. She tucked her arm through mine as we sat close together and peered at the disintegrating programme. The music was thudding techno. I thought about the Chinese dragon festival. But I said nothing to my mother.

'Luce is on last. Bet she's backstage, fussing.'

'Do you know anyone here?'

'I invited everyone in the department and at the gallery. I should've told them there'd be free wine. Then they'd have shown up.'

People were still trying to fit their bums onto benches when the music changed gear and the spots glowed red, orange, white. The peculiar distance which was opening up between my vision and the ordinary things that I had taken for granted suddenly became huge. The spectacle was a mystery. A parade of women, thin as the coathangers which they represented, sauntered past. They had bony shoulders and legs like giraffes. They all held their chins high in the air, haughty and poised, daring us to laugh. Their gestures and expressions were bizarre. They scowled and preened, challenging the audience. The costumes were still more mysterious. The theme was the millennium. What will we all be wearing in the twenty-first century? Orange flares and black boleros, bum-freezer jackets decorated with silver and gilt, epaulettes shimmering like the uniform of a toreador, swirling silver shirts and huge Elizabethan collars, layers of ruffles, waterfalls of silk, heels blocked up like the steps of Mayan palaces, Cinderella's slippers, great black shining beads, bracelets of amber, tiny evening bags on chains, biting tight trousers which ended at the knee, SM leather studs on braces and leather micro-skirts, nipples almost visible beneath the spiked straps.

But is this Luce's collection of embroidered fiery striped red, orange, black beads stitched into tresses trailing from the shoulders and the hems, huge sleeves hanging loose like the costumes of mandarins? And the women her designers had chosen were suddenly quite different from the other models. They were full-breasted, wide-hipped, tall as Rider Haggard's Black Sorcerers of Africa, their long arms rattled with great circles of gold. There was no bride's dress as the denouement, as there always is in conventional collections.

Instead the tallest and most formidable of the women rustled down the stage towards us, turning first to the right and then to the left in a pyramid of rustling ivory silk. She put her hands on her hips and glared at the audience. Her black, black skin was purple dark against the embroidered slick silks. She was not a bride, but a queen. She could not be bought, she ruled. The applause was as much for the majesty and power of the woman as for the intricate robes that cascaded from her shoulders.

'That's it, Luce, think big,' cried Iso in my ear.

And then Luce herself appeared, hand in hand with her designers, prancing forward among their models, the reds and lilacs of her own clothes metamorphosing into green and purple underneath the lights. Luce was transfigured by glory. We bellowed out our roar of praise.

Suddenly I had the prickling sensation that I was being watched. Again I saw the single eye of the iguana which had turned sideways, and begun his natural process of cryptic coloration, the blue retreating on his shingled skin as he began to vanish into the green. But his gaze had settled upon me. I twisted round and looked up. Quite a few people were standing at the back, but I'm sure that he was there. It was Roehm, his huge form dimly looming against the raw brick wall of the theatre. I jumped up and muttered my departure to Iso. She was fixed upon Luce's triumph. I rushed up the aisle towards the door and hunted him down the back row. There was no sign of Roehm. Some of the audience were already leaving, but the foyer wasn't full. I dropped the programme and ran to the front doors. There was an inanimate row of black taxis waiting in the damp night. The street was deserted. I bolted back into the theatre. I even checked the Gents. I was convinced that I had seen him, his giant shadow, his white face, clear against the back wall.

How had he vanished so swiftly, leaving no trace? Puzzled, I pushed against the mass of people leaving the theatre. The techno beat began again. There was no chance of regaining my seat. I waited for a while in the foyer, then saw Liberty pushing her way towards me.

'Hi, babe! They're backstage, drinking champagne. I'm off to get the car. It'll take ages. Keep a glass for me. Climb up stage left and ask for the green room. Wasn't it wonderful? Luce is jubilant.'

I wandered back into the emptying theatre, wondering if I had hallucinated his presence. But he was too solid, too massive to imagine. No, Roehm had been there. He must have been there. But he had deliberately disappeared. He had decided not to speak to us. Luce. It's because of Luce. She's not allowed to know. When Luce is there, we're off limits. I asked where the green room was. But I could hear them, long before I reached the green room.

What struck me as odd was that they were shouting at each other and still drinking champagne. I could hear Luce's dreadful shriek, a roar above the cheerful bubbles.

'He's twenty-five years older than you! What the fuck do you think you're doing, Isobel? Shagging Grandad?'

'Luce. Control yourself. And watch what you're saying. How can that possibly matter?'

'And I suppose you still go in for all that risky sex where you could easily end up dead.'

Luce never lowered her voice. I heard her. I saw her hands and chin wobbling with indignation. My mother's voice was deadly. I had never seen her so angry and so calm.

'Luce, how dare you. May I remind you that Liberty is even younger than I am? And if anyone ought to speak up in defence of perverted sex then it should be you.'

She swallowed a whole half-glass of champagne in one gulp, got up and stalked out, shaking. She never looked at me. I don't think she even noticed that I was there. I sat down next to Luce. She didn't say anything for a minute or two. She was paralysed by distress and rage. I waited, looking at the abandoned costumes hanging round the walls. They sagged, shapeless and foolish, as if the women's bodies that had filled them had suddenly dematerialized. Then, halfway down her second cigarette, Luce burst into tears.

'Shall I go after Iso?' I asked, alarmed.

Luce mopped up the streams and mumbled, 'I just don't want her hurt. I don't want you hurt.'

I couldn't pretend that I didn't know what they were quarrelling about, and things couldn't get any worse, so I decided to enter the fray.

'But you don't know Roehm. He doesn't seem old, though I suppose he is. Anyway, he's rich. You should meet him. Then you'd understand why she loves him.'

Luce looked at me in horror, as if I'd suddenly given her certain evidence that I had been deposited on the planet by visiting aliens.

'Then *you've* already met this monster. Let me tell you, child, that I have no desire whatsoever to meet him.'

'Well, you should.'

Luce and I glared at each other. Liberty suddenly thumped across the threshold, waving her programme.

'Drink up, chaps. I've got the car out the front. And I'm on double yellow. Did you save me some? Where's Isobel?'

Suddenly she noticed that something was horribly wrong. Luce's cheeks were black with running paint.

'Heavens, Luce, what's up?'

I poured myself the last glass of champagne and began to drink it down at speed. I offered Liberty the dregs with a provocative smirk.

'Luce and Iso have been fighting over a man.'

*

We lived in a smokeless zone. I sat in front of an illegal wood fire. An implausible thriller set in Cornwall was running its course on BBC2. There were two possible murderers. One was an ideological vagrant given to meditation sessions on the top of a tor, and the other was a retired lifeguard, who had dedicated his last days to alcohol and embittered disillusionment. He was bristling with possible motives. So it was more likely to be the unemployed vagrant. The porch lights were on. Isobel had not come home.

I heard someone's step on the gravel and the high-pitched ring of the bell as the key turned simultaneously in the lock. Luce. No one else had the keys. I sat waiting in the sitting room, but turned off the sound. A small blue loudhailer with a line through it appeared in the left-hand corner of the screen. My mind went blank.

Luce strode in, rustling with heavy bracelets and chains. She was dressed to kill in reds, blues, greens. Her mouth was a thin line of violet.

'All right, then,' she sat down and stubbed out her cigarette amongst the others festering in a shell left on the bookcase, 'who is he?'

'I told you. He's a scientist. He works in London and somewhere else abroad. He's also got a research institute in the Alps.'

'And how old is he exactly?'

I had no idea. But I had done some calculations.

'He must be over fifty. He said that he remembered his father coming back from the war.'

Luce snorted. She lit another cigarette. I hugged a cushion and noticed that the police were swarming up the tor in search of the philosophical vagrant. Luce stared at the soundless screen, her face impassive.

'He smokes. Like you.'

She stubbed it out at once, in a rage.

'I don't see why you're so angry. Roehm makes her happy.'

I had no idea why I was saying this. I didn't believe that anyone could be happy with a man like Roehm. He was too ambiguous, too large and too terrifying. But I pushed out the patter of clichés into the gap between us.

'Don't you want her to be happy?'

'Not with him!'

Luce snorted with indignation and righteousness. I sat silent for a while. The vagrant was flying across the moor, pursued by dogs. Cut to the rotting boat which the lifeguard kept on the beach.

'He must have another name. He can't just be Roehm, like Heathcliff.'

'She's never called him anything else. I thought it might be his first name.'

'It's not a name at all. Do you know where he's from?'

I volunteered the minimum of hard information. I had no tangible motive to keep the little I knew secret from Luce, but I refused to give up this strange huge man. It was as if Roehm now belonged to me, to us.

'His car is registered in the Haute-Savoie. It's got left-hand drive. It's French.'

Luce gave an irritated shrug.

'Well, that's a start, I suppose. But won't tell us much about him. It could be a company car. And where was this laboratory you said you visited? Inside one of the university hospitals? Off Gower Street? Much use that is, Toby. There are dozens of hospitals off Gower Street and you were born in one of them.'

The embittered lifeguard was salvaging something from the rotting boat. Obviously the murder weapon. I hastily revised the plot in my head. The enlightened vagrant must be innocent.

'Is he English? Toby, are you listening?'

'He doesn't have an accent exactly. He speaks perfect English. But he sounds foreign.'

I wished that she would go away.

'Roehm's not an English name.'

'He mentioned Switzerland,' I suggested unhelpfully. Luce looked gloomily into the fire. She tried another cigarette.

'I've blown it with your mother. She won't even speak to me.'

'She'll get over it.'

'No, she won't.'

We sat silent. I stood up and poked the logs. Immediately the flames ebbed as if someone had hushed them to be quiet.

'Well, you say he's rich. Even if he is old enough to be her father. Has he bought any more of her paintings? And I suppose he might be Swiss. What does he work on?'

'Genetics. It's either plants or animals. He had both in his lab.'

'Oh, great. He probably modifies crops so that when we all think we're eating beetroots we're actually eating bananas.'

'No. It's nothing like that. It's about breeding strains that resist drought, heat and ice.'

'It's the same thing. It's interfering with Nature.'

'But so are insecticides and vaccinations. Luce, be rational.'

She glared at me. Neither of us spoke. The vagrant was brought down by the dogs. I decided that if I were an actor required to perform scenes with slavering Dobermanns I'd demand more money. Then Luce changed tack and spoke with peculiar urgency.

'Look, Toby, Liberty and I are off to New York tomorrow. Your mother won't even say goodbye. She doesn't return my calls. She'd better not find me here. So listen. Here's the deal. This is the hotel where we're staying. That's the number. You put 001 before it. You can leave messages at reception if we're not there. Then here's the number of my friends in Brooklyn Heights. That's for emergencies. If anything goes wrong or if you notice anything odd you must call me at once.'

The entire cast of the thriller began revealing things to one another. Faces contorted in rage, relief, surprise. I stared at the silent denouement, frustrated and mystified.

'What could go wrong?'

'Oh, I don't know. I have a bad feeling about this man, Toby. We know nothing about him. She's not saying anything. She didn't introduce me. Why didn't she?'

'Well, look what happened when she did tell you about him. You went nuclear in seconds.'

For the first time Luce stops, thinks.

'You're right. I did.'

'Maybe you should ask yourself why.'

She stares at me. Hard. There is a long pause. The credits are coming up.

'OK. I'll think about that in America. In the meantime, my dear, you hang on to those numbers and for God's sake ring if you suspect anything. I'm counting on you.'

I looked regretfully at the silent screen and the march-past of unknown names.

'Luce. You'll just have to tell me straight out what it is that you're afraid of.'

'Don't you see? Can't you smell it?' Luce's voice rose. 'I'm afraid he'll kill her.'

*

We had no bonfire for Guy Fawkes that year. The leaves gathered, blown into huge piles on the paths and across the damp lawns. I decided to burn them. It was a windy afternoon and I moved steadily across the garden, raking them into recalcitrant piles, which blew over, away, out of the wheelbarrow, damp handfuls of the dead year. I collected them together with sober concentration. My hands and face were very cold, but it was satisfying work. The dark lawn reappeared, like a fresh green plain, a gambler's table with all the chips cleared. The space became wider, more generous, open. I took some old boxes from the kitchen and built the bonfire among the yew trees by the wall at the end of the garden.

The newspaper was damp. I fumbled with the matches, but the wind took up the enterprise and sent the whole thing exploding into flames with a satisfying rush. I watched the fire rustle and dance, sweeping the waste into the base. I was absorbed and entertained. I did not notice the enclosing dark. The last embers glowed and shimmered beneath me. I was still standing there, leaning on the rake in the twilight, when the lights went on in her studio. I could see perfectly clearly across the dark garden. Roehm was with her.

She came to the back door, looked out and called.

'Toby! Toby!'

I neither moved nor answered. I stood, holding the rake,

hidden among the dark yews, watching her. The bonfire was now merely a heap of glowing ash in the November night. I watched her scratch her shoulder and look down into her herb patch. Roehm was still in the studio, his back towards me, lifting her stacked pictures away from the wall, like a snooping dealer. I saw her enter the studio again. She spoke to him. It was like watching a mime from a great distance. He shrugged. For a while they looked at her paintings, standing close together. She lifted one of the white walls of ice onto the easel. Roehm was not wearing a coat, but a black jacket, which stretched tight across his shoulders as he leaned forward. I saw his profile, the heavy white face and clipped grey hair, as he turned towards her. She reached up and stroked his cheek. This was the first time I had ever seen her touch him. I flinched. A hot prickle of shame ran through me. I shouldn't be watching this. But I went on watching. I stood absolutely still, leaning on the rake.

Roehm turned towards her, just as he had once turned towards me, and kissed her, very slowly, on the mouth. The scene unfolded in slow motion, like a foreign film. I was transfixed in darkness, unable even to see the subtitles. The studio was fully lit, all her spots and lamps were controlled by the main switch. Behind them rose her latest project, a huge canvas, six by four, representing a procession of grey and white pillars, in which the white dominated. But it was not a neutral white, it was a rich, thick white impregnated with rose, yellow, blue. Roehm stubbed out his cigarette in something on her work table. She had her back to me. I saw her hair shimmer in the brightness. He loomed black against her white painting. But I could see his face, concentrated, calm, unhurried. He eased her jacket off her shoulders and dropped it into the cane chair. He was looking directly into her face as he undid each button on her shirt. I watched her head drop as she followed his movements.

I crouched down, supporting myself on the rake, my grip clenched about its metal shaft in the windy dark.

My mother's bare shoulders looked appallingly vulnerable, stripped flesh against the black presence of her lover and the grandeur of her white painting. I had never thought that human flesh could look so fragile and so pale. She shrank to the scale of a mannequin, dwarfed by this man's grasp. I stared at them, horrified. It was as if I was seeing her body revealed for the first time. His spread hand almost covered the expanse of her frail back. I saw his other hand descend to the front buttons of her jeans. He was still looking intently into her face as he stripped her naked. His expression never changed. He was speaking to her.

All I could hear was the wind in the yew trees caressing the lost bank of charred leaves that had blown from the bonfire.

She perched upon the table, leaning backwards. I saw the slit between her buttocks stretch and settle as she arched her back and opened her legs. She had her arms around his neck. It was as if he covered her completely, his darkness bearing down upon her puckered flesh, the two of them framed by the almost white canvas towering behind them. They became part of her painting.

My mother was unconditionally naked and Roehm appeared to be entirely clothed. He loomed over her, monstrous. It was as if he had ceased to be human.

I felt the moment when he penetrated her body because she shuddered and fell back, her shoulders hunched and twitched, as if she was braced against the force of a wave, crashing against her stomach and her thighs.

I freeze, clutching the rake. I savour the shock of his body breaking over me.

Suddenly the whole scene lurches closer, magnified. The lights glare pitiless above them so that he and I can see every crease and fold in her skin. As she pulls back away from his chest, her arms flailing unsteadily, I see one huge hand catch her in the small of the back; his other hand is in her hair. Her thighs ride up the man's body, clasping him inside her. As he moves against her, pushing her open, forcing himself deeper into her sundered flesh, I catch sight of his face, concentrated, calm, unhurried. He draws back from her a little. One hand drops. She clutches at his shoulders. He is touching her genitals, watching her face intently as he does so. She is utterly exposed. She leans her head against his chest. I see her naked face for the first time. She is in pain. Her mouth is open, her eyes closed, her cheek a terrible unearthly shrieking white.

The tears are hot upon my own cold cheeks, my breath is coming in unstable gulps, hanging in the frosty air. My chest is burning, a thudding, stabbing pain as if the air is being forced out of my lungs in violent bursts. I have been underwater for too long. The surface is too far away, we are rising too quickly. This must not end.

I see the moment when she comes. Her whole body surges up against him, then falls away. He has finished with her. I absorb the movement of her back, shoulders, buttocks, as her muscles clench, shudder and relax. A plastic bottle stacked with discarded brushes wobbles and falls silently across the desk. I hear nothing, no words, no cries, nothing. All I see are his hands and face.

I slithered down the rake into the wet slime. As I moved, Roehm looked up, straight out of the windows and across the rising dark lawns. He should have seen nothing but his own reflection in the bright glare. But he saw me. I know that he saw me. He was looking for me. He knew that I was there. My mother's naked body and the shame of her desire for this man had been a calculated spectacle, a special performance staged for another man, the only one left in the audience, still there hunched on the soaked grass, abandoned in darkness, clutching only a rake for a weapon.

4
JEALOUSY

Freud's Wolf Man was a Russian aristocrat. He sought out the famous analyst when his neuroses became too much for him. I imagined the unhappy Count, journeying night and day across snow-covered steppes and arriving in the glittering capital, a world of operettas, chandeliers and diamonds, descending from his carriage and demanding the way to the house in the Berggasse and the small bearded Jew who held the keys to the mind. Did he lie on the legendary couch covered in carpets gazing at the cabinets of goddesses, trying to remember what it felt like to be bathed by strangers, kissed by unknown perfumed women, whipped by his older sister? How can you remember the sensations of infancy? Did the doctor ask leading questions? Did he sit silent, puffing on his solitary cigar, wishing his patients in hell? Did he pound the couch if they got their dreams all wrong? Did he doze off, bored with the second-hand clichés of memory? How, above all, for that was the question which obsessed me, did he persuade them to remember?

Or did he hand them their memories, slice by slice, with the ultimate promise of a cure? That is, the ultimate forgetting. Memory is a pit of terror, haunted by the serpents of embarrassment. Who dares to remember? Memory is the hot burn of shame at our own cruelty and self-indulgence, the pitiful diminutive scale of our own desires, the admission of our impotence. For it was that corrosive vanity of men, the menace of physical impotence, which brought the Count to Vienna, rushing across the snows. He could only prove his virility on the bodies of indifferent whores. And he could only penetrate a woman in one unvarying position. She crouched like a dog on all fours, while he mounted her arse, his balls banging against her buttocks. Did women have to be paid before they would present their vulnerable slits to be pounded and buggered? Was that the problem? Did the virtuous white women of the Count's world refuse to settle on their hands and knees, arses naked in the air, oblivious of the indignity? Was a son and heir beyond him?

Surely this was just a curious, eccentric sexual quirk which made him an uninteresting lover. It did not seem to merit the dangerous passage across the snows. In his dreams the Wolf Man saw his ancestral family residence adorned for Christmas like a tinsel bride, crystal glass decorations spinning rainbows across the mirrors, paintings, carpets, a huge tree set with candles and wooden toys suspended from the branches, lit up in the salon windows. And then on every branch, alert, intent, he saw the white wolves of the steppes, watching him. Wolves, dozens of wolves, perched on every level of the Christmas tree. He awoke, screaming.

What is the significance of the Wolf? Well, in the primal tales we hear as children the Wolf is sexual, predatory. He slinks through the forest, stalking the naive and the unwary. He lets you see that he is there. He waits until you are addicted to his spectral presence, veiled by the white waste among the barren trees. The Wolf belongs to the night side of our desires. The Wolf is always male. And his victims are women.

What kind of sexual crisis evolved in the mind of a man who felt the Wolf's gaze upon him? In the symbolic Christmas forest, the domesticated version of the long slopes of evergreen, curving away for thousands of miles, the Wolves appear, en masse, untamed, their pale gaze intent, fixed. Suddenly the Christmas family festival is not a safe place in which we open presents, share memories, drink toasts, spend six hours sitting at the table. The family is not a safe place.

The doctor in the stiff dark suit ignores the sounds offstage of his domestic arrangements pursuing their own rhythms, and persuades the flaccid Russian Count that he can remember the bars of his cot, where he has been swaddled and laid flat to doze, his stomach full, his arse washed and powdered. He is sleeping and content. He is not yet two years old. He is awoken by a strange sequence of yelps and gurgles. He raises his head and pushes himself up onto his stomach. On the bed next to him, horribly close, for his cot is always placed next to her bed, he sees his mother, naked and bent. She is crouched on all fours. Her mouth is open and she bellows in pain. Behind her, his face blank, insensate, is the man who arrives and departs, the man they name as his father. He is naked, white and hairy. The child watches the father's purple penis pounding the mother's arse. She screams, he screams. He spurts a thin trail of vomit through the bars of his cot. His mother's red, straining face is unearthly, obscene. The child shuts his eyes and yells with all his force.

This is the primal scene.

But why is this more important than the fact that his tomboy sister dressed him up as a girl and whipped him for kicks? Or the fact that his nurse persuaded him to suck her breasts when he was only eight years old, while she pumped his tiny, bald penis in the faint hope of a reaction? Or did he once see the Wolf in the forest and never forgot the sleek lean silver of its swift, loping stride? How can you ever return to the world once you have tasted the wild saliva of the Wolf's kiss? It was this that drove him mad as he tried on all the roles: as an army officer, a gentleman farmer, a bored civil servant, a Russian aristocrat trapped by his class in a historical catastrophe. It was his memory of the Wolf's kiss which mounted the train alongside him and sat upon his shoulder all the way across Europe to the waxy museum cabinet of Dr Sigmund Freud.

And it was this that he held back, even when he appeared to tell all to the splenetic little doctor whose fingers tapped irritably against the leather of the couch. For the good doctor was not fooled. He too had seen the Wolves in the Christmas tree, and he knew why they were there.

*

'What are you reading?'

'Freud.'

'Good heavens, it's in German.'

'He wrote in German. It's better in the original. It's not very difficult.'

'Are you into all that stuff? I mean, you've never read it before, have you?'

'Yes, I have. Just a bit. I've read *The Interpretation of Dreams* in English. This is good. It's all about the meaning of the Wolf. Look. Here's a drawing of what the Wolf Man saw. Wolves sitting in the Christmas tree.'

'How appropriate. I don't mean the wolves. I mean Christmas.'

*

96

Christmas was three weeks away. We drove out to Heathrow. Much against Iso's principled inclinations we had agreed to pick up Luce and Liberty. Their night flight from New York arrived at seven in the morning. But it was grim raining dark, and we had miscalculated the traffic. The M25 rolled along like an accordion played in slow motion. We doubled back, but even the last push coming down off the M4 was irritatingly slow. The lights before us were smeared with rain. We missed the signs and got stuck in the tunnel trying to find Terminal 4. The cars stalled, nose to tail. Iso had difficulty keeping Luce's Volvo ticking over. Liberty had left the thing in our street on the grounds that car theft was unknown outside our house and that Iso could start the beast from time to time and save the battery. But Iso was still furious with Luce and hadn't touched the car once. The engine sputtered, gulped, shut down.

'Don't flood the motor. Leave it a minute.' She was afraid of seeing Luce.

Iso swore. Nothing happened.

'Shall I get out and run for it?'

'No. Don't leave me. If you do this thing will never start again.'

'Well, should I push?'

The engine gagged as she turned the key again and again.

'Fuck this bloody car.'

The Volvo burst into indignant life.

We had to separate at the entry to the short-term car park where the queue had ceased to move at all and desperate late passengers began hauling suitcases out of their boots. I ran through the rain into the terminal building, leaving Iso to do battle with the temperamental Volvo. The arrivals board had LANDED written up beside the flight. Luce came marching out of NOTHING TO DECLARE with her cigarette defiantly alight. She aimed straight for me like a programmed missile.

'Well? Is he still there? Answer me, you little beast! Has she chucked him?'

I deflected the first attack. Most of the terminal building was a no-smoking zone. I confiscated Luce's cigarette before a uniformed supervisor could pounce. He backed off.

'If you mean Roehm, then no, he's still there.'

'Buggering hell!' shouted Luce, sitting down abruptly on the caddy, which I had pushed as close as I dared to the arrivals exit.

'Does Liberty need any help with the bags?'

'Even if she did you can't go in. You're unauthorized personnel. Where's Iso?'

'Trying to find a space in the short-term car park.'

Luce remembered her manners. She swayed to her feet a little shakily and kissed me.

'It's sweet of you both to come and pick us up. God, I hate aeroplanes. We're sitting there in mid-Atlantic, suspended over bottomless depths, the thing isn't even wobbling, nothing but endless black above and beneath and all you can hear is a gentle roar, and I realize that it's stopped. It's just stopped. And Liberty is utterly infuriating. She settles down inside one of those dark blue BA blankets with a little pink cushion and she sleeps like a baby. And when I shake her awake, convinced that the thing is about to fall out of the air, all she can say is, "Stuff it, Luce, you've drunk too many gins." '

I put my arm around my great-aunt.

'Don't worry, Luce. Ten hours' sleep and you'll forget the flight. I hear that the trip was a great success.'

We had received three conciliatory and ecstatic postcards.

'It was while we were there. People in New York tend to forget who you are as soon as you walk out of the room. I just hope that all my negotiating won't go for nothing. I need someone to go out again soon and follow up my contacts, someone to keep pushing the samples and the catalogues, force them to watch videos of the Paris show and then sign here, just above the dots.'

She reached for her cigarettes again.

'New York's amazing. I feel as if I've been living at the same speed as the Keystone cops and now we're back the movie has slowed down. It's another world. They've heard of Europe, but they really aren't that interested. We get the wrong idea about America from the ones that live over here. We think that they're pseudo-Europeans. But they're not. They're all completely deracinated and traumatized because they've noticed that the rest of the world exists. And that it's different. The ones that live in the US have yet to realize the truth. We're aliens! What a shock! That'll keep them in therapy for decades.'

Luce lit up another cigarette with a vindictive flourish. She looked up at me through a little cloud of dragon's breath. She was still thinking about Roehm.

'Does he come to the house?'

'Yes. Not often. Luce, you can't smoke here.'

'How often?'

'Oh, how should I know how often? She has sex with him in the studio.'

Luce smoked an entire cigarette before replying. Then she stood up and gave me a glare that would have mesmerized Medusa.

'And you watched?'

'Yes.'

'I'm in two minds as to whether I should ring the social services or the police.'

'Luce, there's no point. I'm eighteen. You can't say anything to her. She doesn't know I saw.'

Luce suddenly exploded at full volume.

'How dare you watch your mother making love to another man, you infantile pornographer!'

Everybody within earshot stared at us. I felt surprisingly nonchalant. I had intended to shock Luce, and was delighted that my ploy had worked. The tale had the advantage of being true. I looked at her indulgently, as if I was humouring a mad relative who made scenes in public. My motives were obscure, even to myself. I wanted someone else to know what had happened. But my own view of the event had altered radically in the weeks that followed. I was no longer angry, humiliated, ashamed, but strangely excited. The worm of pleasure had entered my skin and begun to burrow and turn. It was as if Roehm had made me a promise and offered me a gift.

'I didn't mean to watch them. I wasn't spying or anything. I was in the garden and they turned on all the lights. The entire neighbourhood was probably watching too. I was a bit freaked out at the time. But I've gotten over it. Luce, I see and hear far worse things at school.'

Luce sat back down on the caddy. Her shoulders sagged. She was exhausted. A wave of tired excited faces began to pour out through the glass doors. We found ourselves surrounded by chauffeurs waving placards: BENSON, ARIANE PLC, GREY WOLF PUBLISHERS, HENDERSON ELECTRONICS, MRS S. GUPTA, pushing their block capitals before them like a bizarre scrabble game. A woman in a wheelchair, being propelled at speed by a British Airways official, ran over my foot. Everything smelt of humid winter rain. Far above us the security announcements faded into a verse of 'God rest you merry, gentlemen ... tidings of comfort and joy.' Here comes Liberty with a spiky, dyke hair cut. She has clearly gone native in Greenwich Village. Her huge hug engulfs me.

'Guess what, kiddo. I went out and got myself a tattoo. D'you want to look?'

*

The doorbell rang at five the next day. It was either grasping carol singers or the local Evangelicals bent on explaining the True Meaning of Christmas. We had dealt with both last year. I paused in the hallway and put on the porch light. The bulb was still alive. Through the organic swirls of green and red Victorian glass, I saw a huge dark shape standing just inside the pergola. Roehm. She hadn't cut back the Virginia creeper, which hung in sad dead strands over the entrance. I saw him framed by dead vegetation as if his presence had caused the world to darken and to die. He knew I was there, watching. I hesitated. He spoke.

'Toby? Open the door.'

It was the sound of his voice that changed everything; measured, firm, expecting nothing but immediate obedience. It was the implicit acknowledgement and recognition in the way he used my name, which made me catch my breath. You're here again. You've come back for me. I was chosen. Addressed. I flung open the door.

'Why didn't you ring me? I wanted to see you.'

He spoke the words. They were burning my mouth. I could never have said them out loud, neither to myself, nor to him.

'I dunno. I should've thanked you for dinner. I thought you might come round.' I faded out. 'She never told me you were expected. Come in anyway.'

He was carrying three bags from Safeway. As he stepped past he kissed my cheeks, lightly, in the French way, the way men kiss one another in France, when they are family or when they have always loved each other.

'Your mother invited me to dinner. But you know what she's like,' he took off his coat and hung it up as if he had lived in the house all his life, 'so I went to Safeway on the way here and bought the food. Now we shall cook it together.'

He lit a cigarette and strolled into the kitchen. I could no longer conceal my pleasure.

'I'm glad you've come. Do you want a drink?'

We went through the wines lodged under the stairs. Some were still in the wine rack, but some were piled up on top of her shoes. Roehm disentangled a bottle from a muddy pair of lace-up boots.

'Juilènas. Did she buy that in France?'

'Present from Françoise, I think.'

'Let's open that. Will she mind?'

'Oh no. She won't even notice.'

'Don't underestimate her. She doesn't miss much.'

I felt rebuked. He acknowledged this at once.

'She doesn't always comment on what she sees. And she isn't always clear. You think she has abandoned you. But nothing could be further from the truth. Toby, if she ever had to choose between us she would choose you.'

The grey eyes met mine. The extraordinary content of this speech and its inappropriateness in the situation never occurred to me. I felt judged and reassured. It was as if he could not only read my feelings, but control them.

Roehm began opening the bottle. The corkscrew snapped apart in his hands.

'Oh dear,' said Roehm calmly, 'it must have had rust fatigue.'

We began a futile search for another bottle opener. In the end Roehm constructed one from a discarded drill, which we unearthed among the archaeological layers of her painting equipment box, and a piece of driftwood she had used as an object in a nautical still life. I felt odd being near to him in the studio. I backed away from the table under the window. Roehm chuckled to himself, but gave no other sign that he knew what I was remembering. He studied the speckled shells, rounded stones, dried starfish and oysters that were carefully arranged on a ripped piece of canvas.

'She doesn't paint traditional subjects,' he said thoughtfully, staring at the beach relics.

'No. But she draws them.'

I flicked open her sketchbook, which lay upon the table. She drew something every day. Sometimes it was domestic, my foot hanging over the edge of the sofa as I lay watching television, the core of an apple left on the draining board, the handle of the stove just below the radio, a vase with a crack which we no longer used for flowers. But here too were all the elements of the classical still life, fruit in a bowl, a pyramid of flour alongside a breadboard, a rolling pin and a wooden spoon, a peach and a pear assaulted by bees, wilted flowers lolling in a glass. She used pencil, inks, charcoal. Roehm looked at each image carefully as if he were recording them and storing them away.

'She tells the students to draw something every day. It helps them to see. You have to learn how to see. Observe, observe perpetually.' I imitated her Do As I Say tones.

Roehm laughed out loud.

'Let's cook,' he said.

We were having trout. He laid out the pink-speckled fish upon the draining board. There were four. I suggested that we should have one each and lay the other in amongst her oceanic *objets trouvés*.

'Not a bad idea,' said Roehm. He washed his hands carefully. 'The subject of every still life is really eternity, death and immortality. So you wouldn't be wrong to do that. If you look at the still lives of the great masters they will often contain dead rabbits or a death's head. But even if you paint the passage of time on the furred nap of a peach your audience will still get the message. All picked fruit rots and dies. It's possible to paint death, even to paint the moment of death itself, but hard to paint its inevitable approach.'

He reached for the potato peeler and we set to work. I noticed something strange about the way he moved about the kitchen. He didn't rummage in drawers or cupboards as guests do when they are trying to help. He didn't look for herbs or utensils. He already knew where they were. So far as I was aware Roehm had never stayed in our house. He had never been there in the mornings. I began to wonder if I had been ignorant of his passage through the household and imagined a secret conspiracy, complete with priest's holes and roof-top exits, to disguise his presence and his departures. But it was impossible. I knew every groan and creak of the doors and stairs. I plotted her every movement across the floors. I had a clear view of the front entrance and the porch roof from my attic. I could hear every word spoken three floors down at the bottom of the staircase. He had never worked in the kitchen. He could not have known the kitchen. But he did.

We peeled the potatoes and lit the gas. Then we made a *mousse au chocolat* for afters. Roehm used four eggs. She only ever used three. He frowned at the state of the fridge.

'Don't you ever defrost this thing, Toby? There are living creatures trapped for ever in the ice.'

I looked at the ice flows, which were now wedged solid either side of the freezer compartment. There was very little space left in the aluminium slot. Ice hung in strange blue folds like double chins beneath an open mouth. There was an odd powder crust of white, sprinkled over the top. Roehm threw out some shrivelled left-over curry and made more space for the mousse. Then he looked into the embedded layers of blue ice.

'Do it soon. Clear out the freezer compartment. Then put bowls of hot water inside the box. Keep renewing them with boiling water. That will loosen these blocks of ice attached to the walls. If you just switch it off and leave the fridge door open it will take for ever.'

I was astounded, not so much by the domestic advice, but by the fact that Roehm was telling me what to do as if I had been one of his laboratory technicians. He assumed that I was responsible for the well-being of the fridge. He was confident that I would obey him. Yet his manner was neither autocratic nor peremptory. He had the authority of a prince: *I have only to speak, and it shall be so.* And I in turn had become his willing subject. His power enclosed me, removing all anxiety. I felt at ease and at home and secure.

'You haven't touched your wine,' said Roehm and handed me the glass.

We worked peacefully together in the kitchen, without saying much to one another, as if the rhythm was habitual. My head was warmed by the wine. Roehm cleared up between the different stages of production. I was obsessively aware of every move he made. He was one of those cooks who worked methodically, avoiding huge piles of vegetable shavings and debris in the sink.

'Here, you can lick the bowl.' Roehm handed over the chocolate remains with a knowing smile. Then he opened the back door to smoke another cigarette. The cold and the dark rushed past him. He leaned against the doorframe, blocking out the night. I sat in the draught by the door, peeling the chocolate off the bowl with the spoon, just to be close to him.

'Your Aunt Luce isn't happy about my connection with you, is she?'

I stopped in mid-stride to the sink. Obviously Iso had spoken to him about the row. But it wasn't that. It was his use of 'you'. Was this the plural, you and Iso? Or was he talking about me and me alone? I wanted 'you' to mean me, but realized that it couldn't do. The frozen frame moved on. I opened the taps.

'Oh, don't worry, it'll blow over.'

Roehm had put the rusty garlic crusher, which he had clearly decided was a health hazard, into the dustbin and begun chopping the stripped cloves into a fine, dense mass. His shirtsleeves were turned back. I stared at the weight of his white arms.

'I think that you're understating the opposition Toby, to spare my feelings.'

I thought about the drive back from the airport. Luce sat silent, chain-smoking. Iso drove like an underpaid gangster in charge of the getaway car, blank-eyed, tight-lipped and treacherous. Liberty and I chattered away in the back and she demonstrated her latest toy, a Psion Revo palmtop, which could access her email in any country. She and Luce were email junkies who gossiped at odd moments during the day; both of them had a flashing envelope in the bottom right-hand corner of their screens, which lit up and beeped when anything arrived. We kept the show going in the back seat, but no one said anything in the front.

'Well, it's just . . . actually I think Luce reckons you're too old for Iso.'

Roehm laughed and prodded all the onions in the basket looking for one that wasn't sprouting or blackened. He threw the rest out.

'She's right there. I'm far too old. Thousands and thousands of years too old. Luce imagines a beautiful young woman with an old man.'

'How old are you?'

Roehm laughed again. He had a strange warm laugh, a laugh that was deeper than his voice, as if it came from somewhere else.

'Old enough to be your grandfather. I'm even older than I look, Toby. My work takes me to so many countries. I'm worn out with travelling. I cross time zones and date lines. It adds years to your life.'

He sighed. He seemed suddenly vulnerable to me. I handed him a bunch of fresh chives. As he took them our fingers touched. I put my arms around him.

'We don't care that you're old. We want you. I want you.'

He returned my hug. The cold grey eyes were terribly close. I had overstepped the mark. Alarm rushed through me like an erupting geyser. But I was also embarrassed by the impertinence of my own gesture, the risk I had taken. I pulled back.

'Don't,' said Roehm, gently, 'I love to hold you.'

But I was again a little afraid of him. His directness did nothing to dismantle his ambiguity. I wanted to retrieve the earlier moment, recover the easy intimacy of cooking, doing something together. I realized that I was unsteady on my feet, as if I had just stepped back from the rim of a precipice. I began to grope for excuses.

'Shall I chop the chives?' I said. He let me go.

'No. I'll do it. I've got the only sharp knife your mother appears to possess.'

'There was another one, but she used it in the studio and now it's caked with paint.'

Roehm washed the chives, put them down on the

chopping board, then set about scrubbing the sink. I smiled at his huge bent shoulders. He did all the things I usually did in the house, without asking or being told. It was both comforting and strange. I liked the confirmation that my hygiene obsessions were both justified and shared and that my clean-food fetishism was not an indication of old-maidishness. But I did not like the uneasy sensation that he was occupying my place.

And yet I was delighted that he had come. His presence changed everything. The kitchen was transformed from a scruffy comfortable room into a vital centre of operations. Simple objects, which I saw everyday, became charged, exciting. My own perceptions, sensations, intensified. I saw things more clearly, smelt the sizzling garlic as if it was already in my mouth. Roehm lit candles in the windows and on the table. The drawn blinds were no longer spotted with paint and weather stains, but decorated with leaping shadows. Her cacti on the window sill appeared larger, animate, intelligent. The wine loosened my tongue. I began to talk to him as if he had always been there, part of us.

Roehm looked inside the oven and stood up, shaking his head.

'The sanitary inspectors would have closed this kitchen down, Toby. Look. She appears to have been cooking her paints.'

He retrieved one of Iso's palettes from underneath the grill. We both laughed at the cracked glass and hardened spots of paint.

'That wasn't there yesterday. We can't cook the fish in there until I've cleaned it.' I snatched up the Brillo pad.

'No, don't bother. We'll cook the fish outside over an open fire. Do you have any barbecue coals?'

Miraculously, we had. But the barbecue, a £10 contraption on special offer from Great Mills, had rusted and listed over to one side and was now a potential fire risk.

'Doesn't matter,' said Roehm, 'all we need are four bricks.'

I retrieved these from the archaeological remains of the rotted shed and we built a little furnace in the still damp night. The outside light had gone, but if we left the kitchen door open we could see what we were doing in the long shaft of light. The sticks and coals were damp, but they flared up at the first touch of flame from Roehm's lighter. It was like a magician's trick. I stared as the flames began to guzzle the sticks. It was as if he had given them a sign, a command.

'How did you do that?' I asked, wondering.

'I learned how to make fires in the army,' said Roehm calmly. 'Scrub the grill, Toby, and find some Bacofoil. I'm going to wrap up the fish.'

We stood outside, watching over the silver packets of fish in the flickering glare of the coals. As usual, Roehm was smoking. I saw his face illuminated from beneath, heavy, unsmiling and powerful, but softened in the gusting flame. He looked down at me intently as I crouched over the fire and said, 'This can't make up for all the times I haven't been with you. There are too many missing years. But if I begin now we can go a little of the way.'

'What do you mean?'

I heard the crash of the front door. And her voice calling, 'Toby? Roehm?'

She yelled out our names in the certainty of finding us together. Then there she stood, still wearing her jacket and scarf, outlined in the back doorway. She took in the scene before her, the two of us around the fire and the smell of fish cooking on the coals. Roehm waited for a moment, unmoving, and they smiled at one another. Then, so slowly that it began to seem a little strange that he should wait so long before moving towards her, he took her in his arms and kissed her. It was not a gentle kiss to welcome her home. He kissed her as if I was not there. He kissed her in the way a man kisses a woman whose entire body is known and possessed. He kissed her as if he owned her. I looked away, frightened and humiliated. Roehm had withdrawn to a great distance, dragging her apart from me. A crevasse opened up between us. I hated him for being there. Then just as suddenly as he had withdrawn, he was beside me again, pulling me to my feet. He looked at Isobel, amused, and offered proof that we were complicit in the enterprise of dinner.

'You're just in time to help us lay the table,' said Roehm.

*

A few days later I found a brown envelope on the mat when I came home from school. It was addressed to Toby and Iso in an odd script which I did not recognize. I opened it at once. There were three tickets folded inside a single sheet of paper.

> *Would you like to come to the opera with me as a Christmas treat?*
> *Roehm*

The tickets had cost £150 each. I studied his handwriting. It was curiously old-fashioned and written in ink, the kind of careful legible script which suggested that he had been taught to write from a copybook, duplicating line after line, following a printed model. The question was at odds with the tickets. How could we refuse? The opera was Weber's *Der Freischütz*. We had never been to the opera. I had never heard of either Weber or the Freischütz. Was it a castle? Or a nobleman? Like the Prussian Junkers? Or some kind of huntsman? Iso was as startled by the price of the tickets as I had been.

'God! Isn't he extravagant? He's already booked seats. We'll have to go.'

She stood there in the hallway, without removing her coat, transfixed by the cost.

'What's a Freischütz, Toby?

'Dunno. I haven't looked it up yet.'

'Find out. You're the one with the Deutsch.'

Luce rang up to invite us out to dinner. The gesture was intended as a peace offering. But she had asked us for the same night as the opera. Iso refused and told Luce what we were doing. She was haughty in her tone and there was a frosty exchange down the line. When I looked at Iso as she put the phone down I saw that she had two grim red spots high up on her cheekbones. The price of her estrangement from Luce was more costly than anything Roehm could ever have bought for her. She was desolate and empty-handed. But she would not give him up. Nor would she ever submit to Luce's angry blackmail.

I caught her wiping her eyes at the sink.

'Don't say anything to me,' she snapped. I backed off.

We spent the afternoon before the opera deciding what to wear. She had a fantastical array of costumes, all made by Luce. She could look like a flapper in orange taffeta with glass and amber beads, topped off with a pergola of feathers, or a gypsy with coins hanging from her breasts. She had slick black sheaths, which clung to her arse and thighs, softened by dripping Indian shawls in purple and green. She had a deep red velvet gown, floor-length, which she tried on that night before the mirror, but which she had never worn. She dressed me up as a lesbian boy in one of Liberty's dashing tuxedos with a lilac bow tie and a green carnation made of silk. Then she shovelled me into a William Morris waistcoat and a pair of spats that pinched. We paraded before her silvered mirrors like forties film stars, preparing for an audition.

I studied her body in the mirror. She was slender rather than thin. Her breasts shook as she pulled the dresses off over her head. The hair under her armpits and covering her sex was dark, like mine, but not as thick. I could see the gentle cleft of her cunt as she pulled off the black silk slip she wore beneath the dresses. It was the first time I had seen her naked since the night of the bonfire. She caught my eye in the mirror. I thought that she would be angry, but she only laughed and performed a frisky pirouette. Her hair flashed across her face and her stomach shook as she danced before me. She was like a schoolgirl, making an obscene gesture at one of her peers, just for the hell of it. She was showing off. Then she held up one of Luce's more daring evening dresses against her white nakedness.

'Oh, I can't wear this. I'd look like Dracula's bride. We'd be arrested.'

The next black dress was one of the prototypes for the models we had seen at the last show. It was constructed out of handmade lace and decorated with shining black sequins. The collar arched stiff around her neck and the sleeves stretched down to heavy points upon her wrists. But the deep V-neck held with a Celtic knot all but opened out across her breasts, revealing their warm weight and the pale blonde line of hair descending towards her groin, which was only visible when she turned at a certain angle towards the light. She could have worn black knickers underneath the dress, but nothing else.

'It looks great,' I said, 'really sexy. But you might pop out at the wrong moment.'

She bounced up and down on the spot, as if she was

skipping, and sure enough the dress stretched back under her armpit and her left breast suddenly leaped forth like the witch at a puppet show. It was made for a woman with less to reveal. We collapsed on her mattress snorting hysterically.

'Luce must have done that on purpose. To get a load of the youthful titties!'

I kicked off the spats and tightened the belt on my Fred Astaire trousers, which Luce had made for her, perfect with pleats and turn-ups. I realized then that I could easily have worn her dresses too. We were so astonishingly alike. We resembled two cut-out dolls, the same size, the same shape, the same colours. She lolled back, her naked breast was still exposed. I leaned over her, ogling like a lecherous seducer. I was aware that I was going too far, trying it on.

'Madame, may I kiss your breast?'

'You can if you like.'

I had expected her to laugh and order me off, out and to hell. But she stretched out, one leg buckled up beneath her, and closed her eyes. The dress smelt of naphthalene. The flickering sequins scratched my cheeks. My hair fell across my eyes as I leaned slowly down and took her nipple in my mouth. I moved my tongue against her dark circle in a long slow curl. The tip hardened and rose to meet my tongue. I felt her hand on the back of my head as she pressed my face against her breast. I sucked her hard, suddenly aware that my penis was burning, pushing against the flies of Fred Astaire. I reached for the naked cleft where her pubic hair darkened and swept downwards, a place I had never knowingly touched. Gently she caught my hand and held it tight. Her eyes were still closed. I tightened my lips on her breast. I felt her weight shift beneath me as her legs parted. She pulled the dress up to the top of her thighs exposing her slit sex. Cautiously I kissed her breast once more, then let it go. She pressed my head down onto her stomach. I caught my breath for a moment. I could see the fine down of her pubic hair, darker at the rim where her body divided with the pink fissure opening beneath. I dared not move too quickly. I dared not speak.

But this was my time, my turn. I need no longer deny or repress the scale of all that I felt for her: all the desire, all the fascination and all the longing. I shifted my weight gently above her and gazed into her open sex. She lifted her hips to greet me. I was astonished at how dark the folds of delicate flesh appeared to be. She was swollen and engorged. I peeled back the hood over her clitoris with my fingertips and began to lick her small protruding mound. My mouth was instantly drenched with a rich salty liquid. Her legs parted still further and she pushed herself against me. I increased the pressure and speed of my movements. But I took my time. I wanted her to desire my touch so much that she would not be able to resist. I wanted her to beg me to make love to her. I wanted her to say yes. She tasted salty and odd. Gradually, her breathing changed and deepened and her stomach heaved. She came quickly in my mouth, crying out to me as she did so. My penis throbbed and burned as I sucked her dilated sex.

I had never desired her so much before. I was in pain.

I knew, even then I knew, that I had to wait until she wanted me to touch her, strip her, enter her body with my own. But now I was certain that we were playing a waiting game. I had only to wait.

She sat up slowly, full of hesitation and regret. Her eyes were black and strange. Not now, not yet.

'We're supposed to be deciding what to wear,' she said reproachfully.

I cupped the liberated breast in my hand, caught her wrist in mine and made her feel the shape of my penis still captured in the pleats and folds of my dancing trousers. She ran her fingers lovingly all along its length then took hold of both my cheeks and kissed me hard on the lips, sliding her tongue into my mouth as she did so. She tasted of paint and garlic. I took a deep breath, then kissed her back, squeezing her nipple between my finger and thumb. I was angry that she had stopped me.

'Why not?' I demanded.

'Because if we start doing that we will never be ready on time.' She stood up. The dress fell to the floor in a torrent of sequins.

'Iso, have we ever done this before?'

I began to remember something irrevocably lost, something that had ceased to chime in my mind, but was still there, like the sound of a bell underwater. Here was a house on the beach, sand on the lino, and the damp smell of collected shells, wet trunks lying in knotted heaps, and a terrible windy night when the surf rose up towards the dunes. I remembered the sound of its crashing slap upon the sand, coming closer and closer. I slept in her arms, my mouth encircling each of her nipples in turn, her salt skin sore against my own, her kisses tasting of the sea. I felt my tiny hairless prick sinking inwards, buried in the warm ravine between her legs as she rocked like a gentle wave beneath me.

'We have, haven't we? When I was much younger and we were on holiday.'

'We always used to sleep together in the great big bed,' she sighed, peering into the wardrobe and pulling out a sober suit of Lincoln green.

'Did you like it when we did?'

She looked at me directly, her face full of tenderness.

'I love you, my sweet. You are my first and only love. I shall always love you.'

I lay flat and gazed at the Indian tent bedspread hanging in folds and coils above me. Here was a great white embroidered elephant and here were Krishna and Rada. Krishna, for some reason best known to himself, was bright blue. I felt delighted and justified. My erection subsided. I had not been deceived. It was I who had changed more radically than she ever had. Yet she accepted me back into her body, whenever I leaned against her belly, her thighs, her breasts. She was the open door. She had never pushed me away, forcing me to leave her, find someone else, grow up. The silk twist she had let down for me had never frayed or broken. It held, tight and strong.

She put on the suit.

'How do I look?'

'Like Robin Hood. You got any red shoes? You always look wonderful in primary colours.'

She preened and turned before the mirror. I gazed at her. She now looked older, more elegant.

'You're so beautiful, the fairest of them all.'

There in the mirror she stood, framed and fixed in red and green as if she was a nineteenth-century portrait of an aristocrat in hunting costume. She was the Wolf Man's mother, ready for the forests and the great sweep of snow. The figure in the mirror bowed low before me.

*

The box at the opera was coated in deep red velvet. Iso's suit shone luminous against the reds. She looked extraordinarily vivid in her lavish fragility of green. She looked as if she was part of the set. Roehm's pale grey eyes never left her face. I watched him feeling irritably in his pockets for the cigarettes he couldn't actually smoke inside the house. I leaned my elbows on the padded rim of the box and watched the incoming hordes. Some people, even those sitting in the stalls, were far more casually dressed than we were. I followed a boy in T-shirt and jeans who was nibbling a Choco-Bar. This was a little disappointing. I gazed at Roehm's white tie and silk lapels with passionate approval. I wanted them both to look elegant and rich.

'You look great. Like one of the James Bond villains.'

Roehm smiled slightly.

'I don't have the white cat.'

'No, but you've got the fag and the eyes.'

'Speaking of which . . .' Roehm got up and went out to smoke on the stairs. When he stood up there was no more room in the box. He handed me the programme.

'Tell your mother what it's all about,' he commanded.

As he left the box he caught my eye. I recognized a sudden glitter of satisfaction in his gaze. I thought, he knows. Somehow, he knows.

The programme was one of those thick information packs got up for the uninitiated which told you all about the first performances and reproduced unreadable posters in Gothic type. I began reading the script Roehm had officially delivered.

' "Weber took five years to compose *Der Freischütz*. He worked on the opera from 1817 to 1821, while he was Royal Saxon Kapellmeister in Dresden. But he chose Berlin, the intellectual capital of Germany, to present his master-piece for the first time. At the first performance on the 18th June 1821, the overture was encored and the first act received with interested bafflement. But the audience rose to their feet at the climax of the Wolf's Glen scene to belt forth their shout of triumph. Here was an opera, which expressed the artistic ambition of Germany. Here were the darkest regions of the psyche bursting forth into the daylight world." '

There were pictures of the first sets. These improbable

facades, which moved in all directions at once, were apparently immensely sophisticated for their time. The Wolf's Glen scene was a tour de force. A wind machine sent all the painted branches into shivering fits and brought a rapturous gasp from that first terrified audience. The torrid effusions of the first critics were excessive, hysterical, bizarre. I read them out to Isobel, who was beginning to fidget.

' "Weber has captured the soul of the German nation. All our longings and dreams are represented here. This is the music that will fan the fires of our patriotism and bring us to a blaze, in which we shall recognize ourselves at last." '

'I didn't think it was political,' she said.

'Germany was becoming one nation then for the first time.' I repeated one of my political history lessons on nineteenth-century German unification. 'There was a common language and to some extent a common culture. Intellectuals used to move around the little princely states with a certain amount of freedom. But some states had savage censorship and some didn't. It says here that Weber was rebelling against the dominance of Italian opera. The Prussian court had an official Italian composer called Spontini, who had once produced gigantic operas for Napoleon, adapted from classical myths. I've never heard of any of them. They were huge affairs, empire stuff. And very expensive. *Freischütz* was based on a German folk tale and developed out of the "Singspiel", which was a native German form. So maybe it was cheaper. Weber was hailed as a national composer who had composed the first national opera. It wasn't political exactly, it just got read in political ways.'

Iso went skimming through the plot.

'It's awful nonsense, Toby. Listen to this. Max is a

huntsman who has to win a shooting competition to earn the right to marry Agathe. He keeps missing. The evil Kaspar suggests that he comes down to the Wolf's Glen and has a word with the satanic demon huntsman, Samiel, who does a nice line in magic bullets. You *have* to buy seven. Six will take out whatever you want to hit but the seventh bullet belongs to Samiel. Max buys in. Anything to get his fingers on Agathe. Meanwhile, the fair virgin maiden is faced with all sorts of silly omens and presentiments, pictures falling off walls and melancholy thoughts. An atmosphere of impending doom builds up, lightened only by the cheerful confidante. A comic role, I suppose. They send her a wreath rather than a bride's crown. *Totenkranz.* That's a wreath, isn't it? She gets a Holy Hermit to make up a crown of white roses for her instead. Have you got that? You've got to remember the sodding hermit because he comes in at the end. Max and Kaspar turn up at the shooting competition armed with the magic bullets. Now what you also have to know is that Kaspar has done some sort of deal with the Demon so that he has to be given *somebody's* soul on the big day. He can't have Agathe because she's so saintly and in the grip of the Hermit. But he can get either Kaspar or Max. So Kaspar fires off all six bullets, leaving the last one for Max. I suppose he thinks that it'll ricochet off one of the trees and do for the aspiring bridegroom. Anyway, here comes the Prince and all the Huntsmen. Full chorus of yokels on stage. Max gets told to shoot the white dove. Heavy symbolism, geddit? White dove! They only ever represent one thing! Don't look so vacant, darling. I keep forgetting that you are mercifully post-Christian. Agathe rushes up yelling, "Max, don't shoot!" So she must have got wind of the bullet. Bang! And she collapses. But so does Kaspar. Samiel must be on stage too. Everyone else is. Chaos.

Climax. Shock. Horror. On comes the Holy Hermit and revives Agathe. Must be a sort of resurrection theme. He tells everyone off for sin. Sentences and judgements all round. Kaspar's dead. Samiel's legged it, presumably clutching said sinner's soul. Hermit abolishes the tradition of the *Freischütz* and calls for general repentance. Entire cast kneels and asks forgiveness from God.'

She banged the programme down on her knees. I was slightly irritated.

'OK, Iso, so you've just proved that nobody goes to operas for the plausibility of the plots.'

'Well, yeah. I've seen operas on television and we watched that film of *La Traviata*. But I've never gone because Luce prefers the theatre.' She stretched out her long green legs. 'She says that the music is destabilizing, whereas you're safe inside the spoken word, however disturbing.'

'But lots of Shakespeare gets turned into opera.'

'Yes, it does. Shakespeare's characters are larger than life anyway. Think of Othello and Lady Macbeth. They're already down there at the footlights, belting out their solos. All you've got to do is set the words to something thunderous.'

She picked up the discarded information pack.

'Look at this guy's costume. He's the Holy Hermit. Like one of the crusties. Weird.'

The one-minute bell rang. Roehm came back into the box. The house was full of muted rustles, whispers and coughs. We looked up from the programme. Roehm's eyes gleamed slightly as he gazed upon the two of us together. Then he bent down and kissed us both, one after another.

'I'm glad you came,' said Roehm, 'I hope that you enjoy the opera.'

You was plural; we were you. He sat down and the chair shuddered. We were inordinately pleased with ourselves. We were the chosen, the elect, engulfed by his sinister gentleness. We belonged to Roehm.

The house lights dimmed and the conductor appeared in the pit to warm and expectant applause. The performance began.

Iso said afterwards that it was a bit like watching a western in which all the characters were labelled, and the bad guy, in this case Kaspar, wears a black hat. The Holy Hermit turned up dressed like Jesus with long hair and sandals in a tatty white shift. Just so that we get the message. He's got religious authority. Right? Agathe wore the immaculate white of chastity and innocence, the crown of crucifixion roses, which guarantees that she'll get up again, satisfactorily resurrected, when the shooting stops. It was ridiculous, preposterous. Yet we watched, enthralled. We were impatient with the interval, anxious for the tale to continue, to be endlessly retold. We already knew the story, yet we could not bear to be separated from the telling and the retelling. The music was the key. It acted upon us in precisely the ways Luce had identified and so thoroughly mistrusted. It was compelling, mysterious, seductive. We ceased to think, to judge. And we were more powerfully entranced by one figure than by any other character.

'*Ihr seid begeistert, meine Kinder,*' said Roehm, laughing at our naive complicity with the traditional characters of fairy tales. We had eyes only for Samiel.

The Demon Huntsman was clad in Lincoln green. He was huge, bigger than Roehm. He wore a floor-length cape of dark, swirling green, green hunting boots and falconer's gauntlets of terrifying amplitude, as if his hands were larger than his arms. A dark patch covered one eye, the other eye glowed cyborg red. Traces of a decomposing skeletal frame were visible through the ravaged green of his costume. He swept silently across the darkened rim of the stage at crucial moments in the action and his voice when he spoke was magnified to a hollow echo.

The Wolf's Glen scene made use of computer-generated images on the backdrop. We saw and heard the satanic hounds loosed in the forest. The creatures flung themselves towards the audience down an elongated tunnel of green shadows. We heard the Demon Huntsman's voice, urging them on, and the call of his horn. I realized with a shiver of fear that they were not dogs, they were wolves.

But this was the truly uncanny, distinctive element in his arresting power; Samiel is a speaking role. The voice, freed from music, challenged the terms of the opera. It set him apart, gave him an eerie horror, which made him unforgettable. Samiel represented power, pure power, summoned and unleashed.

We were thrilled to the core by his threat that he must have someone's soul at dawn, delivered against a rising thunderclap from the drums and cymbals: '*Morgen, Er-oder Du!*'

'He's got the most erotic presence I've ever seen,' whispered Iso. I realized that she wanted to draw the character at once, before any of the details faded.

'I think he's wearing built-up shoes,' said Roehm.

*

As we walked down the streets of Covent Garden towards our dinner and champagne, jubilant and elated, I asked why *Der Freischütz* had been regarded as the essence of the German soul. Roehm nodded grimly.

'It's a version of the Faust myth. Don't you see? Sell your soul to the Devil, but the Lord will intervene through the love of a good woman and you will be granted salvation at the last.'

'No, I don't see.' I wanted to argue back. 'Why should the Germans be obsessed with Faust as a national myth?'

But we had arrived at the restaurant.

Roehm had already ordered our dinner so that we didn't have to wait. We fell upon our rare steaming beef and rich sauce, laced with port and fresh mushrooms. We were slavering unrepentant carnivores. We practically licked our plates. Roehm ate little. He waited until we had finished before he began smoking again. I watched how Iso sat before him, illuminated from within, like an Advent candle, whenever he looked upon her. She was the hand-maid of the Lord, ready and submissive to his will. I was jealous and irritated.

While we were chomping chocolate I returned to the satanic pact which had been the subject of the opera.

'Why's the Faust myth so special for Germany?'

Roehm's pale eyes settled on my face. He didn't answer my question directly.

'The ultimate salvation of Faust is essential to the myth, because it redeems the fact that he is damned for his desire, the desire to suspend time and enter paradise. "*Wenn Ich zu Augenblicke sagen / Verweile doch, Du bist so schön . . .*"'

'What's that mean?' demanded Iso.

'Have you forgotten all your German?' asked Roehm gently. Then he translated the words for her, changing the meaning with his glance.

'When I say to the passing moment, stay with me, you are so beautiful . . .' Iso spread herself out like a peacock.

'You've always maintained that you don't know any German!' My tone was aggressive and accusing. Roehm turned back to me and dismantled my anger with his full attention.

'Are we to be damned for our desires? For wanting more

than the world can ever offer us? For being curious? Longing for knowledge? Or for wanting back the time to relive our lost lives? Faust spends his youth trying to achieve wisdom through study, through books. He never lives, drinks, travels to other lands; he never makes love. What Mephistopheles gives him is his youth and the chance to live again. And think of poor Max. His desire for Agathe is so strong that he will risk his soul to possess her. This is the original sin, not ambition, not curiosity, but desire. It is the sin of Satan, Eve, Faust, the desire for more than our allotted portion. For more life, more love, more time.

'We are willing to be damned for our desires.

'And who is to judge us?

'Desire is what draws us beyond ourselves and our safe, dull lives. Our desires make us greater than we really are.'

'Yes, but—' He still hadn't answered my question.

'Listen Toby,' Roehm cut me off, 'Germany's folk tales were terrifying. Do you remember Grimm? Which you must have read when you were a child?'

'He had the cheerful versions,' put in Iso, snatching the last chocolate.

'Then,' said Roehm strangely, 'you cheated your son and you withheld the most important part of the truth. In the Grimms' original version of *Rotkäppchen*, Red Riding Hood, the little girl and the grandmother are eaten by the Wolf. There is no handsome huntsman, no salvation, no redemption. We like the Faust myth because Faust is punished, as is Max, but eventually he is saved. Our desires may be dangerous, but forgiveness and salvation are at hand. This is comforting, but it is not the truth.'

Iso guzzled down the last of the wine.

'So the truth is that we are swallowed up and damned for all eternity?'

Roehm said nothing.

'Well,' said Iso, and I knew that she was dreaming of the erotic green cadaver of the Demon Huntsman, 'there must be worse fates.'

*

When I came down to breakfast on Sunday morning Roehm was no longer in the house and the panzer had gone. Iso was still fast asleep. But on the easel in the kitchen was her largest sketch pad and there, reproduced in all his uncanny glory, was the figure of Samiel, staring back at me as I filled the kettle. His cape swept the floor, and with a meticulous attention to detail she had drawn the giant hollowed chest and the ghostly ribcage of his living corpse. His face was slightly turned away, only one eye met mine, but the huge dome of his tremendous head loomed perfectly to scale. On the top corner of the page, neatly darkened with cross-hatching, were the barrels of a hunting gun pointing directly out of the picture at the level of the viewer's chest. I put on the coffee machine and sat down at an angle to the image. But she had been too clever for me. Wherever I sat I saw the single eye of the demon, following me around the room, and the barrels of the gun swivelling steadily, taking aim.

*

It was now quite dark by four thirty. I met her at the college lodge, under the illusion that we were going Christmas shopping. Instead she drove straight to the park. The park was locked. Iso stopped just beyond the gates and leaped out.

'What're you doing?' She rummaged in the back of the Renault and a damp wind ruffled my ears.

'Getting the Christmas tree. We want a big one and we can't afford it. Have you noticed the prices? I've had my eye on this one for over a month.'

She rushed towards me, waving an axe. I got the message and set about scaling the fence. The arrowheads on the railings were rusty and dangerous. I crouched on the top, uncertain of the drop.

'Can't we just ask Luce for some dosh?'

'I'm not asking Luce for anything any more, Toby. And our Christmas tree is going to be as big as hers ever is.'

She passed the axe over the fence. I felt the edge. It was cold and clean and sharp.

'How'd you sharpen the axe?' I had last seen her weapon lying abandoned in the woodpile. The handle was loose and the blade covered in rust.

'Did it in the metalwork department at college.'

'Anybody see you doing it?'

'The boys sharpened it for me, nutter. Here, hold tight. They won't get me for forestry. I told them I was going to decapitate my lover.'

I watched her slither over the rails, supple as an athlete, swinging her legs easily into the void, leaping well clear of the pruned stumps on the rose bushes. The park was an eerie orange in the half night. We were more circumspect than we had been on the street. There were occasional raids on the park to clear out the tramps, gays and drug addicts, who sometimes coalesced into an informal community round the summerhouse and the fountain. We slipped between the shadows, whispering, pausing, looking out for the parks police, running quietly down the bare paths. Offstage I heard the passing roar of the cars turning down the slip roads towards the motorway. There was a statue of Edith Cavell, sombre in bronze, her nurse's uniform draped around her, gazing boldly out into a better future for women. We hid behind her skirts, waiting for the all-clear. In winter the parks police only did two or three rounds a night. The furtive homosexuals were, at this season, outnumbered by the pushers and their clients. Between seven and ten was usually a safe time.

Iso's tree was a crucial element in the formal garden. Little box hedges framed its silver elegance and the neatly dug beds formed a curlicue around its base, like a formal swirl, completing a signature on a legal document. Another ornamental pine around the same size balanced the pattern on the far side of the garden. I saw all this in the faded glare of orange and black.

'Iso! You're going to wreck the garden.'

'Nonsense. We'll take the other tree next year. Then it'll be symmetrical.'

She applied the axe to the base of the slender pine, slicing downwards towards the root. The tree's wound gaped open, releasing a faint, sappy smell of resin. The thing shuddered with each violent cut and the crash of the axe seemed to bellow around the park. I begged her to stop. I was convinced that we would be caught. 'You can't cut down trees quietly,' she snapped back. She pulled off her anorak. It was hot work. I watched her oval face, white and concentrated, as she aimed the axe. The tree wavered, then suddenly began to list.

'Catch it,' Iso hissed. I pounded into the flowerbed, leaving huge footprints.

'You can see where I've been.'

'Then burn your shoes later if you're afraid of being caught.'

The tree keeled over, scratching my face and arms. My knees gave way. We battled across the abandoned lawns with the dead tree swishing a long trail through the dew behind us. She climbed over first and pretended to be waiting by the car as a couple walked past. When she signalled that it was safe to approach I heaved the tree upright against the railings. We were now clearly visible in the lights of every car that passed. My hands and face were damp with soft rain.

'Over you go.'

Our attempt to tie the tree onto the Renault's roofrack revealed that the thing was too big for the car. The cut trunk projected over the windscreen like a medieval siege engine. Iso drove off at speed. I watched the fine silver branches banging against the windows on the driver's side as it lurched about on the roof.

'Whoopee! We've got our Christmas tree! Listen, Toby, we're having Christmas at ours. I've invited Luce and Liberty and I've told Liberty that I'll never speak to either of them again if they don't come.'

I looked out of the back window to check that we were not being followed.

'And I've invited Roehm.'

I felt the tree heaving on the roof.

'Iso, was that wise? Luce is still up in arms about Roehm.'

'She'll never come round unless she gets to meet him. You'd have hated him if he hadn't been kind to you.'

But you don't hate men like Roehm. And Roehm was never disinterestedly kind to anyone. I stared at her disturbing confidence. She used all the wrong words. How do you react to a man like Roehm? You have two choices. You either follow him like the disciple who has just received the gospel through a Damascus experience, or you fear him to the core of your being. I hadn't yet decided what to do. And I wanted to feel that I was still capable of a choice.

*

Luce did not take the Christmas at Ours proposal at all well. She scented a plot to win her over to our side and our way of seeing things. But she didn't suspect the coup d'état which Iso had devilishly planned. I negotiated with Liberty over the phone, as if we were the second-rank diplomats at top-level talks, the ones in grey suits with forgettable faces, who were sent in to put out feelers and assess the other party's more intractable positions.

'She'll come, Toby. But she's not happy. And she doesn't like the break with tradition.'

'Tough nuts. Iso's as obstinate as she is. Are you having hell?'

'Yup.'

'Whadda you do?'

'Listen her out. Then push off to chambers and get on with my preparation and paperwork. She sends me five emails a day.'

'Oh no!'

'Yeah, and they all start with stuff like "And another thing, she has never apologized for insulting my sexual preferences . . ."'

'I expect she thinks that we're vicious and ungrateful.'

'I'm afraid so. Luce is crackers, Toby. She thinks that you've gone over to the enemy and that Roehm is the incarnation of evil.'

'Rubbish! All that's happened is that Iso's got a posh foreign boyfriend, who's a bit older than the last one, likes her pictures and has stacks more money.'

This was a dramatic oversimplification of the case, but it was my official version and it was the one in which I most wanted to believe.

'I know,' said Liberty. 'I can't quite believe that Luce is carrying on like this. She sometimes sounds like the demon sister, Katie. We're all perverts who've gone to the damnation bow-wows, etc. etc.'

'We'll have to form a cordon sanitaire around the warring parties.'

'Keep at it. Good luck. So long, kiddo.'

We spent far more than we usually did that Christmas. Iso actually baked an armada of home-made mince pies. We did two trips to Safeway and she insisted on buying potatoes that were all the same size so that they would cook evenly in the oven. Roehm had vanished. I never asked where he was. I assumed that he was abroad. There were no messages left on the answerphone and her hair was blissfully free of cigarette smoke. Then the first of the packages was delivered.

I was lying on the sofa reading Stephen King when the doorbell went. I had to sign for a huge square crate that was appallingly heavy and addressed to both of us. One of the Securicor men helped me to carry it into the kitchen. He left the door open and a mighty gust of cold air ravaged the house. Once I was alone I turned up the thermostat and set about dismantling the package. It was an impenetrable Pandora's Box. The outer carton was embedded in straw and sealed with black tape. Inside was a light wooden structure that appeared to have no hinged lid. It was sealed with staples. I searched for a screwdriver. It was only then that I thought to look at the shipment documents. There was no sender's address, but the box had been sent through a company in Bern. It must have come from Roehm.

Smiling and excited, I splintered the wood and burst in upon the treasure. The contents of the box were packed in fine, shredded coloured strips of paper, which I threw out in handfuls. There were bottles of ginger, marrons glacé, Turkish Delight, exotic spicy chocolates, a litre of Kirsch, and a sinister green phial of Grande Chartreuse. There were even two exquisite tiny vats with curling spouts and glass stoppers sealed in wax, containing olive oil and vinegar seasoned with walnuts. Carefully buried in the surrounding packaging were fragile glass and wooden angels destined for the purloined tree. All the delicacy and excess of Christmas was packed into that magic box. I danced on the ruptured cork tiles with pleasure at the gift, exultant as a spoilt child. I replaced as many of the treasures as I was able to do and rang Iso at the college. It was the last day of term and she was overseeing the studio clean-up and writing her reports.

'Guess what he's sent us . . .'

'He hasn't, has he? . . . Oh, Toby, he shouldn't have.'

'He is coming, isn't he?'

'So he says.'

'Luce's nose will be way out of joint.'

'God! Do you think she'll start a row?'

'If she does, it's her problem. Come home quick. I want to show you everything.'

Two more parcels came before Christmas. One contained twelve bottles of vintage champagne. The last one was slender and official. This was delivered, not through the export company in Switzerland, but from central London. The box within a box was wrapped in Christmas paper, a forest of silver stars. And the label was addressed to me in Roehm's peculiar Gothic script. We laid it reverently beneath the Christmas tree.

Luce and Liberty arrived early on Christmas Eve. They were invited to eat with us and then spend the night at our house. Luce swept over the threshold, dressed in black and white. She looked exactly like Cruella Deville. The house was transformed. Iso had hoovered everywhere and packed all our daily junk into the Glory Hole. The luxuries from Switzerland were laid out on trays. The Christmas tree was alight with real candles. Next to the presents was a large fire extinguisher illegally borrowed from college. The fridge was full of champagne. It looked as if we had suddenly come into money. Luce began to melt.

'Oh, Iso,' she said, the old gentleness surging back into her voice, 'you shouldn't have gone to so much trouble and expense.'

I pulled Liberty aside and dragged her up the stairs.

'Did you know that Roehm's coming? Have you told Luce?'

'Iso warned me. And no, I didn't dare.'

'Shit! What'll we do?'

'Brazen it out. And if she storms off home I'm not going. Where'd you get all that stuff?'

But as she looked at me she guessed and burst out laughing at the realization Luce had been upstaged as Lady Bountiful. Liberty wasn't naive. She knew that Luce used her gifts to control us and to keep us in her debt. It was a complex exchange of love and money. The usual terms of engagement had been breached.

'Brilliant!' Liberty and I giggled all the way back down the stairs.

We were opening the second bottle from Roehm's crate of champagne when I heard the panzer's roar coming down the quiet street. He didn't park where he usually did, but came right up to the front door. I pulled back the curtain so that the monstrous chariot was visible. Iso burst out laughing. The panzer's windscreen was picked out in multi-coloured fairy lights. I flung open the front door and there stood the strange gigantic man who had seduced us both, his arms filled with glittering ribboned parcels.

'Happy Christmas everyone,' said Roehm.

The really extraordinary thing about the whole situation was that nobody shouted, lost their temper, went all frosty or stormed out. Luce went a little whiter under her mask of elegant paint and her pupils narrowed to slits, as if she were a cat facing mortal danger, or a junkie feeling the first rush. But it's very hard to be devastatingly rude to someone twice your size who has just oozed over the threshold bearing armfuls of expensive presents. Roehm was eerily at home in our house. He knew where everything was, even things we thought we'd lost. He was as easy with me as he was with Iso. He shook hands with my aunt and her lover as if he was honoured to meet them both. His courtesy was generous, but not excessive. He waited for everyone else to sit down before lowering his menacing weight into one of our straight-backed chairs. He finished opening the champagne without an explosion. He let the vapour rise from the green mouth before taking the tall glass in his hand. He said very little. He took his time over everything. He stepped outside to smoke, but lit Luce's cigarettes one after the other. He sat back and waited for all of us to come to him.

Iso glared at Luce triumphantly. Roehm's perfect manners had entirely disconcerted my aunt. So did his hospitable silence and his extraordinary size. As I watched her observing him I saw how he had begun to fascinate her, as surely as if he was moving slowly from side to side, his deadly hood extended, presenting a steady unreadable gaze, his concentration fixed, his eyes pale and gleaming.

We did not notice the passing of midnight. We did not hear the bells. The moment of Christmas was upon us, but we were absorbed in ourselves, the little drama of our domestic lives, and the careful rearrangement of our identities around the still figure of Roehm.

I noticed how little he moved and how intently he listened. The cabinet in Vienna again appeared before me. And I wondered if the doctor sat like this, relaxed, concentrated, unmoving, listening as his hapless victims disgorged their past in broken sentences. For that was exactly what we were doing. Roehm provided the stage, the lights, the orchestra and we began to act out our lives before him. Every sentence that began 'Remember when . . .' necessitated, out of sheer politeness, an explanation of the circumstances and the time in which the event occurred. Characters in the action had to be described, the events anchored in landscape. We produced the back story, then the main narrative. We presented our histories to Roehm.

He gave us his full attention, peaceful and encouraging. His attitude towards us, consoling and remote, resembled the priest whose forgiveness, however desired, is merely that of the mediator. We became convinced that we were heard by one greater than the messenger. And in his presence we ceased to be trivial and self-absorbed. Our stories became wittier, more telling, our observations more pertinent and just. We became better people than we were.

As the night drew on we stood up, saving the presents for the coming day. We were warm, drunk, satiated and content. We slept the sleep of the righteous and for once, on that rare Christmas morning, we were at peace with one another and ourselves.

I overheard Luce lecturing Iso in the kitchen. I smelt her cigarettes.

'You mean he went home last night? I don't believe it. And shall we see him today?'

'Well, I still think he's too old for you. But I'm fair-minded enough to admit that he's charming.'

'Just don't get in too deep . . .'

'I must say he's been very generous . . .'

'He must be very fond of you both . . .'

'I have to be frank, Isobel, there aren't many men prepared to take on another man's half-grown child.'

'And there is one thing which I did like. He was very civil to Liberty. I'm always sensitive to that. She's so shy that people often overlook her.'

'Listen, my girl, are you absolutely certain that he's not married? He must have been married at some time in his life. He wears a wedding ring. Rather a lot of rings in fact. At first I thought there were rather too many for a gentleman, but I'm not a snob and academics are often eccentric. Nevertheless, no unmarried man knows his way around a kitchen quite so effortlessly.'

'Well, you damn well should find out. Ask him directly.'

'And what did you give him for Christmas? Oh, one of the larger ice paintings? Shouldn't you have kept that for the next big exhibition?'

'Good morning, Toby darling. And happy Christmas. I'm afraid your charming scientist has left us to open all those presents quite unaided.'

The Christmas tree touched the ceiling, soaring well past the Victorian moulding. We had wedged it in a heavy box with logs, but it remained a little unstable and the needles fell in showers, over the presents, the television, the armchairs, the carpet and the fire extinguisher. It smelt of resin and outdoors. Iso doted on the stolen tree, which was the first one we had ever had. The Swiss decorations spun and shone in the firelight. We sat down in our pyjamas and dressing gowns greedily inspecting the hoard beneath the tree.

We opened Roehm's presents one after another. I think I was the only person who noticed that these gifts were ambiguous, uncanny, even disturbing. They were too perceptive, too well chosen. Iso's raft of expensive oils and brushes in a handsome wooden box appeared conventional enough, but I could read her too well not to register the quality of her joy. They were a brand she coveted but could seldom afford. Each single tube cost over £18. But here, spread out in abundance, were the substances she desired: gold, lapis lazuli, indigo, cobalt blue, vermilion. Liberty discovered a biography by a famous American judge on the Supreme Court, which she had longed to read and been intending to buy when the UK edition came out in the following year. But this was the American hard-cover edition, autographed by the judge herself. She let out a snort of pleasure when she saw the scrawl beneath the printed name.

'My God, guys, how did he know?'

I searched my mind for any conversation I might have had with Roehm, which could have revealed their preferences. I looked hard at Iso, suspecting her of smug complicity, but she too was turning the pages in astonishment.

'And it's just what you wanted? Isn't that weird?'

He had given Luce a case of Rotring draughtsman's pens. Exactly what she used. His presents to the women were expensive, but not exaggeratedly so. There was nothing there that was ingratiating, nothing which they could not graciously accept.

I opened the parcel, which had come for me.

It was an iBook computer in transparent white and pale blue, its innards visible like a dissected animal. This was the most expensive present. It must have cost nearly £2,000. We sat in a circle of exclamation and satisfaction. It was as if Roehm had at last decided to make a formal statement to us all and had absented himself so that we could decode his gesture.

I took myself off upstairs and lit up the computer. The thing let out a pompous chord as it turned from black to pale blue like the coming dawn. Then the creature welcomed me into its system. The black arrow appeared in the top left-hand corner, a deep rush of purple engulfed the screen. The icons appeared one after another on the right-hand side, click, click, click. Outlook Express, Netscape Communicator, Navigator 5, Microsoft Internet Explorer, Sherlock 2. I double-clicked on the hard disc. I had begun to gloat over my new toy.

Then my hand froze over the mouse as my own files began to appear one after the other. My A-level essays, my secret commonplace copy file, my translations of Camus and Pascal, my first attempts at writing, my little pack of card games. Roehm had downloaded everything from my old computer onto the new one. I rushed from file to file checking that my information was safe and uncorrupted.

I stood up, frightened and enraged. When had he done this? When had he been in my room? How long had it taken him? Did Iso help him do this? What had he read? I hurtled back into my Miscellaneous Writing file to see if I had committed any of my feelings about him, or anyone else, to the screen. But there was nothing there that could have given me away. Not yet.

The most clandestine thoughts I had were not about Roehm, but about my mother.

I had my own locked files on the old computer that he would not have been able to access. And now I searched for these, which were hidden behind my password. Double click. But the files opened at once like Ali Baba's secret cave and the usual box demanding my Logon and my secret password never graced the screen. He had followed me to my most secret places. He had casually opened all the doors, then left them ajar so that I should know that he had been there. I sat staring at my own words, which now seemed ragged, infantile and naked in their lost privacy.

I felt manhandled by an intruder. It was as if he had assaulted me. All my pleasure in his gift had gone. I sat there before the gleaming screen and battled with my rising tears.

The kitchen reeked of cinnamon and cloves, baking and red wine, the thin glass ball of Christmas. Only Liberty noticed that something was wrong.

'What's up, Toby?'

'Nothing, nothing.'

I managed a wooden smile.

5

JUSTICE

I stood inside the ice and stared into its strange flesh. I had never examined the ice so closely before. It was not static and fixed in flat white planes as I had imagined, but filled with streaks of moving blue, tiny pockets of grit and bubbles of clear air. It was varied and dynamic, like a changing sky. I wanted to witness its stealthy shifting and stood, getting colder and colder, in the murky passage. There was gravel and sacking on the ice floor to prevent visitors from slipping as they wandered round the cave. It had to be re-cut every year, re-chiselled and re-designed, as the glacier crept, furtive and tense, down the hollowed slopes. I looked at the facile spotlit sculptures of dogs, armchairs, an ice bed, a real four-poster with clever pleated drapes, a sheet of hanging folded ice. Where the substance had been finely worked, it was sheer, clear, free of impurities and strangely sanitized. Only in the walls of the cave, where the halogen lights penetrated the flesh of the glacier, were its muscles clearly visible. And there it seemed alive. I stood staring into the ambiguous depths of frozen cold. I stroked the wet solidity of the glacier and touched its intimate uncanny life.

I was the only visitor to the ice cave. Strangely enough the mountain felt deserted in the winter season. The hotel was shut. The trains, which ground up the valley from Chamonix on a rack-and-pinion railway, ran less frequently. Only the railway buffet was open. I walked down to the open-air cafe where we had spent an afternoon last summer giggling at the contrast between unsuitably dressed tourists carrying poodles and Alpine mountaineers jingling with crampons and ice axes. Half of the huge, semicircular wooden floor which spread out over the glacier had been taken up, so that I now gazed down through a network of iron girders to the snow-covered rocks and pines, hundreds of feet below. The cafe steps were blocked by a wooden barricade and awful warnings of sudden death. I climbed further out beyond Crystal Gallery, also shut, to look across the Mer de Glace. There was no one else on the eagle's nest terrace.

But there were hundreds of tiny sticklike figures on the valley floor, crossing the ice. The glacier buckled into ridges like a dragon's spine, giant crevasses opening where the river rose, arched its massive back and held its breath. As the surface dipped into a smooth concave hollow the voids closed shut. It was as if the creature lay there, breathing once every two hundred years, shifting constantly, but taking care to hide its subtle exhalations. I watched the little groups of figures, riding the glacier, curving and gliding through its sudden gulfs and troughs.

I remembered a huge block-like structure, massive as a Borg cube, which had dominated the dirty tongue of ice in the summer. We had picked it out with our binoculars. We had marvelled at its duplicitous scale. I looked and looked again at the now whitened mass of solid ice. The rock cube had gone. It had been sucked back into the glacier. For a moment I was incredulous. The thing had been over a hundred feet high by my calculations, even allowing for the deceptive distances. I shifted uneasily. My feet were getting colder and colder.

A posse of choughs wheeled and circled over the steps beside the station buffet, searching for *pochettes* of abandoned, greasy chips. They called to one another, a sweet high cry in the cold air. I put some more sunscreen on my nose and watched the black birds swooping down upon a recently abandoned table. I sat down amidst the raiding party and looked up at Les Grands Montets, which were now opposite. I caught a glimpse of the red suits of distant skiers by the hut at the peak. Behind them, falling away down to the Mer de Glace, were sheer walls of rock. I noticed how the light changed dramatically during the short day. Now that the sun was descending, huge gulfs and cliffs fell into blue shadow. The crisp sparkle on fresh snow vanished and a sinister creeping blue swept across the surface of the glacier. I saw, more clearly, the dark shapes of rocks and trees swallowed up, then spat out by the creeping ice.

'Do you want anything? I'm closing.' The waiter was cold and bored.

I stared at my wet boots.

'*Non, merci.*'

He shrugged, then pushed off inside. I heard the clatter of chairs banged down upon tables.

I caught the last train back down the mountain. Four skiers and snowboarders clambered inside after the departing whistle, clutching their dangerous equipment and breathing heavily. They were too tired to talk. They just looked up at the bright white light catching the peaks as we slowly rumbled back down into the discouraging flood of liquid blue mist, which had enveloped Chamonix.

*

It was December 29th. I was buried in the alien world of winter sports without her. We had planned to spend the New Year in France. Françoise had given us the chalet in the woods at Les Praz. But at the last minute Roehm had invited her to Paris. She had packed and gone without hesitation or apology. She had never asked my opinion. I had nothing to say.

Luce and Liberty immediately settled into their winter rhythm of blazing log fires, vats of mulled wine, *ski de fond* expeditions with a very patient instructor who, as far as I could see, was paid not to shout at them, silly horror novels and channel-hopping. The chalet was made of wood. The walls were piles of polished logs, but presumably the structure was lined with cavernous insulation, as it was very warm. Françoise had fleets of aged retainers who cleared up our dirty snow tracks in the hallway and recoated our duvets with soft cotton covers, smelling of lavender. We couldn't understand any of the faithful servants because of their murky local dialect. So Luce left little piles of 100-franc notes under the mirror in the dining room with messages saying, *Merci pour tout*. The notes disappeared and the house was cleaned daily with exaggerated fanaticism.

There wasn't very much to do. So I spent the evenings buried in the sagging sofa reading whichever horror novel the women had just finished. Luce specialized in sinister tales with a religious slant. I had two favourites: *The Footprints of Satan*, a no-holds-barred saga of demonic possession, and a dog-eared quest novel full of religious revelations called *If It Were So, We Would See Jesus*, in which a young boy lost his faith when his mother died, but was comforted by a pederastic priest, who worked with a Twelve-Step Plan for Regaining Your Faith in God. Finally, the boy succumbed to the priest's persuasive blandishments and became convinced that God had helped him to win a rowing competition. They ended up with clasped hands, embraced by the True Fellowship of Christ, forming a Holy Tableau of Revelation. The priest's last words bore an uncanny resemblance to the final passage in a Rider Haggard novel, but I couldn't remember which one. '*Beyond the night the Royal Suns ride on, ever the rainbow shines about the rain. Though they slip through our hands like melted snow the lives we lose shall yet be found immortal, and from the burnt-out fires of our human hopes shall arise a heavenly star. Faith is necessary, for we have not The Presence. Blessed are they that have not seen and yet they have believed.*'

Luce read it, enthralled.

'Fearful guff, really,' she admitted, 'but it brings back my childhood. Your mother doesn't like me talking about the Saints. Especially not to you. But we were brought up in a sect that was even madder than the Moonies. They'd burn homosexuals with gusto if it were legal.

'Are you still moping because your mother's gone?' Luce sounded irritated. 'Really, Toby, you shouldn't let yourself get so tied up in her life. You're eighteen now. I expected you to be the one bringing home a boyfriend.'

I shrank into the sofa and then crept quietly off to bed.

I had carried the menacing iBook with me. It took me a day or so to find a Continental adapter that would allow me to illuminate the thing without running down the batteries. I had become convinced that Roehm had left me a message inside the computer. Otherwise why would he have gone to all that trouble to eliminate my passwords yet give me back my opened secrets? I sat wondering why, if he had something important to tell me, he didn't just say it outright. Nothing, not even my feelings, made sense. Iso would never have looked inside my computer any more than she would have dreamed of examining my excreta or the contents of my intestines, nor, my intuition told me, would she have allowed Roehm to do so. So I had tried another line of attack. Did she know how Roehm had managed to download my files into the new computer? She had looked surprised, perhaps a little puzzled. But she had thought no immediate evil of Roehm. 'Oh, did he? How clever! But how can he have done that? He's never been up to your room, has he? Did you show him your computer? You've always been there when he's come to the house.'

And I thought, No, not always. Once I was watching you from the bottom of the garden.

But I said nothing.

Instead, I began to search the Internet. The answer came easily. Whenever I accessed my empty email box an icon appeared labelled MY FAVOURITE SITES. Most of these were linked to Yahoo shopping offers, classified ads and the Internet Job Centre. But there was one site on the tendentious list, which I had never visited. It sat there hidden like a rabbit trap.

http://www.hautmontagne.irs.org.ch

The white-gloved hand tapped twice upon the doors. I watched the blue line slowly filling at the bottom of the screen. The small black and white ball twirled in dead space. Then the screen opened up before me.

An Alpine glacier is an ice stream that flows down a mountain valley from a catchment area or snowfield. They are to be found in every continent except Australia, mainly in high latitudes, but also in high mountains near the Equator. Some Alpine glaciers are quite thin and cover less than a square kilometre. Many large alpine glaciers are three hundred to nine thousand metres thick. *I spent the following day roaming through the valley. I stood beside* *the sources of the Aveiron, which take their rise in a glacier, that with slow pace is advancing down from the summit of the hills to barricade the valley. The abrupt sides of vast mountains were before me; the icy walls of the glacier overhung me; a few shattered pines were scattered around; and the solemn silence of this glorious presence-chamber of imperial nature was broken only by the brawling waves or the fall of some vast fragment, the thunder sound of the avalanche or the cracking, reverberated along the mountains, of the accumulated ice, which, through the silent working of immutable laws, was ever and anon rent and torn, as if it had been but a plaything in their hands.* An area that has undergone Alpine glaciation shows a characteristic Alpine-type topography and may be called a fretted upland. The landscape becomes sharper and more rugged and has arêtes (sharp-crested ridges), cols (saddle-shaped depressions in ridge crests), horns and other prominences, and glacial troughs and cirques (deep, half bowl shaped basins).*

It is the *anticyclone d'hiver*, −14°C at eight o'clock. The air is thick and still with frost. The front steps are equipped with rutted rubber treads like a Michelin tyre, but they are silk-smooth with ice and treacherous. I cling to the rails as I descend. The cars in the road lie like rigid dinosaurs, pickled in frost. I breathe slowly, for the whole world has solidified into cold. Then we are inside the cable car, clutching our boards and skis. The ski school vans litter the car park. I find myself reading the names painted on their doors: *Evolution 2*, *Fresh Tracks* and *Chalet Snowboard*. There are different styles among the ski uniforms. The snowboarders are more original, in baggier outfits with mad hats. They look like street rappers or breakdancers. Here is a group of them, feinting punches and all chewing gum. The skiers have svelte suits, more tightly clinging, in vivid colours. They are all white, powerful and young, like an alien race, too perfect and too beautiful to have been born in pain like the rest of us. The men and women look the same. Their hair is covered in oil; their faces are greasy. Rainbows flutter in their dark goggles. All the materials of their clothes are synthetic, light and wind-proof. The *moniteur* pushes us in together like animals in a freight car. Someone begins bleating piteously, everyone grins and takes up the chorus. The cable car lurches away from the concrete ledge.

> ALPINE OROGENY This is the name which we apply to the mountain-building event that affected a broad segment of Southern Europe and the Mediterranean region. The event occurred in Middle Tertiary time. This is the time which began 65,000,000 years ago and ended 2,500,000 years ago. The Alpine orogeny produced intense metamorphism of pre-existing rocks, crumpling of rock strata and uplift accompanied by both normal and thrust faulting. This is the immediate cause behind the height of the Alps as we see them and from which the name derives.

We fall silent as the upper town drops suddenly away beneath the cable car. Here are the sheer precipices of snow and the tall pines, grappling for soil, which plummet past us. We rise rapidly. The world diminishes into littleness. My ears explode with the dramatic change in altitude. The light is transformed. From the murky gloom of dark frost in the shadowed valley we rise up through the flat bank of mist and find ourselves in sunlight, a brilliant white light charging the white slopes with an electric flare. The world is illuminated. We all cry out with pleasure, gluttonous for heat, light, the glitter of white crystals and the clean white sheets of fresh snow. And then I am perched on the summit of Le Brévent. The bank of clouds is now hundreds of feet below me. The peaks are in sunlight. Far away I see their rocky black backs arched and plunging in the white sea. I look across to the row of needle peaks in the Mont Blanc range and see the bland curved back of the final peak, simple, undramatic, cautious, presenting no challenge and no threat. I am dazzled by the bright white light and the liquid silence. For I can hear nothing. There is no one else on the terrace, no one else leaning over the barriers, no one else gazing out into the void. I peer at the slick rock precipices plunging into flaccid, empty banks of mist.

Who has brought me to these high places? Why am I here, lonely and cold?

The clue must be lodged in these vast deceptive distances, the frozen drama of waste spaces, the immensity of cobalt blue.

During periods of clear sunny weather, sun cups, cup-shaped hollows usually between 5 and 50 centimetres in depth, may develop. On very high-altitude, low-latitude snow and firn fields these may grow into spectacular narrow blades of ice, up to several metres high, called *penitentes*, or *nieve penitentes*. Rain falling on the snow surface or very high rates of melt may cause meltwater runnels, which are shallow grooves of water running down the slopes.

I am wandering across the surface of the Mer de Glace. The glare is so blinding that I cannot judge the distances. The shifting scale has disoriented me completely. My jacket is not proof against a butchering wind, which is sweeping down from the Glacier Géant. There is a corridor of winds, gusts of ice-air that raise the snow in waist-high flurries before me. I am walking the dragon's spine. There are no markers in the snow. To my left and right a muscle of rock is thrown up from the white flesh of this living thing moving beneath me. The creature is carefully, surreptitiously, flexing its length, white as a dove, subtle as a serpent. Its white hood is spread out before me. The skin of the glacier moves more swiftly than the braided ice far beneath. The thing moves at a metre a day, a cautious, invisible, diurnal creeping stealth that bristles with rocks and stones and trees. I sense the yawning gulfs of ice below and the terrible fragility of my steps.

> Crevasses are common to both the accumulation and ablation zones of mountain glaciers, as well as ice sheets and all other types of glaciers. Transverse crevasses, perpendicular to the flow direction along the centre line of valley glaciers, are caused by extending flow. Splaying crevasses, parallel to the flow in mid-channel, are caused by a transverse expansion of the flow. The drag of the valley walls produces marginal crevasses, which intersect the margin at 45°. Transverse and splaying crevasses curve around to become marginal crevasses near the edge of a valley glacier. Splaying and transverse crevasses may occur together, chopping the glacier surface into discrete blocks or towers, called seracs. Crevasses deepen until the rate of surface stretching is counterbalanced by the rate of plastic flow tending to close the crevasses at depth. Thus crevasse depths are a function of the rate of stretching and the temperature of the ice. Crevasses deeper than fifty metres are rare in temperate mountains, but crevasses up to one hundred metres or more in depth may occur in polar regions. Often the crevasses are concealed by a snow bridge, built by an accumulation of wind-blown snow.

I see the world through her colours: cadmium yellow light, Paynes Gray and unbleached titanium. Suddenly I realize that I am seeing colours broken down into their chemical elements: titanium dioxide coated in iron oxide, complex sodium alumino-silicate containing sulphur, hydrated aluminium silicate and cobalt aluminium oxide. The peaks shudder in sunlight. The world separates from itself . . .

*

. . . then everything fuses again. I plunge into the liquid crystals, terrified, and hard boot the system. The computer screen burps, then fades into black. I lurch back into the safe wooden chair, sick with dizzy nausea from over-exposure in the lost peaks.

What is this?

I stagger to my feet and look into the bathroom mirror. My nose and cheeks are red and stinging, my eyes are bloodshot from the slick whip of the high cold air and the snow glare, which damages your eyes if you don't wear dark glasses or the goggles that curve around your face. My hands were numb with cold and now they are painful and stinging in the central heating's blast. I was not wearing the right clothes. I cannot feel my feet.

I slump back down in front of the evil screen, incredulous. All I had done was access an unknown Web site. It is dark outside and the house is quiet. The sinister, secret ministry of frost leaves its tracks upon the windowpanes. I sit still, blank and unmoving, for over an hour.

Then I brush my teeth and climb into bed, shivering.

Next morning Luce inspects me carefully over the bowls of milky coffee.

'Toby! You must put more cream on your face when you go out. It's madness not to take precautions. Have you looked at your nose? It's bright red and peeling. Isobel will lynch me if you end up a victim of malignant melanoma.

Now go upstairs and put some sunscreen on at once or I'll throw a wobbly.'

'Oh, God, is my nose peeling too?' asks Liberty, alarmed. We have the same pale skin.

'No, dear. I coat you in a plaster varnish. It's a wonder that you haven't solidified into a statuette.'

*

The rhythm of January set in: getting up in the dark, humping wood and coal, mock-A-level exam preparation, difficult German prose translations, Luce battling with a sequence of atrocious colds, Iso's students learning how to do frescoes, the smell of fresh plaster in the kitchen. The days marched past like a succession of grey praying penitents. I started regular driving lessons with a taciturn instructor who made it clear that as soon as his band became successful on the circuit he would give up teaching driving to become a rock star. He wore heavy golden rings. I found myself staring at his rings and remembering. I was filled with the sensation of perpetual expectancy. I was waiting.

Something had begun to happen to me. It was as if the parameters of my world had become fluid and unstable. I had always been solitary, self-contained and independent. But I had been held in place by Isobel. We were like mercury in the porch thermometer; one rose and fell in balance with the other. Now she was absent, withdrawn, even when she was physically there. She had begun to spend more time in the studio. She was working towards another exhibition. She often disappeared at night, without notice, comment or explanation, and I assumed she was with Roehm. When she was not there, I slept badly, fitfully. There were fewer phone calls. I could no longer monitor their private arrangements. I took stock.

I had set eyes upon Roehm precisely seven times in three months, and been continually in his presence three times. I began to imagine him, without choosing to do so. He filled my days, and my dreams. He waited, patient and inevitable, on the edges of my mind. I saw his heavy white face, the giant hands and wrists pale above the black gloves. I saw his fingers with the worn blurred circles of gold and the nails in which the cuticles spread to the tips. An eerie knowledge of his presence persisted in my daily life, no matter how little he was present in the flesh.

When I returned from Chamonix I went back to using my old computer and shut the iBook down. I never accessed the Web site again. Yet I could not forget the uncanny sensation of entering that virtual world of ice. I risked looking up another Web site, which seemed innocent enough, but appeared to refer to the Alps.

http://www.alpinoinfo.com

But there were no mountains or glaciers. Instead there was a man whose life bore an uncanny symmetry.

PROSPERO ALPINO born November 23rd 1553 in Marostica, Italy – died November 23rd 1616 in Padua.

The information also suggested that he might have died on February 6th 1617. But this was not geometrically satisfying. So I ignored it.

He was a physician and botanist who is said to have introduced Europe to coffee and bananas. He was medical adviser to Giorgio Emo, the Venetian Consul in Cairo, and reputed to be the first person to fertilize date palms. He became Professor of Botany at Padua in 1593 where he cultivated oriental plants, which are described in his *De plantis Aegypti liber* (1592). He also studied Egyptian diseases and his life's work was a study of the signs of approaching death, *De praesagienda vita et morte aegro-tontium* (1601) translated into English as *The Presages of Life and Death in Diseases* (1746).

The pleasure of the Internet lies in its random connections. It is like reading an encyclopedia or a dictionary, turning pages at will, allowing the eye to settle like a wasp on anything that shimmers. But this version of the Net, which appeared beneath my fingers, was uncanny because of its coherence. Nothing appeared to be a coincidence. For Prospero Alpino sat upon the plains of Padua in the city where St Antony had preached, with the Alps crouching behind him, dreaming of the flooded Nile, the crumbling pyramids and the palm trees at sunset.

I see a strange heavy figure seated on a stone bench in a garden. I stare at his huge, clean, white hands.

As I glared at the microdot image of Prospero Alpino, based on a contemporary portrait, I felt an uncanny tingle of recognition. Why is this image so strange? Because it is lit with southern light. I have never seen Roehm in daylight. He has always come out of the dark.

*

Her paintings began to change. This put me on the alert. For over two years she had worked on her ice giants, the huge grey and white monoliths in rich textured masses. They were built not in shapes, but in layers, monumental structures of white, strange thick blocks of paint. She used oils for the monoliths, so that there were always three or four in progress at any one time. She let them dry slowly, reworking the surfaces again and again. When she came back from Paris she set the great shapes aside in a reproachful looming stack at the far end of the studio. She spent one whole Sunday banging downstairs, stretching a sequence of smaller canvases, about four feet square. She shifted from oils to fast-drying acrylics. These were cheaper than oils and easier to use. She was beginning to cut corners. She wanted instant results. I watched her preparing the surfaces with a translucent eggshell sheen. The new colours assaulted my habit of white. They were luminous square blocks of red and green. She was no longer painting the pure high flanks of the mountain, but the intricate ambiguity of the forests.

I began to spy on the changing colours in the studio. The surfaces were densely worked as usual, but there was a sharper, glassier finish to the edges. The textures no longer dissolved, whispering to one another. She erased more of the work than she usually did. Smeared blank canvases stood facing the wall, like stupid schoolchildren who had failed to get it right.

She had always drawn figures, in charcoal, pencil, pastel; the nudes in her life-class, or even the self-portraits, which she drew often, staring at the mirror with an obsessive intensity. There were endless sketches of me; watching television, reading, peeling potatoes at the sink, painting the windowsills outside the studio, bending over the daffodils in the garden. But, outside her college projects, she had never, to my certain knowledge, painted figures before. Or at least not with such professional care, not as part of her own work, preparatory for exhibition. This was entirely new.

Something was lurking in the dark blocks of green, a shadow, a hulking shape.

I expected to decipher the massive contours of Roehm.

But when the shape gradually solidified over a period of weeks, I made out, not the white and pale grey face of her lover, but the glowing red eye of the Demon Huntsman. It was Samiel. I did not like the new paintings. They were arresting, but tacky and sensational, like a horror comic. To me, they were simply bizarre. There was also an odd shadowy menace in the pictures which had been entirely absent in the opera. Samiel owned the forests, but he stayed there. If you were looking for trouble and satanic bullets, you could seek him out in the Wolf's Glen. This demon figure was on the loose, wandering about, seeking whom he might devour. I scrubbed at the green and red stains in the sink in an ostentatious flurry of resentment.

She gave me the first finished painting of the sequence in early-February. I had cooked a large lasagne, which would do for two days, and was serving it up when I saw her coming through the studio door angling the painting carefully away from the door frame.

'Here you are. If you like it, this one's yours.'

I had spent hours staring at the thing on the previous evening before she came home. So I didn't even bother to look up, I just went on spooning out the sauce.

'I don't like your new work.'

She stood still for a moment and her angry disappointment hit me like a sudden gust of cold. She set the picture up against the fridge, facing away from us, so that all I could see were the wooden struts of the frame. Then she sat down at the table and pulled her plate towards her. After a while she said,

'Why don't you like them?'

'I just don't. I think they look cheap.'

'Cheap?' Her voice rose a bit.

'Yes. Like a horror film. Cheap and scary.'

We ate in silence. Then she said,

'Well, it's not as if I paint in my own blood like this year's Turner Prize winner.'

I said nothing. We smouldered at one another in a long

champing silence. Then she pushed back her empty plate, stood up and stalked off upstairs. I heard the radio in the bathroom. The picture still leaned against the fridge. I ferried it back into the studio without looking at the image and trying not to touch the damp rim. Then I sat on the stairs with my head in my hands listening to her movements on the boards above me. I could not let the anger grow between us.

I followed her upstairs. She had left the bathroom door ajar. She was running the bath and had turned up the radio.

'Iso?'

She didn't hear me. I pushed the door slightly open in time to see her slipping her shirt carefully over her shoulders. She had her back to me. I caught my breath.

All across the upper part of her back was a sequence of raised welts, forming a livid red pattern, like cross-hatching. The skin was broken and oozing in places. The pattern was perfectly symmetrical, as if she had been sliced open with precision tools.

I rushed back down the stairs and collapsed shaking in the kitchen. My cruelty had appeared in her flesh. I had never touched her, yet my first impulse was to blame myself. Then I remembered Roehm.

I got up and flung open the back door. The cold air, smelling of damp turned earth, hung draped in the door-way. I sicked up the lasagne into the nearest flowerbed and then sat down on the damp back step, shivering and appalled. I had the same unsteady sensation of being paper-thin and unreal that I had had when I stepped inside the uncanny Web site. I waited, paralysed, for the cold air to enter me. My stomach steadied. I glanced back into the kitchen. The soiled plates and the remains of supper still lay upon the table, but the whole thing now looked yellow, ghastly and surreal, like an abandoned traveller's site following an eviction, a waste space littered with rubbish and the echo of violent acts. My fingers and my face were stinging with winter cold. I shut the back door.

When I looked closely at the kitchen again I knew that I was no longer in control of what happened in the house.

*

I rang Liberty on the following day from the phone box outside the school gates. It was covered in stencilled obscenities and still smelt faintly of summer urine. My phone card had twenty-eight units, hoarded, stored. For the first time I realized that I never spent anything. I acquired nothing. I gave nothing away. I listened to my mother's phone calls, but I never made any of my own. Liberty was in her office. She picked up my anxiety at once.

'Let me ring you back.'

'What's put the wind up you so badly, Toby?'

'A Web site?' Incredulous.

'Have you quarrelled with Iso?'

'Well, you don't have to like everything she paints.'

'Don't take on so. She'll get over it. I don't like all of Luce's work and she gets ratty too.'

'Whadda you mean? There's other things. What other things?'

'Toby – is this anything to do with Roehm? It is? How? . . .'

'You saw him sitting on another Web site in Egypt??! Toby, love, you're not making sense. Have you been spending too much time revising?'

'No. I'm not patronizing you. And I don't think that you're going dotty. I just can't get a handle on what's going on . . .'

'Listen, sweetheart, don't go home. Get on the train and come down into town. You can be here by four. And either Luce or I will drive you back. You're all wired up and I can't quite understand what the matter is . . .'

'OK. I'll see you very soon.'

I ran for the train.

Liberty had just been taken on as a pupil at 10 Court Steps in the Temple. She had access to a vast iMac G4 and a parking space shared with another junior barrister. She was also part of an informal drinking club called Bar Dykes, which was women only and aimed to advance everyone's career. I loved going to visit Liberty in chambers. They were lodged in ivy-covered ancient buildings around a garden with the edges of the beds neatly trimmed. Court Steps looked exactly like the Cambridge college where I had been interviewed and appeared to be occupied by many of the same people. Liberty had access to methods and information. I decided to ask for help. Her pupil-master employed two ex-policewomen as private detectives. When they weren't trailing unfaithful husbands, they bred dogs in Essex.

I imagined the two ex-policewomen pursuing Roehm with a brace of pitbull terriers.

Liberty was watching out for me and had warned the security guards that I was coming. One of them already knew my face so that I had no difficulty entering her courtyard kingdom.

But when I found myself sitting safely in her room, clutching a mug of herb tea, and had begun my narrative it all sounded mad, even to me. I could not bring myself to tell Liberty about the marks I had seen upon my mother's body. I felt too guilty and ashamed. Instead I begged her to access the Web site.

http://www.hautmontagne.irs.org.ch

While we were waiting for the computer to process our demands Liberty looked at me suspiciously.

'Toby, is there anything concrete – and by that I mean visible proof – of which you know that would link this Web site to Roehm?'

But before I could answer the screen exploded into life.

So far as I could see it was all there. The images were the same. Here were the forests, the ice peaks. But the language was unintelligible. It was not even a script I recognized. There were strong thick bars across the top of every word, from which hung a sequence of dots and squiggles.

'Have you read this?' Liberty demanded.

'No. It used to be in English and French. I read that.'

'What language is this?'

'I don't know. It isn't Arabic. It could be an Indian language. Maybe Hindi? Or Urdu?'

'Urdu!'

We stared at the opaque mass of text. Liberty frowned and ran her hand through her short hair. She looked like an undertaker.

'Toby, I have no idea what this means, although the pictures suggest that it's about glaciers and chamois. And you say that it went all gelatinous and seemed to suck you in.'

I crumpled in front of her, suddenly infantile and tearful.

'You don't believe me.'

Liberty hugged me and gave me a warm kiss. She smelt of musk and fresh linen.

'Now listen carefully, and concentrate. I want you to tell me every single thing you can remember about Roehm. No matter how small. How you first knew him. When you first saw him. Everything he did, everything he said. I don't yet know what's important. So just talk, Toby. Try to remember. I'll take notes. Don't be put off. Imagine I'm your barrister and you're putting your side of the divorce case. Just tell me everything. Take your time.'

She rang her clerk and her pupil-master. We sat in sealed and legal confidence while I floundered through a swamp of guilt and fear. I left out the key moments: the pub where I had arranged to meet Roehm, my fear that he had assaulted my mother – with her consent. The gaps in my narrative destroyed my credibility, even to myself. But there was one thing I could describe in detail, because it implicated no one else, and that was my journey across the ice. The sheer walls of blue cold were real to me. The peace and immensity of the mountains became steadily more intelligible, and, as each day followed another, closer. When I had finished Liberty gave me a long look. It was as if she guessed the details of what I had not said.

'I know that something's horribly wrong and that it's got something to do with that man. Listen, my dear, I'll have a word with my head of chambers. Leave it all to me. And don't be so demoralized. I do believe you.'

She rang me, late in the afternoon on the next day.

'Toby?'

'Hello, Liberty.'

'Your mum there?'

'No.'

'Good. Listen. I've been making some enquiries. But I don't want her finding out.'

'What sort of enquiries?'

But I knew what she was going to say.

'About Roehm.'

'You ringing from work?'

'Yes.'

'I've rung UCH,' Liberty continued, 'they know about the lab, but the people who work there aren't on their payroll. It's a government project jointly financed by a Swiss foundation about which I can find out nothing whatsoever. They didn't know Roehm's name when I asked if he was the director.'

'He had his own key. He let himself in.'

'So he must have had a security key and security clearance.'

I couldn't remember any security at all.

'There were animals in the lab. Live animals. Monkeys, rats, birds.'

I remembered the sad and fearful eyes of the creatures that shrank from Roehm's dark passing.

'Which is probably why it's so secret. They're scared of the animal rights brigade.'

Liberty paused.

'Could you find the entrance again?'

'I shouldn't think so. It was dark. I was a bit drunk.'

We both breathed into our respective mouthpieces.

'I've tried the phones. All the numbers he's rung from go through the UCH switchboard. The mobile phone is run through Europhone, one of the smaller groups, Pluto-phones. But he doesn't have a private number on a fixed line. He's not even ex-directory.'

'What about the Web site?'

'Ah, your famous discovery – www.hautmontagne.irs. org.ch? Look into your computer, little cousin.'

Liberty's tone was ironic, frustrated.

'Why?'

'It's disappeared. There's a notice in English. This Web site is under reconstruction. Please call back later.'

'It wasn't even in French or English any more. It probably wouldn't have helped.'

'But it would have been useful to know what language it was written in when we looked.'

'It wasn't a language I recognized. And certainly not one I've ever seen on the Net.'

There was a pause between us.

'Liberty. I've got an idea.'

'What?'

'Have him followed.'

'I've thought of that. The girls are all ready to go. I rang them up. But I'd have to pay for it. I can't tell Luce. She's beginning to come round. She thinks Roehm might be OK after all. And we'd look like right plonkers if he is above board.'

'But he isn't.'

'Why do you say that?'

'Why're you so suspicious? Why did you believe me? I had difficulty believing myself.'

She took a deep breath.

'Because, Toby, my sweet, he leaves no trace. This may come as a shock to you, but I smelt a rat early on. And I've only ever seen him once. The car registration doesn't exist. I've checked. The tax disc is fraudulent. The insurance refers back to the vanished Web site. They're on-line insurers, based in the Haute-Savoie. The labels in his posh clothes come from no known designer, nor even a private tailor. Oh yes, I even looked inside his pockets, and apart from his cigarettes, there's nothing. Not even a Kleenex. I don't recognize his after-shave and he always pays in cash. He must do. Toby, this man has neither chequebook nor credit cards. He therefore cannot possibly be a fully paid-up member of the patriarchy. No one hides their tracks so carefully and turns out to be honest.'

'So you think he's a crook? Or a spy?'

'I've no idea. I don't think any more. I just fear that Iso

may be getting herself mixed up in something weird. Or dangerous. Toby, the man is nebulous as an apparition.'

But Roehm seemed too substantial, too fleshy and too solid to fit this description. He felt more real than I did. And it was this fact which frightened me most. I had persistent feelings of unreality, as if my familiar surroundings were fake. I was living in front of a row of one-dimensional facades, which resembled the lots at Universal Studios. I was made of painted paper, fraudulent. But Roehm was real, like the gunfighter in *Westworld*; he might come swinging through the saloon doors at any time.

Iso withdrew from me during the grey days of frost. I hunted for crocuses in the garden, anything that might give her pleasure. I tried to cook suppers that did not rely on a central dish of junk food surrounded by chips. She was perfectly pleasant, but she avoided confiding in me. I felt the distance between us widen, inevitable as an expanding glacier. I circled the house like a buzzard, lonely, angry, bored. If I had had more courage I would have gone out with other people, but my *noli me tangere* policy at school had been all too effective. I had no close friends. The only person I trusted was Liberty.

I bought Iso a cheeky padded red heart for Valentine's Day and hid it underneath her letters, among the Luxurious Glass Conservatory offers and invitations to view Knock Down Curtain bargains. I watched her turn it over, puzzled. Then she picked up her knife from the breakfast table and slit the unaddressed envelope open. I saw a slim line of butter, skimming the rim. I watched her pale face change, lighten.

'Oh, look!' She was smiling. Then she said, 'It's from you, Toby, isn't it?' And she didn't even try to hide her disappointed indifference. She didn't bother to read the message.

She had lit the match. I crumpled, shrivelled, then blazed

up. Months of jealousy and suppressed terror that I was at last losing her detonated inside me like a landmine. Neither my feelings nor my behaviour were especially dignified. I leaped up from the table and flung my coffee cup at the fridge. The result was spectacular. Far more coffee than could ever have been in the cup drenched the front of the fridge and the cork tiles. The cup itself shattered into thousands of shards, which flew round the kitchen like shrapnel. I felt one sting my cheek. The noise exploded before us like a bomb in a litter bin.

I was transformed into a gigantic green monster, the Incredible Hulk, and I was screaming,

'You fucking bitch! You fucking sex-crazed stinking bitch! Is that all you've got to say to me? I live here. With you. Remember? And I've sent you a Valentine every year since I was in primary school. And you've kept them all. So what's different now? You are. You're the one who's changed. You're . . .'

I ran out of steam and stood there, white and shaking.

'Shut up, Toby and sit down,' she yelled, her mouth taut. The adrenaline suddenly returned.

'No, I fucking won't sit down. I don't have to listen to you any more.'

'No, you don't. You're eighteen years old, even if you are acting like an infant, and you're free to walk out that door any day you choose.'

'Are you throwing me out?' I hit an unfortunate top note, like an opera star on a bad day. I was terrified of losing face and bursting into tears. She sat down, and let me sweat it out. Then she spoke, her voice deadly.

'Listen, Toby. I know perfectly well what this jealous scene is all about. I've put up with your sulks and tantrums for months. I've ignored your silences and prying. I've paid no attention to the fact that you've behaved like a perverted voyeur. I've waited for you to grow up and come to your senses. And since it's clear that you're not going to I may as well put all my cards on the table. I have a lover and I want him. Can't you grasp that? Or is it beyond you? I want to sleep with him and I want to spend time with him. If he asks me to marry him I shall say yes.'

By the time she got to the end of this speech she was banging on the table and shouting like a demented auction-eer with the last lot to sell.

'Have you understood me? I've chosen Roehm.'

There was one second of white-faced hesitation between us. Then I grabbed the front of her flannel shirt and hauled her upright. Two of the buttons tore off. She was so startled that she did not resist me. We were face to face. I ripped her old painting shirt open and the well-washed material gave way at once. Her breasts shuddered beneath my hands as I spun her round and yanked the shirt up her back. She fought back like a cornered stoat, jammed her elbow into my ribs and sent one of the chairs flying. A plate slithered off the table; it did not break but rocked back and forth on the cork floor. Then she punched me in the face. I sent her spinning backwards.

'Is that what you want? You want a man who does that to you?'

She staggered against the fridge and her upper arm came away from the surface sticky with dripping coffee.

'Fucking hell, Toby.'

She was afraid of me. But now I too was afraid of her. I had glimpsed her back. It was smooth, white, lightly freckled, her bony shoulder blades elegant and perfect. She did not have the shadow of a mark upon her. She stood trembling, half-naked in front of me. My penis was hot and swollen against the buttons of my jeans.

'I'm . . . I didn't . . .'

'Get out of here. Get out,' she screeched. Her entire body flinched and shrank. She was breathless.

*

I packed the minimum and set off across town. She didn't have to order me out of the house. I wanted to put the miles between us. I couldn't look at her again. I was unable to cry or to speak. The day was murky and grey, the light pinched. I sat on the train and the tube holding my collection of short stories by Thomas Mann in front of me without being able to see clearly. My legs no longer obeyed my brain. I had to sit down after every hundred yards and catch my breath, as if I was scaling a vertical rock face. I was white with cold. I minced unsteadily down the slippery pavements towards Luce's house. I saw the spotlights on in her studio, but she must have been on the phone. It was a moment or two before she opened the door.

'My God, Toby! Why aren't you at school? Oh my sweet boy, what on earth has happened to you?'

The bruise on my cheekbone was red and swelling. Her blow was being slowly coloured into the flesh.

I don't think either of us ever did explain exactly what had happened. Luce spent several hours on the phone to her and came down the stairs with her eyes and jaw set, intent and savage as a cannibal. Liberty made up an ice pack to deal with the swelling. She didn't ask too many questions either.

'Looks like you're staying with us for a while, kiddo.'

I learned that Iso rang Luce every night to see how I was. But she didn't ask to speak to me and I had nothing to say. My black eye was vivid and glamorous. Liberty was impressed.

'She gave you a superb shiner, babe. Even Luce can't pack a punch like that. You must have asked for it something terrible.'

And in the weeks that followed I came to realize that I had been living under siege. I no longer waited in the kitchen, angry and sullen, for her daily return. I no longer behaved like an amateur spy, checking the post and the phone calls. I no longer lay awake at night, listening. I ceased going through the dustbins, bent on gathering evidence. I no longer ached with the pain of separation from the woman I had always loved too much, without measure or restraint. I had made our lives a hell of claustrophobic tension, unaware of the monster I had become. I stayed home from school during the rest of that first week away and slept for almost three days. I was exhausted, finished.

In the absence of detailed explanations Luce assumed that we had passed through a domestic crisis, understandable in the circumstances, and that we simply needed time, for Iso to regain her equilibrium and for me to think better of the whole thing. I wasn't allowed to cook in Luce's kitchen and spent my time upstairs revising for my mocks or watching TV. Liberty was more suspicious. We were rarely alone, but after a week or so she came upstairs to call me for supper and took advantage of the moment.

'All this was about Roehm, wasn't it?'

'Yes.'

'When did you last see him?'

'In the flesh? Christmas Eve.'

'Well, listen. I put the girls onto him and fuck the cost. And they've drawn a complete blank. We can't even find out what his first name is, for Christ's sake. It's as if he didn't exist. And we imagined him.'

'That's ridiculous.'

'I know. The girls think he works for MI6. The problem is that we haven't even got a photograph.'

'But he looks so strange. All you have to do is describe him.'

'But, Toby, even the manager of L'Escargot had trouble placing him.'

'I can't understand that. Everybody knew who he was when we went in there.'

'Well, they obviously didn't.'

Pause.

'Liberty. There's one other place you could ask. In Old Compton Street. A club called Veritable Cuir.'

'He's never queer.'

'I think he is.'

She gasped. Then she said, 'Well, that takes the biscuit. Did he take you there?'

'No. But he said he might.'

'Has he ever made a pass at you?'

'No. Well, sort of.'

'SUPPER!' We heard Luce shouting downstairs. 'What are you two doing up there?'

Liberty hardly listened to Luce over supper. She just sat there, staring at me.

I had to travel all the way across London and then out west to get to school. It could take over two hours. If my classes were at inconvenient times I was often late or just missed them altogether. Luce read me a lecture about educational opportunities and My Future, so I guessed that the school had started ringing Iso. It was nearly three weeks after the row and my anger and alienation began to subside. I had slept, dreamless, for nine hours every night. Liberty had frog-marched me out to the Heath every day for punishing runs. I had put on weight. I looked better, happier. But I missed my mother. I missed my room, my computer, the daily smells of the house, my Django Reinhardt and Stephane Grappelli CDs. Luce and Liberty lived in a germ-free habitat, scoured by Mr Muscle, which made me feel scruffy and underdressed. I didn't discuss my movements with them. The timing was coincidental. I did not plan. I suddenly decided to go home.

It was a grim, cold day at school. The pipes had frozen in the boys' loos and we entertained a row of puzzled plumbers trying to thaw out a joint with a blowtorch. Snow was forecast for that night. Our French teacher sent us home early. She had a long way to drive and we were fed up to the back teeth with Gide and his Arab boys. I slunk out of the kitchen gate by the dustbins, so that the staff on duty in the front hall wouldn't see me go, and set off home. It's about forty minutes on foot. At first I marched along cheerfully, convinced that the tension between Iso and myself was like a lanced boil. The pus had drained and dried. We could resume our old rapport. I simply suppressed the ugly and uncanny aspects of my last days in the house. I had been overwrought, wired up, exhausted. Something had sucked me into a dark corridor of hysterical jealousy and had distorted the daily scale of things. I had imagined the welts on her back. I must have done. Because when I looked again they weren't there. Roehm was just a big, busy man, who travelled a lot. He probably wouldn't continue to be part of her life for much longer. And the iBook could remain switched off and packed up under my bed. When the weather was better I'd put an ad in *On Line*, delete all my files, and then sell the thing. After that I need never open it again.

I turned the corner into our road. The trees hung in frail white strands of frost. The grass on the lawns was spiky with white ice. The world was frozen and still. I noticed a black patch of dead Michaelmas daisies that had never been cut back lolling among the decomposing white heaps of exhausted plants. The winter held its breath. There were no lights in the house.

I noticed that something was wrong as soon as the door thudded shut behind me. There was a strange fluttering in the air. The red light winked on the answerphone. Two messages. The house was ice-cold. The central heating had either broken down or been switched off. I turned on the hall light. Nothing happened. I went straight through to the kitchen. There was frost on the inside of the windows. I stared at the spider's web of cold extending in circular patterns, projecting away from the thick point of frozen damp. My breath hung in a white cloud. The remains of a congealed meal lay like a corpse upon the table. The sink was full of unwashed dishes. The washing machine had turned itself off but had not been unloaded. The orange switch glowed. Cycle complete. Unthinking, I switched it off. It was the second thing I had touched in the quiet, vacant house. It was ice-cold.

The strange chill of warning rushed into my fingertips. The car was gone, but she was never home before six or seven, even if she drove straight back from college. I watched the winter dark rushing up the frost-covered lawns. Then I turned back to the hall and pressed the answerphone, PLAY MESSAGES.

Hello? This is a message for Isobel Hawk. Would you please ring the painting studio at the College of Art as soon as you can. Thank you.

Click. Next message. Same voice.

This is an urgent message for Isobel Hawk. Please contact the college. If you are ill we need to know as soon as possible.

I stood in the half-dark of the cold house. Horrified. I picked up the phone to ring Luce. When had Iso last contacted her? But as I picked up the receiver I noticed my mother's writing on the pad next to the phone. A name. Meersburg. Half an address. Bismarckplatz. A number. 0 75 32 43 11 12. While I had been living in the house I had checked the pad several times a day and written down all the numbers I didn't recognize, then rung directory enquiries after she had gone to work. Unhesitatingly, I tore the paper off the pad and put it in my pocket. Then the implications of the message from her college seeped through into my incompetent calculations. *If you are ill we need to know as soon as possible.* I bounded up the stairs two at a time and burst into her room.

Only the illuminated plastic banana actually worked and it was by now quite dark. I was left standing in the eerie shaft of light from the stairs landing, like an assassin caught in the act.

Someone was lying in her bed.

I took two steps backwards. My heel caught on the skirting board. I stood still for a moment, listening. The figure in the bed looked like one of the giant toppled statues of Communism abandoned in the parks after the Change, a stone Lenin, no longer feared, no longer loved.

'Roehm?' My voice sounded fragile in the stale cold air. The inert still figure was on its side, gigantic and helpless as a beached whale. I didn't need to go any closer. 'Are you OK? Wake up.'

The thing did not move. I did not dare approach. Was he breathing? Was he dead?

'Roehm?' My voice was pitched too high. He neither stirred nor groaned.

I peered at the body in the bed. Through the dim shadows I saw that he was covered by her duvet, but that beneath he was fully clothed in a black shirt and a black jacket. His face was pressed into the pillow. I shifted out of the light. The eyes were slightly, just slightly open. I turned and ran back down the stairs, leaving the bedroom door ajar. I picked up the phone. Then I had no idea whom to ring. 999? The police? Ambulance? The emergency services? Which ones? Luce? The Art College?

I wanted my mother. Where are you, Isobel?

I plucked the torn wisp of Post It out of my pocket and rang Meersburg. A German voice answered at once.

'*Grüss Gott. Zum wilden Jäger. Rezeption?*'

I plunged in.

'*Darf Ich mit Frau Isobel Hawk sprechen, bitte?*'

'*Moment mal, bitte.*'

There was a rustle of paper. Then the voice returned.

'*Sie kommt erst morgen Abend an.*' The woman must have registered my accent for she switched to English.

'Can I help you? Would you like to leave a message?'

'*Nein, danke. Aber geben Sie mir bitte Ihre Adresse in Meersburg.*'

A laborious five minutes of spelling out the place and postcode followed. Iso was heading for the Bodensee in south Germany.

My necessary course of action opened out before me. I thudded back upstairs, no longer afraid of the beached shark in the bed. I collected my Post Office savings account book and my passport. I packed a small bag of warm clothes. I dropped my satchel by my desk. I packed my French and German set texts. Then I left everything ready in the darkened hallway.

I did not plan. It came to me, as if I was performing a part in a play. But it was quite deliberate. *I meant to do it.* I rushed back upstairs clutching a wrench. Then I heaved a pile of towels out of the airing cupboard in the bathroom and soaked them in the bath. Fearless and rapid, I strode back into her bedroom, barely glancing at the hulked shape, and wedged the wet towels round all the windows, shutting out the icy draughts. Then I disconnected the heater from its roots with two mighty tugs and turned on the gas.

6
FLIGHT

The night train, mid-week, was not full. I didn't want to squander my precious and dwindling hoard of cash on a sleeper, so I stretched out across three seats under my coat. My feet dangled into the aisle. No one bothered me. But I could not sleep. Instead I watched the pounding dark and listened, rigid, for every station to be announced as we rushed towards the East, and towards Germany. I was in flight, but I was not even terribly sure what I had done. Was this what it was like, to be on the run? Surely people who committed great crimes made more sensible plans before moving into action. But, as I reflected on the villainy which filled the *Mail on Sunday*, most of it seemed to be spontaneous, random, as if each of us could be seized, at any time, by a sudden rush of violent desire, which led straight into atrocities on an unimaginable scale. I had deliberately attempted to murder someone. Something had happened to that huge man who had all but destroyed our lives, and without calling the hospital, our GP, or even my relations, I had knowingly finished him off.

Would the gas run out? Would the neighbours smell it outside? I had left no warnings. What would happen?

Secretly, I hoped that the house would explode, leaving a mass of domestic wreckage. The body would never be found, we would claim the insurance and begin our lives again. Even the hideous green pictures of the Demon in his forest kingdom would be consumed by flame. I lay scrunched on the narrow blue seats filling out my fantasy with colours, as if I was painting a catastrophe by numbers. If Roehm had left no trace of his origins when he came to us, he would leave no trace of his passing. Did he have a staff in his research institute? Would they be delighted by this sudden liberation? The lifting of the tyrant's hand? Or would they make phone calls? Ask questions?

A murky dawn shuddered in the winter sky. I heard my own quickened breathing above the rhythmic hiss of the ICE train. I had looked at its slick white lines, mercifully free of graffiti, and been bewildered by the sloping logo. My ticket explained the banal acrostics – ICE, Inter City Express. But for one paranoid moment I had suspected Roehm's hand even in this. The metaphor was too close to his nature, and his cold breath. He was far ahead of me, somewhere along the lines, waiting in the tunnels, in the mountains, wandering the ice.

A darker sequence of images ensued. If the neighbours smelt gas, called the emergency services and then broke into the house, we would be the prime suspects. Both of us. It was our house and we were gone, leaving a corpse in a bed on the first floor.

I shut down the images. The narrative had become too frightening. Who would come looking for us? It would be the German police. A front man in plain clothes with a bulge under his arm and then the uniformed men in green, clutching lightweight rifles with night sights. It was therefore imperative that we went to them before they came to us. And then I realized, long after the act, that I had had a plan of sorts. Or an intention. I had wanted to stand between my mother and everything that threatened to do her harm. If she had acted against Roehm then it was crucial that I should deliver the coup de grâce and take the blame. It was also urgent that I should find her and confess, first to her and then to the police. It was a normal thing for a teenage boy to murder his mother's lover. My case would not even make the headlines. I was bristling with easy Oedipal motives that everyone would recognize. After all, the fantasy was even celebrated in our culture. I conjured up Sophocles, Hamlet and Freud. Then I began to imagine the courtroom drama and the plea in mitigation. I saw Luce in black and Liberty sitting beside me before the judge. No jury is necessary if you plead guilty. Just explain all the circumstances and wait for the sentence.

The train slowed a little in the grim grey light. I heard a strange, convulsive hiss. The only other occupant of the compartment was a middle-aged man in a shabby coat who smelt strongly of alcohol. His cheeks were dark with over-night shadow. I sat up and looked out.

The trees were decorated with frost. There were icicles hanging from the eaves. The pines were licked with white and in all the world there was no longer any winter green. We were swaddled in white ice, a crisp aggressive frost which burned your throat and left unsightly drops seeping from your nose. I pulled my coat around me and listened to the clanging bell at the level crossings. All I wanted was to find her.

I opened my book. My marker was still on the same page I had been pretending to read, crouched next to a coffee machine, twelve hours earlier, at Waterloo Station: *The Collected Short Stories of Thomas Mann*. 'Mario und der Zauberer' – Mario and the Magician. It was a peculiar tale of hypnotism and humiliation set in an Italian holiday resort. A sinister hypnotist selected members of the audience and forced them to make fools of themselves. He was cruel and unashamed. He revelled in his power. His victim, the hapless Mario who was a waiter in the Grand Hotel, finally put an irreproachable bullet through the monster's brains.

No one could describe it as a crime.

An eerie sense of recognition blossomed at the back of my mind as I finished the tale and laid down the book. I had been reading, not a summary of what I had done, but a warning. The tale was an allegory of Fascism. It was also about killing the father. And it had no certain end.

I pasted my face to the window. We were almost in Cologne. It was time to change trains.

I took simple precautions. I kept my woollen ski hat pulled down over my blonde hair. Fair hair is easy to spot at a distance. I stayed where the crowd was thickest. I kept close to trailers that were piled with luggage. I hid behind people carrying skis. I avoided the masses who stood by the barrier, staring at the faces, watching. Above all, I did not hesitate. Even when I was uncertain of my next move, I walked fast, with my shoulders straight and steady. Everyone who hesitates or cowers appears to be guilty. I was learning the techniques of disappearance. I was on the run.

In a peculiar way it was exhilarating. After weeks of depression, separation and inaction, sinking beneath my stifled longing for her, I was at last free again. Bizarre as the situation was, at least it felt like an adventure. If the train connections worked I would reach Offenburg in the dark. I then had to get to Konstanz and cross the Bodensee to Meersburg on the ferry. I changed more money into Deutschmarks at the station and watched uneasily as the woman tapped my passport number into her computer.

It never occurred to me then that our movements were astonishingly simple to trace. All the calls from our phone, and from every other phone in England, were generated by computer. The police had only to summon up the numbers of the last two calls, which I had carefully cancelled on the screen as a precaution, to find the hotel on the Bodensee. Iso had checked in under her real name. We had not vanished into the winter Continent. We had barely drawn a curtain across our intended destinations.

I thought about Roehm, about the man rather than the dead hulk in the bed, for the first time as the ferry cast off across the dark waters of the Bodensee. The boat was full of people sitting in their cars, listening to their radios, and workers going home from the city. Giant spotlights illuminated our path across the icy water. The winds coming off the great lake had the savagery of an ice axe sinking into flesh. Everyone turned their backs to the gust. I felt unclothed and frightened. Roehm came back to me in the ice blast, his cold, white face, his lizard skin, his chilling touch. He was made of cold. He had come to us when the leaves were turning and the days were shortening, as the year sank towards the longest night. He felt suddenly near to me on the vast lake of black lapping cold, in the slap of small waves on the ferry's hull. It was as if he was beside me, before me, as if I were passing through a shadow yet always, always, moving towards him. The sensation was disturbing, but I was not really afraid. In fact I was strangely comforted, for the dead do not abandon their killers, but become part of them.

Had he been there I would have spoken to him, without jealousy or resentment. And he would have listened, attentive, reflective, engaged by my stories and my views, but not intrusively curious. He possessed the art of listening. Who are you? Why did you come to us? I had the bizarre sensation that Roehm was in fact two people. There was a giant man, powerful, aristocratic, and generous in his manners, a prince travelling incognito without his entourage, and the other, the ambiguous, erotic presence whose seductive lure was a foretaste of perdition. He had revealed aspects of myself to me with the sinister acumen of a psychoanalyst who has heard it all before. But these were the stories that I did not wish to hear, whose consequences left me terribly afraid. The insidious knowledge that stuck in my throat was that he had forced me to choose between my mother and whatever it was that he did in fact represent. I had chosen her, thinking that I was choosing love, the security of her body against mine, continuity with our shared past, a safe world for the two of us. But if I had not chosen her the only option I would ever have had, through all the years to come, would have been Roehm himself. There was no world elsewhere.

Why had my life turned to rock crystal between the two of them? Other people grow up, leave home, pass beyond their parents or the adults in their lives. Yet Isobel had remained dependent upon her aunt Luce, the woman who had paid for her, educated her, formed her thinking, encouraged her gifts, brought her up. And Luce had clung to Isobel like a desperate tick, afraid of something unspecified that lurked in our vicinity, always present, out of our line of vision. Luce would ring Isobel every day. Why? Why was this necessary? Were we being protected or policed? Why were we unable to let each other go?

I had refused to share all other lives but hers. I had resisted intrusion like a crouching panther. I had watched over her goings out and her comings in. I had never allowed her to escape my grasp.

Yet she had calmly stepped away across the floor to dance with another man. And had never looked back.

Standing on the night ferry, gazing at the long columns of light, steady on the water, the choppy cold and endless dark stretching away, above and below, I clambered back through the last five months of tension and betrayal. I remembered all the nights lying awake, waiting for her to come home, all the sly prying which had turned me into a spy, the sexual Charybdis of triangular desire, the moment when he had offered her to me, the moment when he had made me long for him. But above all I remembered the uncanny sensation, which came and went like the flutter of a moth, that it was not the woman that he wanted but the boy, and that he had seduced the mother to possess the son. I whispered his name into the strange night wind with its horizontal edge of cold: Where are you? What did you want? The rumble of the ferry engine, the faint tinkle of music and news from half a dozen car radios, the stamp of someone else walking the deck to keep warm, this was all I could hear in the freezing night.

Zum wilden Jäger was an orange, square palazzo built directly on the water's edge. There was a garden with Italian arrangements of fountains and terraces all frozen into winter ice. The floodlights from the gardens picked out the green shutters and white moulded swirls surmounting the windows, all the elegant austerity of early Baroque detail. A battered wisteria coiled around the building like a dead snake. Someone had laid grit upon the steps. The town rose up the slope behind me. I saw steep rows of vines between the villas, strung out upon wires, stretched leafless and twisted like torture victims. The Renault was nowhere to be seen. I looked round once, then marched straight through the double doors.

It was an expensive hotel. We never stayed in expensive hotels. I sashayed up the monogrammed carpet to a glass and marble edifice, which was occupied by a young woman wearing a uniform with the same monogram that littered the carpet. Behind her were dozens of wooden pigeonholes with suspended golden keys. The hotel was nearly empty.

I launched the attack in English.

'I'm looking for Isobel Hawk. Is she here?'

'Yes. She's in her room.' She picked up the internal phone. 'Who shall I say is here?'

'Tobias Hawk.'

'Ahhhh . . .' She was visibly relieved. 'Frau Hawk? Your husband is in reception.'

The woman almost dropped the phone. But even I could hear that my mother had begun screaming.

'Which room is she in? Quick.' I raced for the stairs.

'*Zwölf. Im ersten Stock.*'

The hotel was decked out in religious kitsch. I nearly knocked over a festive altar to the Virgin Mary as I flung myself round the corner of the landing. I heard thumps and crashes from behind her door. She was moving all the furniture she could displace into a barricade. I hammered on the green wood, yelling.

'Iso! Iso! It's me. It's Toby. I'm on my own. Let me in.'

My voice sounded hollow in the empty, overheated passage. Her sobbing was audible through the door. The number twelve was painted on a ceramic plaque, wreathed in violets. I eyeballed the offensive flowers.

'Iso! Can you hear me?'

The furniture scraped and crashed. Something heavy hit the floor with an evil thud. Then the door flew open and she leaped straight into my arms. I held her tightly and looked round the room, which had apparently been ransacked by mad burglars. She had shifted a huge chest of drawers and both chairs across the entrance. Armed with the strength of pure terror she had managed to shift the massive, painted wardrobe.

'Iso, it's OK. It's all over. It's finished. Listen to me. I went back to our house. Yesterday. He was there in the bed. As if he was in a coma or something. I plugged all the windows and turned on the gas tap. Then I got out and came to find you. You didn't kill him. I did. Do you understand that? Roehm is dead. And I killed him.'

She was crying uncontrollably. I persuaded her to sit down on the edge of the bed. She was wearing a dirty checked shirt and nothing else. The sheets were a knotted jumble, as if she had been fighting with the bedclothes.

'Iso, have you eaten anything? Anything at all? Have you slept? What's happening to you?'

We stared into one another's faces, red-eyed, hunted. She smelt stale and unwashed. Her hair drooped in lank strands.

'Iso, I'm going to run a bath for both of us.'

But she clung to me whenever I moved. She was unable to speak. I talked to her quietly, gently. Her eyes were huge, the pupils blank. I rearranged the furniture while she sat on the bed and watched, saying nothing and not offering to help. I could scarcely move the wardrobe. She had hauled it halfway across the room. She followed me into the bathroom, which was a symphony of white towels and pink tiles. I poured oils and scented foam into the bath and turned the taps on full. She was still crying silently. The shutters leading onto the balcony were closed. The only light came from the yellow tube above the basin. She sat shivering in the half-light. And still, she didn't speak.

I began, slowly, quietly, to undo the buttons on her shirt. She flinched.

— I won't hurt you. I promise. I'm here to take care of you. Not to make any more demands on you.

— Iso, I love you. You know how much I love you. I

want to make up for being cruel. I promise that I will never knowingly hurt you again. Give me another chance.

— Let me touch you.

— I won't hurt you.

— Why don't you want the light on?

— What's this on your shoulder?

— My God, Iso! Your back is like a ploughed field. Did Roehm do this to you? When?

— And what with?

— Iso, these are old scars. I've never seen these. What in God's name has been happening to you?

— Why are you shaking your head? What do you mean? Don't ask? Don't look? I can hardly help seeing this. It's visible at sixty paces. He can't have done this to you without your knowing about it. He can't have done it without your consent.

— Why are you shaking your head? Why can't you speak? Has he cut your tongue out?

— You must have felt this? You must have felt *something.*

— All right. I'm not trying to bully you.

— No. You can have the first bath. I won't go away. I'll sit here.

— Look at me. Let me touch you.

— Have you got any more of this cream?

— Don't wriggle. Don't pull away.

— Oh, for God's sake Iso, relax. I've done this for you a hundred times. The cream's not that cold. Let me rub it in a bit more. You've got huge white blobs all along your spine. It's antiseptic. I've washed my hands.

— If you don't mind me saying so, you've got very thin.

— It's as if he's eaten you up.

— Of course it's his fault. He did it.

— Is that any better?

— Breathe.

— Relax a little. That's much better. Now stretch out. You can turn over. I've finished.

— How can you possibly be afraid of me?

— You know me. You've always known me. I belong to you.

— Let me touch you.

— Iso, you've got to talk to me.

— You look dreadful. Really ill.

— Are you cold? You're shivering.

— Then get back into bed. Do you want something hot to drink?

— You do? What? Tea? Chocolate? How about tea and whisky? They must have some sort of room service. Even in the middle of the night. OK. I won't be long. Please don't start crying again. And don't barricade the door.

— It's all right. It's me. I wasn't long, was I?

— Look, this has got sugar in it. Lots of sugar. God, you look as if you haven't slept for weeks. It's OK, it's OK. I'm here now. Hang on. Don't cry. Drink this.

— There.

— Let me touch you.

— There.

— And there.

— Don't hold your breath.

— Talk to me.

— Don't turn away.

— Let me touch you again.

— Take this off.

— Kiss me.

— Are you warm enough?

— Talk to me, please.
— I love you. I've always loved you. Only ever you.
— I love seeing you smile like that.
— Go on smiling.
— Move your knee.
— I can't be too heavy. I'm the same weight as you.
— Let me touch you.
— Iso, come back to me.
— We have the same face.
— Talk to me, Iso. Talk to me.
— Iso, look at me.

— You have to talk to me now.
— Iso, who is Roehm? Why is he part of our lives? Why did he come between us? Nothing ever did before. You never allowed anyone to come between us. We loved each other and no one else mattered. Where did he come from? Iso, I know nothing about this man. Who is he? Talk to me.

7

BODENSEE

You're right. I should talk to you more. Sometimes you know what I'm thinking, even when I don't say anything. But there are things you can't know. I forget that you're a man now, not a child. You're an adult. You're over eighteen. It's as if you're catching up with me. I don't feel that much older than you are. You can just about drive. You take responsibility for things. It's as if we're becoming brother and sister, no longer mother and son. That woman downstairs thinks you're my husband. I shouldn't laugh. But isn't it odd? Given that we look so alike? Still, they do say that couples get to look like each other. Or like their pets. Luce says it's uncanny, the way we look alike. And I think it is too. I've missed you terribly. I feel like a jigsaw and you're the missing piece. There have always been two of us. You, me. We never had pets. Not even a cat. You never asked for one. When everybody else's children asked for rabbits and guinea pigs, you weren't the slightest bit interested. I always took that to mean that you were happy with me, just me. Silly, isn't it? It could have meant you loathed rabbits.

I never had pets either. My parents forbade it. Pets are

supposed to help you develop attachments and affections, to practise love. Most children try to assassinate their small furry animals and begin by dissecting their teddies.

Maybe I'm not good at loving correctly. I never imagined myself as a parent, and certainly not as a mother. I wasn't going to treat you the way my parents had treated me. I was locked up. Never allowed to go out with my friends. Hardly allowed to have friends. My parents decided who was suitable. My father used to haul them in and interrogate them on their incomes and morals, even the girls. As if he were working for the Gestapo. My mother sat in on the interviews. Not many passed the test. I stared at the men in church. And wondered how on earth I would ever meet one that I liked.

School was the only time I ever managed to escape from them. How I longed for the beginning of term! My father took me to the very gates in the car every morning and my mother used to pick me up. She was always there, waiting. After three-thirty the car was parked halfway down the street, as if the school was under perpetual surveillance. I once managed to skip the last period and get to the shop and back before she arrived. She never knew. I felt as if I'd gotten away with ram-raiding. Unbelievable really, everybody else was doing drugs and having sex. What did I do? Pray, sing hymns, serve soft drinks. My father said grace every night before we sat down to tinned soup, tough meat, two veg, and pineapple chunks. And do you wonder why Luce and I brought you up as an atheist who visits expensive French restaurants?

I've never talked about the Saints, have I? So it's one of the things you don't know.

My parents belonged to the Communion of Saints. I was washed in the Blood of the Lamb and destined to labour in the Lord's vineyard. Don't laugh. It changed everything. When they were hardly older than you are now they were missionaries. They were sent to Africa when I was very small. I can hardly remember my first years. Just the banana trees. There was always a new shoot my height in the brown crackly folds of the old tree. We came back from Africa when I was five. Mother had accumulated some beautiful things she was given at the school where she taught and by the people among whom we had lived. They had nothing. But still, they never came to us empty-handed. We returned loaded with gifts: extraordinary small seats carved from black wood and decorated with images of birds, grain-sieves with painted leaves and lizards on the rim, strings of beads and silver bracelets, brilliant, woven coloured baskets, toys made from hard wood with eerie symbols in labyrinths. Our house was exotic, different from everyone else's house. Then the former minister of our new congregation told my mother that her pagan grave goods were covered in magic symbols that would lure us away from the love of the Lord. And so she burned the lot. A huge black pyre of Africa. I cried and cried. She told me they were evil things, which could not disturb me any more. But they were gifts that were given with love. It seems to me that she tried to destroy everything I ever loved.

We didn't have a television. I wasn't allowed to listen to the radio. Before I was sixteen I had never been to the cinema. I didn't have a gramophone, no discs, no tapes, no records. And my mother checked my library books, before they were date-stamped.

My father was given the Haywood congregation as a reward for the horrors he was supposed to have endured in Africa. He went back to his old profession as an account-ant. They all had jobs, even the missionaries. The Saints took up their places in the world. We were God's Spies, working undercover, the Lord's Legions, created just a little lower than the angels. And so we lived in a leafy suburb and owned an Austin Maxi. He cleaned the car and she cleaned the house. Now you know why I never clean either. We didn't own much in the way of furniture. Inside it was very spartan and very clean. That was their method of expressing Christian austerity. We were not supposed to be attached to the things of this world. But you couldn't boast about your righteousness. You had to fast in secret. So we presented a middle-class facade which concealed a righteous interior. A barren interior.

On Sundays there was a lunch party for the gathered saints. Sandwiches and fruit juice. No wine. We only took communion once a year. And even then the wine was grape juice from the Coop. Wine was the nectar of Satan. Yes, of course some of them drank in secret. One of the elders even had to be dried out in detox. And we all prayed for him like mad as one of the fallen that needed the whisper of grace. We prayed for his soul on swollen knees, but no one went to visit him.

I can't explain the flavour of the saints. You'll have to ask Luce. She used to be one of them. They didn't vote on the grounds that if they were marching to Zion why should they care for earthly powers and principalities? But if they had voted it would have been Tory.

We didn't have central heating and the dining room was only used for Sunday lunches. Mother laid a coal fire early on Sunday morning and kneeled down before it with a newspaper to increase the draught. When I was a small child I thought this ritual formed part of her Sunday prayers. The smell of musty air in that room never altered. And the Saints had their own odours, mostly mothballs and carbolic soap. They all looked brushed and scrubbed, the women with their hair tied up tightly and their faces naked of adornments. Sometimes the men stood up in their coats indoors, clutching their paper plates and sandwiches, as if they were about to leave.

Those Sunday lunches said it all. The hushed crunch of chicken and salad sandwiches, pious talk or whispered gossip, concentrated fruit juice replete with E-numbers and colouring, mixed in jugs with ice. Mother had dozens of little lace doilies with beads stitched round the edge. And she covered each jug with one of these before we set off for church. The napkins, which she bought in cheap plastic packs of 1,000, turned into mulch in your hands and instant compost if they came in contact with water. Everything was cheap, mean, small. I couldn't stand their mean-mindedness. They were always ready to think the worst of anyone. So much for the compassion of the Lord. Even their prayers consisted of instructions to the Almighty, explaining where He had gone wrong and what He ought to do to put things right.

The Saints intermarried. We were a bit like the Sikhs who shared our streets in that part of London. The Sikhs and the Saints, passing one another mistrustfully, when they had so much in common. They were all facing a sexual sea change in the mores of their daughters. No one who lived in those times could have been completely protected from the wind of freedom. The Saints were not especially fertile. Most couples only had one child. So if some of us defected there was a dramatic diminution of numbers from which to select suitable marriage fodder. I dare say Mother had her eye on several likely boys. I was taken to supervised dances; embarrassing affairs where we all stood against the walls staring at each other, waltzed badly and then went home with our parents at ten o'clock. But it took courage to leave. The Saints were a secure haven and we were mightily indoctrinated with tales of Satan's Progress in the outside world. We were prisoners who feared the world beyond the bars.

The Saints believed in Satan, Satan as a roaring lion who stalketh about seeking whom he may devour. I never quite knew how literal this was. Satan was responsible for contemporary evils like rock and roll, the television and *A Clockwork Orange*. He seemed to utilize insidious forms of agency rather than risk any overt appearances. But I sincerely believe that my mother was on the watch for a seductive chap with cloven hooves and horns. Perfectly visible to the naked eye, if you looked closely.

We were antinomians. Do you know what that means? You don't? Well, it's simple. It's a bit like justification by faith, not by works. Oh, that's no clearer? Listen, Toby, I was washed in the Blood of the Lamb. So I'm clean. It doesn't matter what I do. I've been saved for all eternity. I shall sit upon the right hand of God in the Heavenly City.

Of course it's all nonsense. But it's what we believed. Well, if we were safe in Abraham's bosom why were we always on the lookout for the Evil One? It wasn't consistent. Mother used to explain it like this. We were all like Adam and Eve, created perfect, but with our own free will. Sufficient to have stood, yet free to fall. To fall? It means to fall from Grace. We could choose to renounce God's Covenant at any time. Doesn't that sound magical? Freedom? Choice? I longed to fall from Grace. But it couldn't just happen. You had to *do* something. And I was too locked into their systems to imagine anything else, any other way to be. I had the habit of obedience.

But is that true? No, it isn't quite. I wasn't too crushed to paint. They didn't want me to study art. I was supposed to do modern languages or Maths. I'm not sure how either of these would be helpful if I were destined to the Higher Calling and to become a missionary in Africa. I suppose they could have sent me to a French-speaking bit. Anyway, I painted them. I painted strange portraits of the Saints. It was a quiet form of revenge, I suppose. Saying my piece in the language I could speak best. But I left those in the cupboard at school. The art mistress came to see my parents at home. She begged them to allow me to do Art GCSE. They made her sit in the dining room, which was cold without the Sunday fire. She sat on the edge of her chair and they never offered to take her coat. I remember that interview. It was very funny in a way. My art mistress was called Miss Shirley. She was a bit like Liberty, short hair and strong hands. She explained that I was potentially very good and deserved the training. They demurred. Art was at best a form of self-indulgence and at worst a pagan imitation of the Lord's works. Oh no, pleaded Miss Shirley, art is the handmaid of religion. She mounted a huge argument which took in Russian icons, medieval manuscripts, every known form of ecclesiastical fresco, the Sistine Chapel, Piero Della Francesco, Velázquez and Van Gogh's shoes. Mother put it all down to Satan's inventiveness, but my father was almost convinced. He did think that sacred art had its uses. He had taken advantage of a picture book in Africa, to teach the story of our Lord's mission and sacrifice to illiterate children, who then spent the afternoons crucifying each other to see if it hurt. But he never knew about that. And so I was allowed to do my art GCSE, but it had to be an extra, not a substitute for something more useful, like geography.

You'd have kicked over the traces, Toby. And in my way I did too.

I wished for three things. I even prayed for them. I wanted to look different. I wanted to wear different clothes. And I wanted a man to make love to me. Maybe that's what every naive adolescent girl wants. But I wanted these things with a passion that was almost unbalanced. I wanted to be someone else, someone cool, streetwise, canny, sexy. I wasn't afraid of whatever was out there, beyond the bars. I wanted to learn the world.

There was a school trip to Germany. At the end of April, not long before our school exams. It was a language course in south Germany, on the Bodensee: lessons in the morning and coach trips to tourist sights or long healthy walks through the forests in the afternoons. All safe back at the hostel and tucked up in our rooms by ten o'clock. It sounded like the Hitler Youth. But I wasn't fooled. Freedom. I could smell it, taste it almost – freedom. I didn't really know where the Bodensee was in Germany, but I didn't care. I signed up. I said they'd given their permission. But of course they hadn't. I was trying it on. The German teacher rang them up. We did have a telephone, but it was in their bedroom and I wasn't allowed to make calls. My mother went nuclear straight away. She said it was out of the question. But my teacher took my part. She said that they were holding me back. I wasn't doing as well as I could have done because I was never allowed to take part in school activities. That cut no ice with my mother. But her next line of attack certainly did. She told them that there were bursaries available. And that was too much for Mother. Her high-mindedness was being interpreted as poverty. Pride got the better of her. I was allowed to go.

I think my parents knew that it would be something of a turning point, but not in the way they imagined. Mother actually cried when they delivered me up to my German teacher at the station. She made me promise not to forget my prayers. And on no account was I to approach any of the churches. Rome was far more dangerous than all the wildernesses of Africa.

The trip turned out to be a poisoned chalice. I'd never

been out to a cafe with a gang of girls for an evening, let alone abroad for over a week. I was in for a shock.

I had been forced to put up with quite a bit of teasing at school. They called me Swot or Inkpot in the second form. I was the only girl with a real pen and a bottle of Quink. They also called me Lizard. But oddly enough this was not an insult. One of our first school readers had a wise lizard that knew all the answers and sent the children off on interesting adventures. Like the Lizard I was clever and could do the maths and Latin. I helped them out with prose translations and theorems in geometry. I was useful. And I wasn't out there all tarted up on the disco floor, wiggling my arse at their boyfriends. So I wasn't a threat. Now I was out of place, out of my depth. I looked odd. Difference gets masked by school uniforms, but in civvies I was the only one in a Harris tweed skirt to just below the knee and lace-up Hush Puppies. I had that scrubbed sort of face that screams Virgin. I didn't start conversations. I sat on my own and looked out of the window as the coach rolled away towards Dover. By the time we got to Calais they'd settled on my new name and the general line of attack. They jeered at my hair. And they gave me a new nickname. They called me the Nun.

My hair was really long then, one long blonde plait right down to the small of my back. No one else had hair that long. It did look strange. As if I was suffering from Rapunzel syndrome. But now I think that they picked on that because it was my distinguishing feature. If I'd had spots or been fat they'd have persecuted me for those instead. They made up nasty songs, which they chanted to tunes from *The Sound of Music*, of which, of course, I'd never heard. Then they pissed themselves laughing. My German teacher never quite realized whom all this was aimed at, and anyway it was all going on in the back of the coach and she was sitting up at the front, gripping the map. That journey was purgatory. I've earned more years of grace for enduring that coach trip than all the tortures of my subsequent life put together. For the first time I had tried to join the group and found the gates barred by a mass of schoolgirls all standing there with drawn swords. I didn't cry in front of them. Not a drop. That was a mistake. They'd have let up if I'd cried.

We stopped, long after dark, at a hotel near Strasbourg. And by the second night we were there.

We took possession of an entire *Jugendherberge*. There were *Schleppdecken* sitting on the beds, arranged in two double pyramids like a king's crown. Everything was eerily clean and white, as if we had moved into an asylum. My period came on in the night and I awoke in a pond of fresh blood. That was the end. I sicked up my breakfast in the lavatory and was confined to my room for the rest of the day. My teacher was sympathetic, but she was busy organizing the language classes. The pack backed off. The Nun's sick. Poor old cretinous Nun. Leave her alone.

My roommate looked incredulously at my bulky pack of STs. The Saints weren't allowed to use tampons. Fuck that, Nun. Here, try these. You just take them out of the wrapping and shove them up. Not directly upwards. Backwards, towards your bum. Go on. It might even give you a thrill. I spent the morning crying into fresh sheets and pillows. They all went off to see the Schloss Neuschwanstein in the afternoon. I got up and walked down to the lake.

I remember it all, the still water and the quiet day. The mud smelt of late spring. Fresh reeds were rising from the wet banks. There were moorhens nesting under the jetty. That part of the Bodensee was a wildlife reserve. And I sat there all afternoon, sniffling. Not even the moorhens were afraid of me.

Then I saw him, rowing slowly towards me, a simple painted rowing boat and a giant man cradling the oars.

Roehm looked much the same as he does now, not so heavy perhaps, but much the same. He hasn't changed. He was leaning on the oars, watching me. I had the distinct impression that he was rowing in towards the jetty with the single intention of speaking to me. Have you noticed how he addresses you by your name? Roehm always makes you feel chosen. It's part of his endless, sinister charm. There was a slow dip and splash as he came, the rowlocks creaking in their sockets. He looked up. His face was white, strange, hairless, as if he never shaved. I remember his rings. He wore golden rings, too many for an ordinary man. It was as if he belonged to many different secret societies and wore a seal for each one. I stared at his rings. I knew he was old enough to be my father. But still, I stared at his face, fascinated. The boat slowed and hovered, unsteady in the shallows. He leaned on his oars, looking into my face, waiting.

I wasn't sure what language to use. I had to be the one to speak first. How did I know that? It was a question of permission. Almost an invitation. Roehm could not come ashore unless I invited him to do so. I knelt on the jetty and stretched out my hand for the rope.

'Thank you.'

Those were the first words I heard him say. His voice is the same. *Un de ces voix*, as Françoise describes it. She always comments on his voice. Maybe that's all she knows. I can't remember if she's ever seen him. I caught the rope and pulled him towards me. The boat bumped against the jetty and the moorhens scuttled for cover in the reeds. He shipped oars and reached inside his jacket. He wore a black suit, a white shirt with the top buttons undone, as if he had been wearing a tie, but had hauled it off. He was oddly overdressed for a boating expedition.

'Are you English?' I asked, curious. I sat on the jetty above him, my legs swinging, looking down into the boat. Roehm lit a cigarette and looked up at me. He had shiny, city shoes.

'No. Would you like a cigarette?'

I shook my head.

'Your parents won't let you smoke.' It was a simple statement of fact, something he already knew.

'They won't let me do anything,' I snapped bitterly.

Roehm laughed, that wonderful, eerie, resonating laugh.

'Then I'm glad they're not here.'

'So am I.'

And I smiled at him from my perch above. Roehm always seems to know more about you than you've ever told him. Have you noticed that? He puts you at your ease. I knelt on the jetty and reached out for his hand. I had no fear of him. His face was terribly still. He took my hand. I let out a cry. His hand was so cold. I thought it was his rings, the chilly gold of his rings.

'I'm sorry,' he said, rising, 'I'm unusually cold. You are beautifully warm.'

This was a compliment, a caress. He swung himself onto the jetty beside me and the boat sank alarmingly beneath him. We sat side by side, looking across the lake. He held my hand secure on his lap. I felt the icy gold of his rings.

'You have something to give me. And I have something to give to you.' He delivered these lines as an utterly factual, undramatic statement. Even in my innocence I thought that he was a bit extraordinary.

'What?'

'You'll see.'

There was silence. A ragged chevron of ducks banked away over the lake, their necks outstretched, calling into the watery sun.

'What is your name?'

'Isobel. And yours?'

'Roehm.'

I sat wondering at his name. Was he Mr Roehm? Or did he have just one name, like Heathcliff, or Madonna? He heard me thinking.

'Just Roehm. It's easy to remember. What do you hate most?'

'My hair.'

I banged my heels indignantly on the struts of the jetty.

'They won't let me cut my hair. All the other girls have waxed spikes. Dyed orange and green sometimes. And I sit here like Julie Andrews. They say I look like Julie Andrews. Do you know what they call me? The Nun! I hate it. If I had short hair they wouldn't laugh so much and I'd look more normal. My clothes are awful enough. Especially my shoes. Who wears Hush Puppies with lace-ups? Only health visitors or your dead grandmother. But the plait is the first thing they see.'

I turned to face him and grimaced, my mouth sulky and hard. He squeezed my hand. I felt like his accomplice being trained for my special mission, whatever it was.

'Would you like to have it all cut off?'

'Well, maybe not all of it. But I wouldn't dare. My parents would never forgive me. It says in the Bible that a woman's hair is her crowning glory, so I can't have it cut.'

'Hmmm. Yes. But St Paul was addressing a first-century audience. If he was preaching now he might think that it was nothing but vanity.'

I was puzzled by his accent. He spoke perfect English

but was obviously foreign. Remember that I was only sixteen. Or nearly sixteen. I felt safe as houses. I never suspected Roehm. He seemed reliable, even protective. And I was very struck by his innovative biblical interpretations.

He took me to the most expensive hairdressers' in the town. We walked in as if he had already made the appointment. It was air-conditioned. I noticed the purged chill in the stale air. The room stank of artificial hairsprays. There were long lines of black chairs receding endlessly. Some of them were occupied by women in expensive clothes with old faces and liver-spotted hands; their lank thin hair hung defeated, festering on their ears and shoulders. I hesitated in front of the desk and leaned back against Roehm.

'Are you nervous? Have you changed your mind?'

His voice against my cheek was subtle as a kiss.

'Oh no. I want it off. All of it.'

'Farewell the crowning glory. It is a little old-fashioned.'

A young woman slid towards us across the marble tiles. Roehm twisted the plait around my throat.

'Here is my Rapunzel,' he said in English. The girl looked confused. I winced.

She ushered me to one of the black chairs. I saw myself suddenly in the great gilt-framed pool of glass. I was an English schoolgirl in a white shirt and green cardigan, pleated navy skirt, knee-high white socks, lace-up flatties, my cheeks a little sunburnt, my nose freckled and gleaming. I looked at least five years younger than I was. Even my breasts looked hard and small. Roehm lifted the offending plait and kissed the nape of my neck. I felt his tongue on the last vertebra just below my collar.

'Don't worry. I'll buy you new clothes.'

The woman carrying a pile of gold and white towels took in the suggestive curl of his kiss and stood still, shocked. She had assumed that I was his daughter. I blushed, shrinking into the chair. Roehm won back the ground, easy, charming, speaking fluent German, explaining how he wanted her to cut my hair, shorter here, above the ears, layer the top, a bit of energy, to give her height. But keep the plait entire. I shall hoard it up, to remember her childhood. When I hold it again I shall remember her, as she is now, freckled cheeks, white arms and this long thin torrent of gold. He meets my eyes in the mirror.

'I want to keep my plait,' I said, suddenly perverse. I was afraid of him owning anything of mine.

Roehm cuffed my cheek and laughed. He said nothing. Then he turned to the hairdresser who had already swaddled me in towels and was glaring sadistically at the plait.

'I'll return in an hour.'

The old women had begun to stare at him. Graceful as a dancing master, he strode away down the long marble room passing from mirror to mirror, drawing each glance into the frame and then beyond, staring after his huge shoulders, white jowls and giant hands, with the great bands of heavy gold. I watched him go. Then I noticed the scissors approaching my head. My attention snapped back to the woman's hands. Roehm had gone.

I looked very different with my hair bobbed short. I've worn it like that ever since. I see no reason to change. I looked older, taller. I sat with the plait in a large envelope on my lap.

'Here it is.' I offered the thing to Roehm when he appeared in the doorway.

'I thought that you wanted to keep it.'

'Well, I don't now. You have it.'

I never saw what he did with it. The plait mysteriously disappeared. We walked down the pedestrian streets peering into clothes shops. Everything gleamed. There was no rubbish under the benches. The geraniums in pots lolled sideways as if they had been drugged. Roehm was smoking. He held me firmly with his other hand and my flesh burned with the imprint of his cold rings.

'You'll have to choose, Isobel. I have no idea what the young girls are wearing these days.'

'Don't you notice?' I wanted at least two obscene tight black tops and skin-tight black jeans or a micro-skirt with patterned black tights. I wanted, at last, to be seen.

'No. I never notice these things.'

I chose a black leather jacket, with patterned studs. It was fabulously expensive. I thought, He's my lover. He can pay.

Roehm smiled slightly.

The shops paraded clothes for fat middle-aged women. So how did he know which passage to turn down, which square to traverse, how to find the tiny little caves which contained fake silver trinkets and elastic flesh-gripping tops? One of the boutiques was so small he couldn't fit into the space, so he waited outside as I frisked and pranced in the sunshine, parading one set of black clothes after another. The skin-tight tops showed off my breasts, made them seem bigger, softer. He only looked into my face, and at my smile rimmed by the swinging blonde bob of short hair. He made me feel Hollywood beautiful.

I danced back to the hostel carrying bags of new clothes, which I hid in my suitcase. I couldn't hide the fact that my plait had gone. At first my German teacher was appalled.

'Isobel! What have you done?'

'As you see.'

'Well . . .' She smothered a laugh.

'What will your parents say?'

'Look, the Nun's had her plait off.'

'That's better.'

'You look almost normal, Lizard.'

200

I glittered with pleasure.

'Got a few things too. Want to see?'

The dormitory was all admiration at my conquest and my purchases.

'This your sugar daddy's hand-out?'

'He likes giving me things.'

I am very haughty. I let the money do the talking.

Pause.

'Cool.'

I have had two of my three wishes.

I lay awake that night and hatched my plan. Deceit came easily. I had to cry off the school trip. I had to find Roehm again.

I wilted theatrically during the language lessons, and then lied about my period pains, which had in fact all but disappeared. The other girls were in on it. They seconded my performance. My German teacher wasn't quite taken in. The shrinking violet had done a bunk the day before. She listened to my faded excuses, but didn't insist. I wasn't one of the usual suspects.

I don't quite know what I felt about Roehm then. Gratitude, certainly. Curiosity? Fascination? I was a village girl, come to the city, seeing the serpent dance for the first time. I wanted to see him again. I felt like the woman of Samaria. I had been standing by the water when I had met a man who told me all I ever was and all I ever did. For the first time someone had given me his attention, had looked at me carefully, closely. I was known and recognized. Was I in love with him? Does it matter? I wanted to feel those eyes upon me.

Once the school coach had safely disappeared I dressed up in the sexiest of the clothes he had bought me and then ran all the way through the narrow streets down to the lake.

Roehm was waiting for me at the end of the jetty where I had first seen him. He was standing on the grey-baked planks, looking out over the water. I saw the smoke rising above the bulrushes, static in the afternoon glare. He turned to look at me.

'Well, Isobel,' was all he said, and he stretched out his arms towards me.

I rushed into his embrace.

He was unnervingly cold to my touch. His cheeks and hands were cold.

'You're very beautiful.'

'You're cold.'

He laughed.

'Warm me up, then.'

He put his arm around my waist and carried me away to a sunny patch of damp grass enclosed by the reeds. The daisies flattened under his jacket as he set me gently down, still looking only into my face. I was stirred to the core by the intensity of that gaze. No man had ever looked at me like that before. And so he began to strip me of all my glittering borrowed robes. He never took his eyes off my face. I felt his cold hands on my breasts, my arms, my back, but all I saw were his cold grey eyes. He began to kiss me, my cheeks, my throat, my mouth. His lips were cold and dry. My whole body was shaking with pleasure. Then I remembered the illegal tampon in my vagina.

Nothing could have been more unromantic.

Roehm roared with laughter.

'You are the most charming, beautiful, perverse little virgin I have ever known,' he said, licking my ear.

I was almost in tears.

'It's not my fault that I'm a virgin,' I snapped.

Roehm held me fast in his cold hands and parted my thighs.

Was that the first time?

I never saw his body. He never removed a stitch of his own clothing. But I was naked, white, utterly safe in his embrace. He gave me nothing but joy and a huge sense of space, all the kingdoms of this world stretched out before me. I can still feel the cold passion of his kisses in every pore of my skin. He made all things seem possible. I had had my third wish.

How did he know where we were staying? He must have followed me. On the last day before we left he passed a message to me through one of the kitchen staff. Just an address in town and a time. Recreation time, after *Abend-brot*. We were allowed out for a couple of hours. But we had to stick together and be back by ten thirty. The German teacher issued dire threats of punishments which would come into force if we returned drunk or late. I was now a schoolgirl with accomplices. I set out with them. We were all going to *Zum wilden Jäger*, a *Gasthof* by the lake with candles on the tables and fairy lights in the Italian gardens. I agreed to meet them there, just in time to walk back all together.

'Don't be late, Lizard, or we'll all get done.'

'Have a good time.'

'Give him a kiss for me.'

I gave them the slip and launched myself off down the festive streets. It was a public holiday. I was surrounded by people laughing, carrying balloons. I could hear music from the carousel, the sound of the mechanical organ billowing across the traffic in the warm night. The address was a quiet, modern hotel.

No one could say it was rape.

I was there, wasn't I, alone in a hotel room with a man old enough to be my father, a man I hardly knew. I had already let him kiss, suck and stroke every centimetre of my adolescent body. And loved him for it. I was there again, wanting more. I was saying yes, yes, yes, as if I was shrieking my consent out of the window, over the geranium boxes and into the streets. I offered him my body as if I was acting out a clue in a charade. I wanted his macabre marriage ceremony. With my body I thee worship. I actually believed that I knew what this meant. I wanted him to touch me again, with his hands, with his lips. I was too innocent, too trusting, too disarmed.

There was a curious slatted light in the room from the closed shutters. Roehm stood there, staring at me from inside a blue smoking cloud. He waited just long enough to alarm me. I sat on the edge of the bed, naked and shining, beautifully bobbed and cropped for his afternoon sacrifice. He stepped out of his swirling cloud into the bands of hard light, picked me up in his arms, turning me sharply onto my stomach and pushing me down into the bed.

My groin was wet with the expectation of his kisses that never came.

Again, I never saw his body. I felt the chill of a zip, the sharp press of buttons on his waistcoat. He forced my face into the pillows.

He never hit me, but there were bruises on my arms and thighs, huge purple marks from his clenched fingers, yellowing for weeks afterwards. I was careful. No one but the mirror ever saw them. When he pushed inside me I felt as if I was being torn open with a giant iron bar. I was utterly silent and so was he. I didn't cry out. I couldn't. My face was crushed against the fresh laundered scent of clean linen. My breath came in huge gulps. It was all I could hear. I could no longer imagine him. All I could feel was his brutal weight and the unhesitating accuracy of the pain that rose into my intestines, my stomach. He intended to hurt me. I was being ripped open, laid waste.

I must have passed out. I can't remember the event itself. All I can remember now is how it ended. There was an icy slime down the inside of my legs, and a hammering pain in every part of my body. I couldn't move. Or look up. I heard his voice, *un de ces voix*, remember? It was like a postscript, telling me that our bargain was complete and that he had given me everything that he had originally promised.

'Thank you.'

This was the last thing he said. Then he was gone.

I sat up. There was blood, my blood everywhere, all over the sheets. My mother brought me up never to soil anything. If I ever did I was ashamed. And she made me feel the full extent of my shame. How I scrubbed at those sheets in the tiny bathroom! The stains remained. I got dressed and slunk out, humiliated, traumatized, unable to speak. The woman downstairs was in the bar. She didn't see me. I left the key in the door.

I couldn't run. Every bit of me ached and burned. I walked back stiffly through the crowds. The *Stadtfest* had reached its apotheosis, drunk and roaring. The tourists were swaying along in time to old Beach Boys hits being played by the *Stadtkapelle* band. I hid by the *Gasthof* dustbins and waited for nearly an hour until I saw my classmates standing on the steps, looking out for me. They all thought that it was perfectly understandable that I should have been crying. We were leaving. I wouldn't be seeing my sugar daddy again. Still, I'd done well out of the transaction. Bravo, Lizard. Cheer up. Pull one as rich as that and it's a sure thing you'll hook another. They backed me up. They lied for me.

'Lizard's got a headache.'

I went to bed with two paracetamols.

And do you know, I was fine the next morning. Back on

my feet. Super cool. Lizard's a real ice maiden. She's got nerve, cut her hair, got new gear, put two fingers in the air to her pious parents. Here's looking at you, suckers. For the first time in my life I was admired by my peers. And at last I was one of them. I sat in the back of the coach with my former tormentors and held court all the way home.

So that's what Roehm had done for me. He had given me my freedom. He gave me a different world.

There was no concealing the metamorphosis from my parents. My hair was cut short for all the world to see. But I looked my father in the eye as I climbed off the coach. I wasn't going to waver now. Not in front of the others. My classmates were giggling. But apart from the hair there was nothing else visible. The Saints never contemplated bodies anyway. I just pulled my sleeves well down over my upper arms, so that no one could see the bruises, and climbed into the Maxi. My parents sat there in the front, tight-lipped. They waited until the front door was shut behind them before putting their all into chastising the prodigal returned. There was no rejoicing in heaven over lost sheep. The Saints just reached for their rifles.

'How could you do this to us?'

'I was so ashamed.'

'We are very disappointed in you, Isobel.'

'Go to your room. We'll call you when we have decided what should be done with you.'

I hid on the landing and listened to them. I would never have done this before the trip to Germany. Their main concern was whether to face it out in church and admit their daughter's disobedience or force me to wear a wig. I went into my room and, for the first time in my life, I locked the door. It took a while to work out where to hide my new clothes where she wouldn't find them: bottom drawer inside the cupboard under the sanitary towels and inside the bag with my swimming things underneath the bed. I couldn't find anywhere to hide the black platform soles so I stuffed them into my satchel. I eventually buried them in my locker at school.

The wig turned out to be too complex. So the story they settled on was that I had been led astray by the Sisters of Sodom. I told them that my school friends had clubbed together and pooled their pocket money to liquidate the plait. I confessed to nothing. I never wept. I never said I was sorry. I refused to repent. They summoned God to take away my heart of stone and replace it with a more convenient and biddable heart, one that they could control.

I dreamed about Roehm. Every night. I never dreamed of him making love to me. I saw him in the boat, rowing towards me, his gaze fertile and intent. And I saw myself, as if I were two people, stretching out my hand towards him.

Miss Shirley was the first to notice that I was pregnant. It started seven weeks later, at the end of the summer term. I had missed one period, but prudently destroyed the requisite number of sanitary towels so that my mother would suspect nothing. Do you know, I think I believed that if I covered it up, kept quiet, said nothing, the foetus would somehow disperse, be absorbed back into the place where it had begun, the soiled sheets, cobbled streets, the pale, painted gables and the lake of dark water. I was sick in my art double period, first thing Friday morning. I sicked up a mound of Shredded Wheat and buttered toast. The nausea rose up in an explosion when I smelt the turps and I only just made it to the sink.

'Ughhhh . . .'

'Lizard's puked.'

'Hold on, I'll call Miss Shirley.'

'Get her a glass of water.'

'No point. She'll just sick that up too.'

Miss Shirley's eyes were huge and dark. She sat me down beside her desk and held my hand while I sniffed into a Kleenex. She didn't call the school nurse. I noticed that she didn't send for the nurse.

'Isobel, is this the first time that you've been sick like this?'

I shook my head. Gulped. Sniffed.

She gazed at me sympathetically, then got up and shut the door on her Friday class, which had gathered to ogle the sickening Lizard.

'Isobel, have you considered the possibility that you might be pregnant?'

I shook my head even more violently.

'I don't like to pry but you do seem quite different to me and you have all the symptoms of early pregnancy.'

I looked up, panic-stricken.

'Different? How? What do you mean?'

To my horror she pulled her chair closer to mine and brushed her hands across my breasts. I looked down at them as if for the first time. They were no longer small, crushed, hard as limes; they were swollen and tender, becoming heavier with every day.

I burst into tears. She rocked me in her arms until I returned to the state of uneasy sniffling. Then she sat me down in front of an earthenware jug and a bowl of lemons. I took refuge in the peaceful geometry of still life.

Miss Shirley spent the rest of the lesson on the phone.

I said nothing to my parents, but someone must have. On Saturday morning when I came down to breakfast they were sitting silent in the kitchen. My mother had been crying. Her face was puffy and swollen. Her eyes were hooded slits. She looked like a bloated snake. My father's face was set and grim. There was no question of breakfast. He did the talking.

'Sit down, Isobel.'

I sat down and faced him out.

'I see that you have hardened your heart still further against the Lord's Grace.'

I said nothing.

'And this disgusting massacre of your beautiful hair was but the outward sign of your inward corruption.'

I began to feel sick.

'We will have to make special arrangements to deal with your condition.'

I threw up a thin trail of yellow vomit onto their cheap tablecloth. My mother howled aloud, an odd animal sound, a gust of rage and tears. I rushed upstairs and locked my door upon them.

At the Sunday lunch they said that I had come down with a bad dose of flu. There was one week of school to run, but they told me that school was finished, over. I was stained with Satan's fingers. The Lamb wept in the Highest. I had caused his wounds to bleed afresh. The angels sorrowed over the fallen one and the powers of the pit wriggled for joy. If I did not repent and confess I was beyond redemption. In any case I was to be placed in an institution for the Ruined and the Lost. The child would be given up for adoption and I was to be taught humility, obedience, discipline, remorse. It was all arranged.

I had one single thought and my course of action was perfectly clear. I had to get to my school locker before they did and recover my black platform soles. These shoes represented one treasured piece of the Bodensee adventure which my parents would never possess.

I got up early on Monday morning, stole some money

from my mother's purse and caught the bus into town. I walked up the hill to the school for the first time. The security guard let me in because I was carrying my satchel and wearing my school uniform. I collected my forbidden shoes and retreated to the Art Room. Then I ran out of ideas. Sitting there in my usual place, feeling lost and hungry, I began to imagine my parents waking up, hammering at my door, finding me gone, weeping with sorrow and contrition at their own severity, realizing that they had driven me out. I floundered in muddled self-pity. You've never loved me. All you love is yourselves. When I die, you'll be sorry. Etc. I had my head down on the table weeping when Miss Shirley came in at twenty past eight to set up the classroom.

'Isobel!'

'They're going to send me away and lock me up. I'm to be kept in an institution. They said I'll never paint another picture or go to school ever again. They say I'm a Daughter of Satan.'

I howled into the quiet corridors of the empty school.

Miss Shirley gripped my shoulders firmly with a man's strength.

'Nonsense, Isobel. We aren't living in the Middle Ages. No one is going to lock you up. Sit up. Look at me.'

Sniff.

'You aren't the first girl in this school to get herself into trouble and you won't be the last. But you're a bit special. And I've already taken steps. I've rung your aunt Luce.'

'My aunt who?'

'Your aunt Luce. Lucille. Your mother's sister.'

'I didn't know my mother had a sister.'

Miss Shirley stared. Then roared with laughter.

'Then I'd better get her here right now so that you can meet her at last.'

And it was as well that she did. My parents had already rung the school and told the headmistress that they were removing their daughter from her educational cesspit of iniquity. They were on their way to fetch me. But before they could get there I had been bundled out of the dining-room service entrance into the staff car park. Miss Shirley denied all knowledge of my means of escape, but even so she received a written reprimand and was threatened with dismissal. But that didn't stop her. She banged the door behind her and then held up the enemy forces in the art room.

And in front of me stood the original fairy godmother, a tall tapestried woman in a floating purple shawl with high block-heeled shoes and buckled straps across the foot. She had a haughty, bony face with very white make-up and plucked eyebrows. She looked nothing like my mother.

'I'm not a trick of Satan, child. I'm your aunt Luce. And you're going to live with me from now on.'

'You didn't even know that your mother has a sister, did you? Well, she still does, even if she won't admit to me. I went to the bad a long time ago. People like Katie shouldn't have children. They need dolls or robots. Objects that don't shit or have sex. And she's so fastidious I wonder how she even managed to change your nappies.'

'Your haircut's great. How'd you get away with that? Needs a trim. We'll do it tomorrow. This is the car. Get in. I'll come back for your things. Knowing Katie she'll probably leave a pile on the doorstep. It's not your father, dear. He wouldn't throw you out. He probably welcomes sinners. Thinks we're a challenge. This is all your mother's doing. And she'll have told herself it's all because she loves you. I say, don't cry. We'll be OK together. Here, have a Kleenex.'

'How did I know what was going on? Your art mistress.

She's a close friend. It was my way of keeping an eye on you. I couldn't interfere. I never interfere. Anyway, you might have turned out to be an insufferable, self-righteous little cow just like my sister. In which case they'd have been welcome to you. But it's clear that the genes have gone sideways. Shirley tells me that you're very talented and very clever. You ought to have been my daughter. If I'd had children they'd have been dolts.'

'Good God, child, where did you get those awful shoes? You look as if you've developed two club feet.'

'I live miles away on the other side of town. You need never see them again if you don't want to. I'm an atheist and I don't go to church, so you'll be spared all the righteousness. I'll find you another school for the autumn. You can still be bang on course for your O levels next year. I've booked you a hospital appointment. Well, it's a private clinic. We'll have to pay, but we can jump the queue. You can't be more than three months gone, but we'll still have to move fast. It's a perfectly simple operation. You'll be out the same day.'

'Of course you can't have the baby. It's out of the question. You aren't even sixteen yet. I won't allow you to wreck your life. But we'll have to be honest with each other. Hold on, it's a red light. I'm going through.'

'Now, Isobel, I don't make judgements, God knows. But I must be kept informed. Who is the father and where did this happen? Speak up.'

8
FIRE

'Put on the *haut parleur*. Then we can both hear what she says.'

'OK. It's ringing.'

'Luce?'

'*Iso! And it's about time too. Where the bloody hell are you? And where have you been?*'

'Luce, I'm not in England. I'm in Germany.'

'*Germany? What on earth are you doing in Germany? Are you ill? The college have been ringing me to find out where you are. Your answerphone is full of desperate messages. Have you any idea where Toby is?*'

'Yes. He's here with me.'

'*Oh, thank God for that. His school has been on the line too. He's always skipped some classes, but not all of them. What are you doing? You can't be on holiday. It's term time. Come back at once.*'

'We will. We're going to. Luce, I've got something to tell you. It's very important.'

'*What?*'

'Roehm is dead.'

'Now I know that you're quite out of your mind. Roehm's no more dead than you are, thank God. He was round here last night. Looking for you.'

9
ICE

We fled south the same night. I drove illegally and fast into the frosty dark. My driving test was two months away, but Iso's hands were shaking too much to change gear. She had difficulty reading the map. After several cups of black coffee at one of the motorway service stations outside Bern, she finally felt strong enough to take over. She shouted at me if I dozed off beside her, but, long before dawn, we were both too exhausted to drive any further and fell helplessly asleep in a lay-by, clutching each other across the gear stick and the brake. We awoke, stiff, pathetic and red-eyed as the rush hour traffic began, a dense stream of oncoming yellow lights. We took it in turns to piss in the ditch, shameless, uncaring who saw us. Then we plunged onwards.

Tense as bank robbers at petrol stations, keeping close to walls, we filled the Renault up to the gunwales every time, just in case it became too dangerous to stop. Irrational and terrified, we rumbled into the breaking day, our heads aching, our senses befuddled by lack of sleep.

'Iso,' I begged, 'we must stop. We'll crash or something.'

Finally she agreed. We had reached the great lake at the edge of the Alps.

'We must make a plan,' I said.

'We've got to sleep,' she groaned.

So we stopped at an old hotel which had cleared the ice from its steps. I looked up at the Italian structure with pale green shutters. Would we be safe here? We were in his country, a strange expensive place which we did not know and where he moved with ease. On the other hand perhaps he would never think to look for us in Switzerland.

'We should hide the Renault,' I said.

'Oh God, what for? He can probably see through walls.' Iso staggered up the steps clutching her carpet bag.

We looked like tramps. I thought that the hotel would throw us out. We saw well-groomed, wealthy people sitting down to breakfast, and waiters in black and white lined up behind them. But Iso's gold Barclaycard did the talking. And so we teetered up the stairs, to a huge double room with a balcony and a lake view. Frost had sealed the windows.

'Did you check us in as husband and wife?'

'I didn't say anything. I just demanded a double room. Look, Toby, don't go out alone. Not even into the hotel. Keep the door locked. Don't leave my side even for a second. I'm going to have a bath. Then I must go to sleep. I can't drive another kilometre without sleep.'

We locked the shutters and shut out the light, snuggled into a mass of clean, white pillows, and curled up, back to front, like spoons laid in velvet. Iso fell asleep at once. Exhaustion was more powerful than fear.

When I placed my head on my pillow I did not sleep, nor could I be said to think. My imagination, unbidden, possessed and guided me, gifting the successive images, which rose in my mind with a vividness far beyond the usual bounds of reverie. He was with us, he was present in the room, spread across the floor-length drapes, the high moulded ceilings. His giant shape blotted out the fainter shadows. He possessed and occupied the corners and crevices of space. He loomed from the folds and undulations of the artificial dark, as if he were transformed to liquid cold, a smooth rush of nitrogen. Roehm had become one with the ice world. His touch was upon our faces. He would be with us always. He had become our master.

I opened my eyes in terror. The idea so possessed my mind that a thrill of fear ran through me, and I wished to exchange the ghastly image of my imagination for the realities around me. I see them still: the very room, the dark parquet, the closed shutters with the moonlight struggling through and the sense I had that the glassy lake and the white high Alps were beyond.

Iso breathed deeply and peacefully beside me, lost in sleep. It was as if Roehm cradled her in his arms with a father's tenderness. We had slept for over ten hours. We had lost a day. I was again buffeted by the strangeness of our situation and completely disoriented by the fact that the daily banality of our lives had been so utterly destroyed. My shoulder bag was full of school books, but not enough clean clothes. The steady world of school, home, supper and TV had vanished. We were wandering across the Continent on the run from a man who was either our visiting angel or the monster we had desired.

'Iso. Wake up. You've been asleep for a whole day.'

She stirred, her face bleary with sleep. But when she saw me her eyes cleared, and she smiled.

'I'm terribly hungry,' she said.

We assaulted a cordon bleu meal in the hotel restaurant and guzzled a bottle of Chablis. The restaurant did not pipe music down our gullets. We ate in time to the distinguished clink and rustle of stiff linen napkins and real silver. The decor was at odds with our appetites. The waiters were amused.

'Another day here and we'll be bankrupt.'

'Iso, that's the least of our worries. What can he do if he finds us?'

'I don't know. He might kill us both. But somehow I don't think so. We just have to hide. Lie low. We're safest together.'

'Won't he set the police on us? Have us arrested?'

'Roehm! The police? No, never. He'd never go to the police.'

I stared at her certainty. How did she know that? I assumed that we were fleeing before an implacable band of official uniforms, all linked by computer, rabid for victory, like Eliot Ness and the Untouchables.

'Look,' said Iso, 'we're safest when we're surrounded by other people. And I get nervous when we're not. Let's go out.'

We marched down the lighted arctic streets looking for crowds. I suggested the cinema, but she was afraid of the dark. Inexorably we sailed through the portals of the Casino. Here were the lights, huge chandeliers of nineteenth-century Venetian glass, fluttering in the rising heat. Here were the hushed thick carpets, and the muted scrabble of the gaming tables, the rattle of the ball on wood and the swirling wheel. The croupiers wore evening dress and white gloves. *Bonsoir, Mesdames et Messieurs.* They chanted the gambler's swift litany of adrenaline and despair. *Faîtes vos jeux. Rien ne va plus.* The atmosphere of passionate concentration suggested a collective examination. Everyone played against the clock even though they had settled in for the rest of the night.

The less luxurious section of the casino designated for

the impecunious and the underdressed was packed with slot machines. Glitterboxes, taller than a man, these machines resembled the illuminated pages of the Internet: jumbled flashy cartoon iconography, crocodiles, chipmunks, yellow chimes, spaceships and planetary rings, black hats and guns, icons of the Wild West, all thumping steadily. Some machines appeared to be luckier than others, and collected queues of people waiting to play. A pink light, like a gay police siren, topped every machine. When the punter hit the jackpot the thing lit up and flashed, a torrent of metallic music like a counterfeit jukebox poured out and the rush of jettons pounding into the metal tray beneath caught the imagination of the crowd, who played on with redoubled energy. I was baffled by the passion of the players and the actual process of working the machines. The system could not have been complex for each gambler hammered his or her machine with unselfconscious and rapid expertise, as if they were all carrying out a complex sequence of repairs. It appeared to come naturally.

There was no money in the machines. You had to exchange cash for a child's sand bucket full of jettons, with pink chips that were easily swallowed by the slots. You were playing with children's toys. The game therefore had no consequences. This must have been part of the explanation, for people sat hypnotized on their stools before us, losing fortunes with avid complacency.

A cash dispenser, accepting all known credit cards, was suggestively placed on the right-hand side of the bar. We arrived in the casino at around ten o'clock. It felt like three in the morning. The place smelt of darkness and people who moved in the night. The muted lights could not compete with the tacky glitter of the machines. A row of them sported card games where you could play blackjack against yourself – and the machine. Isobel was fascinated by a line of floating dinosaurs on the PREHISTORIC MONSTER MASH. You had to understand the codes. Three pterodactyls were not worth as much as two velociraptors, but if you managed to hold a *Tyrannosaurus rex* in the middle and doubled your stake you could win the Jurassic Jackpot.

She lurched onto the stool and handed me two 500-franc notes.

'Here, get me some jettons. I want to have a go. Quick. I can't squat here without playing.'

I pushed into the jetton queue while she studied the form.

Iso was a natural at gambling. She poured money into the thing, carelessly, ceaselessly. She became the rhythm of her machine. She was placing her bet against life itself. She played as if someone was standing over her with a stopwatch. Within five minutes she had won 4,000 francs. I supplied her with buckets of jettons.

'I'll have to lose this slowly,' she grinned, beginning to pour a fresh stack of pink chips into the mouth of the monster.

'Why not stop when you're winning?'

'Don't be such an arsehole, Toby. The point is to lose.'

I shrugged, unable to understand the fascination or the thrill.

'Why don't you play?'

'I can't. I'm under age.'

'I think that rule only applies to the roulette tables. We aren't dressed for the main *salles*; you'd look funny in jeans. Doesn't matter on the machines. Anyway, no one'll ask to see your passport. Go get yourself some chips.'

She handed me a wad of notes.

'I'll get a drink,' I said and pushed off through the mass, leaving her pummelling the machine, which thudded and clattered in the half-dark. She was absorbed, cheerful and content.

I had a good view of the main floor of the casino from my perch in the bar. Each table was a little island, like an upturned hull in a green sea, with people in evening dress, clutching the rim. It looked like the aftermath of the *Titanic*. The croupiers all stood poised above the green. They seemed contemptuous of the punters, their white-gloved hands deft as those of a professional puppet master. Their set faces never changed. They worked to a concentrated rhythm and I calculated that they needed to keep the speed of the wheel steady at the roulette tables, so many spins per hour, so that the house went on winning, rapidly, inexorably. I began counting; the average was forty spins per hour. The point is to lose. How could Isobel see that so clearly and yet go on playing? I had lived a safe life. She had invested in our safe lives. And now, stripped of her job and our daily domesticity, my mother made what seemed, quite inexplicably, to be the easy choice: to live at risk.

I watched the wooden rods scraping the green baize tables. *Faîtes vos jeux. Rien ne va plus.* The muffled repetition of the script continued in the background, like a congregation repeating the prayers. I studied the faces of the staff, all dressed in black and white, starched, bizarre. The women wore simple sleeveless black dresses, black stockings and high heels. They watched impassive, indifferent to the concentrated passion on display before them. My mind was blurred with alcohol and unease.

Then I felt that someone was watching me.

I had already been given the once-over by staff and punters alike. My jeans, sweatshirt and trainers had already attracted disapproving stares from the bar waiters, which I had cheekily ignored. It was clear that the bouncer in the bar had wanted to send me straight back to the slot machines, where no one was wearing a tiara. But he had lost interest and was no longer glaring as if I was an unsightly blob in the decor. Someone else was watching me. There was someone out there, someone further away. I felt my face and shoulders growing colder. I looked across the floor.

He was standing next to one of the security staff by the entrance. Either he was disguised as one of the croupiers, or he really was one of them: evening dress, black bow tie, short clipped grey hair, his massive shoulders steady and inevitable. As I watched he slowly raised his cigarette to his mouth. I felt the familiar gesture in my muscles, all along the surface of my skin, I felt his cold breath sucked in, contained for a moment, exhaled – but I was too far away to see his eyes. My body became ice cold. I stood fixed, gazing intently; I could not be mistaken. His gigantic stature, the ease with which he took possession of all the space around him. This was the father I had kissed and attempted to kill. We were now standing at the crossroads with the plush green space of passion and chance between us. I considered the being who had cast me among mankind. He had sought me out, this man, the man my mother had loved, who had the will and the power to effect his own purposes of horror. He seemed to be a vampire of my own creating, my own spirit let loose from the grave and forced to destroy the person who was most dear to me. Roehm.

I leaped off the bar stool and launched myself into the mass of gamblers. I pushed and jostled the shifting stream of wealth and ageing jewelled elegance. The irritated punters huffed, glared and swore. One of the bouncers stepped forward. But I was heading straight towards him – and the door. If I had not rushed outside I would have been thrown out. I flung myself across the marble foyer, past the guarded cloakroom, the piano and the potted palms, out of the double doors and into the white night of snapping frost. Where are you? Come back, come back. On the bald, quiet boulevard the flowerbeds lay turned and dead, the barren trees opaque with frost, the blank lake, eerie, white and still. The cars passed before me with a slick, damp hiss. The mountains hung perpendicular against the black. The pavement and the steps were empty. He was gone.

I decided at once to say nothing to Isobel. When I crept back among the noisy clatter of the machines I saw her sitting jubilant among the dinosaurs, watching the jettons pumping into her lap, over her feet, onto the floor. The music chanted victory and the whirling pink lights bubbled and flashed. She had won, again and again and again.

'Iso, let's go back to the hotel.'

'I suppose we'd better. It'll take me three days to lose this lot.'

One of the house officials dimly helped her to load up her loot into buckets. There was no way she could have cheated the machines. She was just lucky.

'How much have you won?'

We waited for the jettons to be counted up by the rapid, red-nailed fingers of the cashier.

'Oh, about £11,000. All told.'

'What?'

'I was playing one hundred quid a shot. If you win when you're playing for high stakes then you really can win a lot of money. I was gambling with Roehm's cash. The money that was paid over to me by the gallery in Germany – for my ice pictures.'

'It seems he can't lose.' I did not attempt to hide my anger.

'What's the matter with you?'

'Nothing. I just hate this place. It's like being in hell. The croupiers look like undertakers.'

'OK. We'll go,' said Isobel.

*

We awoke to the clear winter day. The Mont Blanc tunnel was still shut after the fire, years before, but the pass above Martigny was kept open into France. It was too cold to snow. We formed a plan of sorts. Françoise had given us the chalet in January and was not coming back down from Paris until Easter. We rang the neighbour who did the cleaning and told her that we were coming back. She didn't pose any questions at all, she simply reassured us that she would turn the central heating on and make up the beds. We had secured a refuge. Iso decided that the best thing to do was to hide out in Chamonix for a week or so, then ring Luce again. She was calmer, in charge again. There was no sign of the police. Obscurely I was still expecting to be arrested. Isobel knew that this was impossible. I could not fathom what she knew. But she never suspected that I might have seen Roehm.

I felt more secure in the daylight world. It seemed oddly unsurprising that Roehm should have appeared in the casino. He moved in the night. I was not afraid of him, we were too intimately bound to one another for me to fear him, but I was afraid of what he might do. His motives and his movements were inscrutable, unknowable. I could not even guess at them. But it was as if I was taking up a role in a script that was already written. All I had to do, even if I could never grasp Roehm's part in the script, was discover the point we had reached in the story. The son could kill the father, but the father could never raise a hand against his son. My mother was, obscurely, no longer part of the geometrical figure. She had been written out of the plot. I watched her with tenderness, but from a terrible distance. I had lost all my need to touch her. It was as if her body were a lush field I had already crossed, and now she lay, fallow and abandoned, miles and miles behind me.

Iso had not obviously changed. But she was thinner, fragile. I watched her blonde head jerking sideways as she changed lanes, yanking on the gears. She was running away from the man whom she had once loved, but no longer did, dragging me with her. I was unwillingly clutching her spindle wrist, looking back.

The Renault's engine stammered and gasped in second gear as we inched up the crawler lanes, around the hairpin bends. We scrabbled on the recent grit, strewn across the frosty asphalt. When the road ceased to be dual carriage-way we collected long trails of irate motorists behind us. I stopped looking at the serpent made of cars and gazed up at the mountains.

The Alps above loomed like a gigantic granite castle, turrets, ramparts, parapets and pinnacles. The sky at mid-day was solid and sharpened, ice-axe cold. Even the melting streams on the steep road were half-hearted. Where the earth lay in shadow the ice remained, shining, immobile. I gazed at the high rock faces and their uneven surfaces of cracks, ribs and ridges. As my eyes traversed the cliffs I saw two tiny red dots, impossibly attached to the rock face, overhanging a grim vertiginous drop. They moved, centi-metre by centimetre, across and then up. I shaded my gaze and fixed them in my sights, like a sniper. For almost twenty minutes as we too crawled up the lower snow slopes of the mountains I could see the climbers, high above us, executing a series of terrifying shifts and steps in slow motion, like dancers suspended over nothingness. Then we turned into the last bend; a gigantic spur of golden granite swept clear of snow by the wind hid them from view.

I remembered what Roehm had told me about the mountains. The mountains are the most beautiful pure space I have ever known. The ice fields, snow, sheer rock, the avalanches and the storms, they bring you face to face with your own limits. You are stripped of all pettiness. The mountain reduces you to simplicity. That's a very liberating thing. I brooded on the mountaineers. They were as obsessive and concentrated as gamblers. Chamonix was filled with them in summer. They were rarer birds in winter, but could still be spotted, roped together, plodding across the glaciers or clanking on the tiles in the post office. I had seen them close up in January. We had been sitting next to a gaggle of mountaineers in one of the cafes. They were drinking sugary tea, surrounded by heaps of material, layers of discarded clothes, nylon ropes, ice axes, crampons, drying out on the floor, and apparently talking in tongues. They discussed nothing but the weather, the climbs they had mastered, the rock faces they intended to assault. They smelt musty and wet. Their fingers were like steel claws. They were all men.

Luce had scooped the chocolate off her cappuccino and sneered at their bulky thighs and shoulders.

'Don't eavesdrop, Toby. And don't stare. It only encourages them.'

We stalked out of the cafe. She turned to me and growled, 'If you have any mountaineering ambitions, you can forget them at once. I will not have you scaling sheer cliffs with a lot of macho psychopaths.'

I had been bemused by the strength of her reactions, but now, upon reflection, gazing at the untouchable purity of the mountains, the desire to embrace them did not seem irrational or mad. We descended through the snow walls of the valley of Vallorcine towards Argentière. The chalets were hooded in snow with long ice spikes suspended from the roofs. Many of the houses were shut up. I looked out for the smoking chimneys and dirty gritted driveways. But the valleys were largely deserted. The French *vacances de ski* were over. There was a lull in the holiday market. It was low season.

All the other cars had snow tyres. Ours were almost bald. Iso drove perilously close to the centre of the road where there was no ice and the fresh sand gave her worn tyres some grip. This was safe enough when we could see a long way ahead, but terrifying on the bends. There was little traffic crossing into France. I rubbed a clear patch in our smoky windows and looked out down the long drops of fresh snow, spattered with outcrops of rock, and random clumps of dark pine. The world had been redrawn with elegance and lucidity, reduced to single elements, ice, rock, pine, snow. High up, I watched the buzzards circling. Their wingspan was huge, unnatural. They turned and turned, riding the thermals in the upper air.

The light sky was fading, becoming paler in the milky afternoon and only the highest peaks were still lit by late sun when we trundled round the last bends into Chamonix. We paused at the Spa. I stood guard over the car while Iso rushed round the shelves. The very normality of what we were doing, buying supper, along with everybody else, was enough to reassure me. The yellow buses were still running, the green cable cars, packed with skiers, were descending from La Flegère, the chalet shutters were open, and the house was warm. Everything seemed stable, familiar; we were on safe ground. We lit the fire, filled up the kettle, turned on the television and sat down in our remote cocoon, to smile at one another.

We spent the first day spread across the sofas, lazy as successful crooks who had pulled off a daring robbery and could now afford to chill out, counting the loot. The temperature rose and it began to snow. We felt comfortable and secure. I built up the fire and made us herb teas sweetened with honey. The snow curtained the widows and increased the silence. I found one of Luce's discarded novels, which she had abandoned seven weeks before. *Behold, Thou Shalt Find Me* . . . The title continued inside after three suggestive dots . . . *Even on the Roof of the World*. This was an American production, produced by Christian Vision Books. The cover said it all: two young men, roped together with snaky coils, exhausted and gasping on a snow cliff. They were both reaching out towards a bright light just in front of them on a mountain peak. It was aimed at twelve- to sixteen-year olds. The author was Bill Tyler III, Ph.D. I read the back.

> Simon Peters has one overriding ambition, even as a boy, to climb Everest, the world's highest mountain. Everything else comes second, his Mom and Dad, his pals at school, even Candy, the girl he takes out to the Drive-In Diner. Then he meets Jeremy, who runs the local mountaineering club, and the chance to scramble up something more than boulders seems within his grasp . . .
> Will satisfied ambition bring him happiness?
> What is the longing that drives him on?
> Will Simon ever question his motives, his vision, or himself?

I settled down to read. I remembered the mountaineers I had seen traversing the granite cleft and wolfed down the book in the spirit of research. The setting was supposedly contemporary, but the references to diners, high-school prom queens, dilemmas about who to invite to the hop and

Bill Haley made the entire scenario seem dated and alien. Simon was banal, blonde and driven by a mad desire to ascend summits, an inexplicable lust for conquest which appeared to come from nowhere. Jeremy was his roommate at college, and together they swarmed up every fearsome mountain that Utah had to offer, attracted the notice of a world-class mountaineer who just so happened to abseil past them as they were performing a spectacular feat of hare-brained courage, and eventually managed to attach themselves to an Everest expedition. It was stretching credulity to the limit to suggest that they would ever have been allowed out of base camp.

'Iso, can just anyone go up Everest?'

She was reading back issues of *Hello!* magazine.

'Yup. There are queues waiting to be hauled up to the summit. They take parties of people who've only ever climbed Hampstead Heath, charge them thousands, feed them oxygen out of bottles and supply them with Andrex. There's a route over the peaks in Nepal that's called the Andrex Trail, where you pick your way through human turds and soft paper, smeared with shit. What on earth are you reading?'

'One of Luce's religious novels.'

'Luce is mad.'

But the book became utterly gripping as soon as the initiates confronted their magic mountain. Everest did not apparently present any insuperable technical difficulties to an experienced climber who was used to ice. There were more difficult climbs just above us in the long range of Alpine peaks, some of which were legendary, like the Eiger and the Matterhorn. What was unique about Everest was the altitude. The highest altitude at which people can live and work is 16,000 feet. The level of oxygen in the air is half that at sea level. Above 16,000 feet the blood can no longer compensate for the reduced level of oxygen. Above 26,000 feet you are entering the death zone. Here in the white waste the process of physical degeneration sets in. The brain struggles to control the affliction known as hypoxia. No one can survive for long in these altitudes. You will inevitably die. You begin to die. What fascinated me were the psychic consequences of this lack of oxygen. Climbers began to hallucinate. They saw dead comrades climbing alongside them, they held intense conversations with people who weren't there. They saw things.

The inevitable freak storm enveloped Everest. Cut off from their team, one of whom hurtled past them, swept away by an avalanche, and unable to reach Camp III, my heroes faced a night on the savage mountain without oxygen. They dug out a shelter in the snow drifts. As they tried to keep themselves awake all night, for if you fall asleep you lose consciousness and never come round again, they both became aware of a third climber sharing their ice cave. He offered to lead them down the mountain. They followed this strange figure, who had knowledge and authority, but seemed insufficiently equipped to risk such fierce extremes of temperature and the angry wind. The unknown climber talked to them constantly, encouraging them, brushing fresh snow from the ladder fixed on one of the ascents. He secured their climbing harnesses, eased them over the sloping rocks, which hung like smooth, downward-pointing tiles. He appeared to be both ahead of them and beside them as they plodded through thick snow on the South Col. No harm would come to them. His breath warmed their hands and faces. He did not carry oxygen cylinders. He wore neither goggles nor mask. They would never forget his voice.

When they finally fell into the tents of the despairing research scientists, sitting hopelessly by the radio at advanced base, they discovered that they were the only ones of the original team of six to have returned from the summit. The mysterious third climber who had sought them out in their ice cave as they struggled against sleep had, of course, vanished. Their survival was a miracle. They were changed men.

Suddenly they no longer congratulated themselves on their prowess and achievements. At a stroke they learned humility, modesty and the Fear of the Lord. There were no prizes for guessing who it was that had stepped out of the storm upon Everest.

I recounted this unlikely ending to Isobel who read three pages and then slammed down the book.

'What about the other four climbers who were plucked off the rock face or froze to death on lost ledges?' she demanded. 'Weren't they good enough to be saved? Did Jesus wipe them out just for fun?'

'I don't think Bill Tyler's got that far in his Handbook of Theology.'

'Fucking bullshit,' muttered Isobel.

*

I thought that she was regaining her feistiness, confidence and good spirits, but she woke in the night and shook me awake.

'Toby! Toby! There's something outside.'

Bleary with sleep, I opened the shutters and gazed out across trackless snow and frozen shrubs. The night was clear. I could see nothing, nothing whatever in the biting white cold. Far above us the long march of the Midi needles glowered in the white night. There was nothing there.

'It's OK. You're just jumpy. Do you want me to make you a drink?'

But she shrank back down beneath the duvet, grizzling

a little, like a fretful child. The tension was too much for her. I lay awake, wondering at the tale she had told me. I decided then that we had to find Roehm. If he wasn't going to report us to the police for attempted murder, or at the very least assault, then maybe we should turn ourselves in. We had to settle things with him and escape from this permanent net of fear. My mother had said that the encounter with Roehm at the Bodensee had been violent and painful, but had an ironic consequence. It had spelt one simple, precious thing, which, all her life, had been denied, freedom. She had escaped the claustrophobic bigotry of my grandparents. She had crash-landed in a secure and wealthy home. She had found Luce. She had not been abandoned. She had never had to struggle. She had been paid for, supported and loved. My mother's life as a painter had been made possible. She had not buried her talent in the sand. She had used her gift. And the biggest, richest sale of her paintings had been to a single collector, the man who had set her free: Roehm.

The timing of his return had been uncanny. He arrived precisely at the moment when she was ready for him, the moment when she was successful, strong and confident. But how had he persuaded her to accept him? Had it made any difference to her that he was the father of her son? She had never actually spoken the words: *This man is your father*. She had simply led me to believe that it was so. He came when she had the courage and the fearlessness to walk straight back into his sinister embrace. What had she wanted from him? Or, for this was the puzzle which returned to me, what had been the nature of the pact between them?

She had let Roehm take her back into his arms. I did not judge my mother for doing this very foolish thing.

I watched over her, thin, cowering and fearful, beneath

layers of duvet and blankets. There was a fairy-tale pattern to her tale. She was a child who had made three wishes. Her wishes had been fulfilled. What was the unspoken part of the contract? I have something to give you. And you have something to give me. She had given Roehm a son. He had waited eighteen years and then returned when I had come of age.

I shook her gently. Her shoulder stuck out like a snow crag, sheer, steep, white. We slept with the night light on. She was only dozing.

'You never told her, did you?'

'Who?'

'Luce.'

'Told her what?'

'About the Bodensee. About Roehm.'

Iso shook her head, her eyes smeared with sleep. But her voice was still sharp.

'No, of course not. And neither will you. Oh, for Christ's sake, Toby, we've already had one fright. Shut off the light. We're torturing ourselves needlessly. Go to sleep.'

*

On the morning of the second day her old obsessions returned. We mustn't separate. We have to find other people. Crowds. We're only safe in crowds. It was on the tip of my tongue to say that I'd seen him. But had I done so I would also have had to tell her that I had not fled, but that I flung myself after him. I would have had to tell her that I wanted nothing more than to confront him, and to insist upon my right to be acknowledged. I wanted him to give me my birthright, or whatever it was that lay in his power to give.

The *anticyclone d'hiver* was upon us, −14°C at eight o'clock. The air was thick and still with frost. The front steps were equipped with rutted rubber treads like a Michelin tyre, but they were silk-smooth with ice and treacherous. We clung to the rails as we descended. The cars in the road lay like rigid dinosaurs, pickled in frost. We breathed slowly, for the whole world had solidified into cold. The unyielding, chilled air made us light-headed as we slithered to the bus stop. The snow on the roads congealed into dirty blocks, but whatever escaped the traffic sparkled, crisp, fresh, last night's snow frozen hard to the earlier layers, as yet untouched by the sun. Tramping past us on the sidewalks, the coloured ranks of snow-boarders were buoyant with celebration. There was fresh powder, *hors piste*. We were surrounded by fanatical con-versations. Iso was encouraged by the huge queue waiting to ascend the Aiguille du Midi.

'That's a tourist thing to do. It's what everybody does. Let's do that.'

There were gangs of skiers planning to descend the Vallée Blanche and a band of mountaineers equipped for overnight survival on the glaciers. The weather was perfect; clear, white, still. Yesterday's snow was dense and solid, the surface flaking into tiny crystals. A delicate crust clung to my gloves. We sat, encircled by stamping excited people, who were gazing up at the descending green cabin, almost invisible against the dark sweep of pines on the lower slopes. The machinery creaked and groaned. Although she had at first been glad to get out of the house Iso was restless with unease. She gazed at each face in turn as if daring Roehm to reveal himself. Her fur cap shaded her eyes, but when she took off her dark glasses I saw the shadows and the lines beneath. She was anxious, strained. She too was waiting.

There was no room inside the cable car to move in any direction. The windows immediately fogged up with our collective breath. Iso leaned against the outside rail as the thing jerked straight upwards, clearing the road in seconds. As we drew closer to the flesh of the mountain I could see the tracks of animals in the wall of snow. Chamois? Or foxes? What creature could negotiate the precipice with such ease? The surface of the upper cliffs, which, from the terrace below, had appeared to be a single massive sheer wall of rock and ice, now developed cracks, ribs, outcrops and overhangs, folds and crevices, all choked with ice. Someone opened the window and the mountain breathed in upon us. The air was dry and cold.

We changed cable cars halfway up. The second stage of the ascent was terrifying.

'Don't look down,' I said.

Far below, Chamonix became an orderly arrangement of shaded boxes, like the internal grid in a computer, squares packed neatly around the black circuits. We suddenly crossed the descending line of shadow and found ourselves in the sun among the snow peaks. Spread out before us, the valleys stretching away into France succeeded one another in a white phalanx of snow folds, one after another, each peak drawn with a chisel against the blue. The black needles hardened into giant spires with sloping snowfields coating their foreheads. We looked out at the distant range, astonished by the dramatic alteration in our perspective. We were suspended in air, thousands of feet up. I turned away to examine the rock.

Then I saw him across the hats and heads of the packed cabin. Roehm was gazing at me steadily. He was dressed as one of the mountaineers. It was broad daylight and full sun. His heavy smooth cheek, his strong face and pale gaze were barely twelve feet away. As the cabin jerked and paused, before bumping up the last stage of the ascent, we stood looking into one another's eyes. He was wearing a dark red hat with earflaps tied over the top. His black coat was made of thick tweed. I saw hemp ropes coiled about his shoulder. No one else carried those. I tried to take him in at once. I couldn't. There was too much of him there. He had already occupied too much of me. I gazed into this man's hooded eyes. Everyone was present on the stage. The curtain had gone up on the action. The play could begin.

But what was my role? My lines? Who was waiting in the wings, following the text, ready to prompt me now? I stood tongue-tied, gazing at the Minotaur, who returned my stare, unhurried, amused. His gaze was slow, obscene.

I formulated a curious sentence in my mind, each word carved and precise as if written on a gravestone. *This man is my father.* And then there it was, engraved on the murky windows behind him. I savoured his dense black presence, at once so enthralling and so monstrous. *This man is my father.* I tried to make sense of the triangle we formed in the crowded cable car. There she stands, gazing out at the far peaks, looking away from us, into infinity. She does not know that he is here, with us. Roehm stands before the sentence I have written on the windows. The sentence remains, fixed, accusatory, but without concrete meaning and suddenly repeating itself without end. *This man, this man.* I felt the colour draining away from my face.

The cabin banged against the buffer, then slid back. We all shouted in fright and protest, tumbling into one another, standing on each other's boots and equipment. The cable had slipped. We had docked too quickly and the ratchet had been unable to hold us. My elbow gouged Isobel's ribs and she yelped in pain. The thing swung for a moment over the cement void. Then rose gently back to the platform. I steadied myself and searched for Roehm. The far doors had opened and the frightened group of people were pouring out.

He must have left in the first wave. I pushed rudely against the intervening mass.

'*Attendez!*' One of the skiers resisted my aggressive shove.

I fell back, rebuked.

Isobel stamped her boots on the concrete with relief.

'Terrifying ride,' she said.

I staggered to the edge of the dissipating mass, searching for the massive shoulders and the dark red hat, but there was no sign of him in the crowds pouring across the bridge of wooden slats over the void.

'Where are you going?' demanded Isobel.

I pushed on to the ice tunnel and the outside ledge above the Glacier Géant. The mountaineers had all strode off in that direction. A terrible ice wind rushed up from the huge gulf of white on the inner range. There was a razor ridge protected by a rope handrail leading down to the surface of the glacier. A queue of skiers and snowboarders were waiting to descend. I heard one of the guides saying, 'If you must fall off, fall to the right. It's only four hundred feet. If you fall off to the left it's seven thousand feet down.'

'Why have you come out here?'

Isobel suddenly noticed the long range of glittering peaks and the gigantic pyramid of the Matterhorn in the distance. She stopped dead and gasped.

'Oh! It's amazing,' she cried.

I snatched her shoulders and forced her to look at me.

'Iso. I've seen him. He's here, with us.'

*

When we finally got back to the chalet she locked herself in the lavatory and sicked up the little that she had eaten that day. She didn't say much. She shrivelled into herself. She was exhausted.

We had searched the platforms and terraces of the Aiguille du Midi, gulping thin, brittle air as we raced up the steps. We hovered in the restaurants. We lurked outside the gents. We even interrogated the guides and staff who manned the cable car. No one had ever seen a man who looked like Roehm. I described his clothes and the equipment he had been carrying. There was only one guide who really listened to us. His opinion was categorical. No experienced mountaineer ever went out onto the ice in winter without a windproof Gore-Tex survival suit. He would never have been allowed past the *moniteur* on watch at the ridge.

'If he wasn't carrying an ice axe and crampons then he was under-equipped for the glacier,' said the guide, clearly anticipating a forced call-out of the emergency services.

It was no longer clear to me whether we were fleeing from Roehm or hunting him down. Iso's unhesitating reaction had been the same as mine. He must not escape. We must speak to him. But he had evaded our grasp. Finally we had to accept that we would not find him. Iso sat down on the ice steps in the brilliant glare and wept bitterly. People stared at her and tiptoed past. I offered her hot drinks and handkerchiefs. Nothing could console her. She sat crouched on the ice, the snot running from her nose. We were being stalked, watched. Roehm was toying with us, circling his game, waiting for the moment when his hand was secure, and he could not miss.

I put my arms around my mother, but she would not be held and she would not be comforted. Her lips were white with cold and fear. Her voice was unstable, gasping, as if she were being strangled.

'He's waiting. You have to make the first move. He can't come near you unless you invite him to approach you. You have to be alone. Then he'll be there. Waiting.'

I gazed at her, uncomprehending. Her lip curled and the next words emerged in a register that was somewhere between a snarl and a shriek.

'Don't you see? He hasn't come back for me. He's come for you.'

Morgan-Er oder Du.

I lit a fire and made her a bowl of herb tea, apple and cinnamon, soaked in honey, to remove the taste of vomit. But she hardly touched it. She sat staring at the burning logs, sunk into blank, red-eyed resignation. I cooked myself some sausages and chips but ate them in the kitchen. For the last four days she had barely let me out of her sight. Now she no longer cared. I stuck the solitary plate in the dishwasher and sat down beside her.

'You tried to kill him, didn't you?'

'Of course.' She shrugged.

'How?'

'Do you really want to know?'

'Yes.'

'Poison. Women always kill their lovers in the kitchen. I gave him a cocktail of weedkiller and barbiturates. Masked by gazpacho. I got the idea out of a movie by Almodóvar.'

'And he drank it?' I was incredulous.

'He knew what I was doing. He drank it like a toast to me.'

'Then why didn't he die?'

'God knows. Roehm has the constitution of an ogre in a fairy tale. It probably didn't even give him constipation.'

I sat staring at the fire in silence. Then I said, 'Iso, was it Roehm who came for us? That day when we hid in the coat cupboard at Luce's house?'

'Roehm? Coming for us?'

'Yes. I was about four or five. I can't have been older. I saw his shoes through the holes on the bottom of the door.'

'You remember that? No, of course it wasn't Roehm. I never saw him again until the day of your eighteenth birthday. It began in October. I was buying your present. The new bike. When I came out of the shop he was there, waiting for me. He paid for the bike. He insisted.'

'Then who was that man who came for us?'

'My father. He was coming to take you away from me.'

Her voice broke and she began to wail. I tried to comfort her. But I saw now that we were trapped. The pattern was almost complete.

'What does he want?'

She shuddered. I put my arms around her.

'What do we have to do?'

'We have to give up running. He's beaten us. We can either sit here and wait or we can go out. If we can find somewhere in this ice wilderness where there are no people – then he'll come.'

This didn't make sense to me. I had seen Roehm in the midst of crowds. But she was too weary and distraught to be contradicted.

'Iso, we have to end this.'

'With Roehm, there is no end.'

I didn't understand her.

*

The next day was white and still. We caught the first train up the valley to Montanvert. Iso allowed herself to be led. She was crushed, silent, acquiescent. Her skin was pasty, discoloured. She had dried and shrunk, like the carcass of a fruit consumed. There were children playing on the slatted bench beside her. She ignored them. Other people pressed against the windows, marvelling at the views, craning their necks, lifting their heads towards the sun. She sat mute and unmoving, eaten up with cold. I chafed her icy hands. She let me touch her, indifferent, dry-eyed. She was past hate, past fear. She was waiting for Roehm.

When we reached the station a small band of Italians followed us down in the red cable car to the ice caves. We found ourselves in their company. They were waving brochures excitedly and longing to see the ice dog that had been carved out of the glacier that year. They looked at Iso sympathetically, as if she had suffered a bereavement. We dropped back. I inspected the soles of Iso's boots. They were light, with deep treads. We decided to risk the ice.

At first it was hard going. We sank into loose snow and struggled to move forward, wavering, clutching one another. I was terrified that we would vanish down an invisible crevasse, or that our combined weight would prove too much for the frail snow bridges that we could not even see. We sat perched for a while gasping for breath on a rock that overlooks the sea of ice. The surface was very uneven; we slithered into hollows, then found ourselves facing sheer curtains of vertical ice. All the routes we picked out were blocked; we sank back, baffled, struggling to find another way. At last we crossed the frozen tracks of the skiers descending to Chamonix. The going was then a little steadier. Our boots no longer sank with every step. We trudged across the vast river of ice, pausing, gasping, gazing up at the glittering white peaks, which shone in the sunlight above the clouds. Before us rose the bare face of perpendicular rock. We could go no further.

Iso sank down upon a boulder and rubbed her face. She had never looked so weary or so old. The glare blinded me. I could not judge the distances. My jacket proved inadequate against a butchering wind which came sweeping down the mountain corridor of ice. We were caught in the passage of the ice winds, which blew the snow into waist-high flurries before us. We were now astride the dragon's spine where there were no further markers in the snow. I could still see the tiny brown square of the hotel far away on the other side of the valley and the light glinting on the descending red cable cars, swaying down to the ice caves. Our only stable point was a muscle of rock thrown up from the white flesh of the living thing beneath us. I looked out across the white hood of the serpent.

Suddenly I beheld the figure of a man, at some distance, advancing towards us with superhuman speed. He bounded over the crevices in the ice among which we had walked with caution; his stature also, as he approached, seemed to exceed that of a man. And at his side, intent, unswerving, moving across the blown snow with uncanny swiftness, loped the lean grey streak of the wolf. A mist came over my eyes.

Then Iso's gloved claw clamped into my arm.

She was screaming, a high fine note in the emaciated air. The wind blew a flurry of powdered snow directly into my face. I was unable to see anything.

'Look, look, look!'

Her voice splintered and cracked.

Beneath us, clearly visible, sightless eyes gazing upwards, was the body of a man, cast in ice. Through the smoky glaze I saw the great white face and the fixed pale stare. It was Roehm. Terrified, I clutched my mother, but I did not look down. I looked out across the sea of ice towards the huge gasping craters on the glacier. But as the wind dropped and the gust of blown snow settled on the blue shadows I had a clear view all the way across the waste spaces of the ice world. And where I had seen a man, a figure greater than a man, there was nothing. There was no one there.

We stopped the leader of a team of skiers who were

swooping down the improvised piste at the centre of the glacier. Their guide had a cell phone and all the emergency numbers in his head. He summoned up the rescue helicopter and the Gendarmerie de l'Haut Montagne. Then he skimmed across the snow to the smooth curve in the frozen river where we had seen the corpse. He stood for a long time peering into the ice. We were surrounded by breathless, curious skiers, anxious to view our discovery, as if we were archaeologists revealing an important find. Isobel was trembling. They helped us back across the white wastes, guiding our steps. I can remember every detail of the voyage out, but our return to Montanvert remains blurred. Dense blocks of white light baffled our sight. Isobel's fingers bruised my arm, despite my layers of wool and down. I bought her a double cognac in the station buffet. Melted ice ran from our clothes and boots, soaking the chairs, puddling the floors. My mother was wild-eyed and incoherent. She was drinking her second glass of firewater when the police came to take us back down the mountain. She insisted in faltering French that she had to make a *déposition*. I heard one of the police officers quietly refer to her as '*la folle*'. And she did indeed sound mad once we were seated in the cream offices of the gendarmerie and she began to insist that not only did she know the man in the ice, but that she had killed him. She tried to calm herself and speak in short sentences.

'His name is Roehm. He is the father of my son. And I murdered him.'

The officer in charge of our case was Inspector Georges Daubert. He was not a local man. He had a thin aristocratic face. He stared at Isobel.

'*Vous êtes britannique?* Do you have your passport?'

'Excuse me, I need to make a full statement—' she began.

He cut her off. 'First – your passport. Thank you. Date of birth? Full address? Your address here in Chamonix?'

And so it went on.

How old is your son?

Where was he born?

Vous parlez Français? Vous aussi? Bien.

Your reason for visiting Chamonix?

Isobel explained that we were on the run after our failed murder attempts.

The inspector wrote down 'tourism'.

Then he ticked us off for venturing out onto the Mer de Glace in midwinter without a guide, proper clothes or equipment.

'You could be killed. Easily,' he said in English, 'it is very irresponsible. Why do you think that you know this body in the ice?' he asked, genuinely puzzled.

'We recognized him,' Iso gasped, tormented by hysterical anxiety at the way we were being treated, as if we were exhibitionists or lunatics.

'And did you recognize him too?' The inspector swivelled towards me.

'Yes. Well, I thought so. But in fact . . .' I hesitated, then came out with it anyway, 'just before my mother cried out I saw him coming towards us. Over the ice.'

Georges Daubert stared at me. He was clearly wondering how altitude sickness could set in at less than two thousand metres.

'I will arrange a taxi for you. I think that you had better go home. Please leave me a phone number where you can be contacted.'

As we climbed into the cab we saw the red helicopter descending towards the hospital.

*

We were called back to the police station two days later, 'just to clarify a few details'. We took the bus into town. Isobel was convinced that, at last, we would be taken into custody and locked up. She left a message for Françoise with the car keys. But when she declared that she was quite prepared to be arrested and would sign her confession at once Georges Daubert roared at her in irritation.

'Arrest you? Whatever for? *Vous êtes cinglé ou quoi?*

'*Écoutez-moi bien.* We now have a positive identification. The body in the ice is that of Gustave Roehm, the Swiss alpinist. He was lost on the mountain in 1786 during the first successful ascent of Mont Blanc. It is a very significant, scientific discovery. The body is very well preserved, most of the fatty tissue has been converted into grave wax. Only the hands have been completely mummified. They are like leather, yellow and hard as a dried cod. He appears to have had enormous hands. We know who he was from the instruments he was carrying. Usually the ice tears corpses into pieces over time. The sheering action of the ice as it flows downhill will dismember them. We find buttons, boots, a jawbone. It is very rare, indeed it is almost miraculous, to find a body intact.

'I don't know what you thought you saw. The body we have recovered is almost unblemished. But we have identified him from his notebook and equipment, which you cannot possibly have seen.

'*Madame, je suis desolé,* but neither you nor your son can have been his murderers. However convinced you are to the contrary. He has been dead for over two hundred years.

'As you have been so distressed I have concealed your names from the journalists.

'May I advise you to go home. Now go home!'

His voice rose to an angry bark.

We were whisked out of the pale cream rooms, past filing cabinets and photocopiers, and abandoned on the front steps.

'What can we do? Where shall we go?'

I heard my mother's shriek as if she were hailing me from a great distance.

I knew then that we would never escape from Roehm. To pass from a normal nature to him one must cross 'the deadly space between'. And we had passed over that delicate snow bridge. He was in our blood, our bones. His hooded pale-grey gaze watched what we saw from behind our own eyes. Roehm had come back to us, brought us together in the hotel on the Bodensee, and withdrawn again. But his hand was stealthy at our backs. He was always there. We had become his creatures.

*

He had been watching me as I turned on the gas. He had followed me across the crowded ramps of Waterloo Station. He had sat beside me, all the way south to Konstanz on the padded blue seats of the electric train. He had watched over me while I slept, lulled by the insistent hiss. He was there on the ferry across the dark water. He had touched the woman's back with my hands. He was present in my body when I entered her, his lips and mine were clamped to her unresisting breasts like a succubus. We were consuming her, inexorably, with our perverted desire, breaking down her body from within. And when her beauty was exhausted, I was next.

The steep flight of steps sparkled with fresh snow. Someone had scraped a narrow path through the ice, which descended in a long curve, like a ballroom staircase on the set of an opera. The road before us was empty. On either side of the street, cars lay buried in the white drifts.

'What can we do? Where shall we go?'

My mother's empty questions meant nothing to me any more. We stood dazzled by great slabs of blue and white light, hesitant before the graceful curving stair. Far above us the needle peaks glittered in the clear air. I looked down. The light exploded at our feet.

ACKNOWLEDGEMENTS

I wish to thank the following people and institutions for their help and support, financial and moral, while I was writing this novel. I worked at Ledig House in New York State and would like to thank David Knowles, the executive Director, and the staff: Kathleen Triem, Peter Franck, Genevieve and Paris, Josie and Lauren, and all the other residents, who were there with me. Hawthornden Castle near Edinburgh in Scotland provided the ideal, silent setting for concentrated work and I am grateful to the Director, the Administrator, the Trustees and the staff at the Castle itself for the productive time I spent there.

Thank you to my brother Richard Duncker, who was my guide in Chamonix, and to Alison Fell for her superb novel *Mer de Glace*, which I carried with me on the ice. Sheila Duncker is, as always, my first reader, but she is involved in every stage of my work and I am very grateful. Thank you to everyone at A. M. Heath and at Picador, especially Peter Straus, Nicholas Blake, Sara Fisher. Thank you, above all, to Victoria Hobbs.

There are several deliberate quotations in this text from the most famous passages in Mary Shelley's *Frankenstein* and from her 1831 Preface. They are to be found in Chapter 5 and Chapter 9. The Saints are based on the Protestant sect described in Patricia Beer's autobiography of her childhood, *Mrs Beer's House*, and on one occasion I have quoted her words verbatim.